Let Spirits Soar!

Other Literary Works
by Johann M. Moser

Verse

Most Ancient of All Splendors

Late Autumn at Dumbarton Oaks
And Other Poems

Farewell . . . and If Forever
And Other Poems

Prose

The Ivory Fount
A Novel

Love of the Blossoming Hills
New England Stories and Sketches

Tutelary Presences
And Other Stories

The Song of the Eternal Aeons
A Phantasmagoria

Translations

O Holy Night
An Anthology of Classic Nativity Verse

Devoutly I Adore Thee
Prayers and Hymns of St. Thomas Aquinas

(with Robert Anderson)

Let Spirits Soar!

Poems and Stories
from the works of
Johann M. Moser
selected and edited by
John Barger

The Diamond Ledge Press
Sandwich, New Hampshire

978-1-964001-27-2 (hardback)
978-1-964001-28-9 (paperback)
978-1-964001-29-6 (ebook)

Library of Congress Control Number: 2026935369

Contents

Harry Wiedenhausen. 1

"Je te veux" 13

"The Triumph of the Human Spirit". 15

Old Gander's Weeping 36

Berceuse. 38

Leander Baxter and the Foxtowne Races 41

The Story of My Life 69

"Good Night, Sweet Prince" 79

Canso d'Amor 80

Maura Briscoe 83

Maître Renart's Shrovetide Confession 97

Aunt Jennie's Christmas Pie 101

Estampie 133

Wobbly Jane 135

Pup. 143

Galileo: A Letter to His Daughter. 145

Three "Friends" 151

Two Sisters 167

Le Danse du Diable 181

A Lament: for Gilgamesh of Uruk. 204

The Bulls of Bashan 206

Bordeaux, A.D. 408 208

Brünnhilde. 213

Leviathan 221

The Stonemason: A Journal 235

Quixote in Paradise 257

Waiting for the Night-Train 261

Envoi 262

Sources of the Stories and Poems 264

About the Author 266

Let Spirits Soar!

Harry Wiedenhausen

"Good-for-nothing lout!"

That's what Juliana Wiedenhausen howled at her husband when she kicked him out of house and home. Harry, whatever else he may have thought about the slightly awkward situation he now found himself in, was puzzled, not by the substance but by the tone of her — in fact, quite warranted — reproach.

"By God," he mumbled to himself. "She's right. But I thought that's what she liked about me."

And in what sense was it a reproach, anyway? He was proud to be what he was. "Amused, complacent," as our old bard of Camden, Walt Whitman himself, might say, Harry took everything in stride. He always did.

So there he was — flushed out of domicile, marriage, a way of life, it seemed — everything Juliana and he had shared so seamlessly the past thirty-five years. You would have thought that his own dear spouse, steeped in the crucible of his luminous imagination for all that time, could rise to a more eloquent dismissal than that. Grand and beautiful years they'd had together — easy, relaxed, playful, intimate, and yet not so intimate that each partner was not able live a life of his or her own: Juliana devoted as she was to her innumerable pastimes and forays; Harry devoted as he was to being something of a fixture at the Dolphin Beach Club, where, in its plush lounge facing out over the sea, he presided over the supreme languor of Florida afternoons.

But something had changed. Maybe it would be unreasonable to expect less, now that prosaic little Gregoire, with his sandals slapping ever fitfully over the terrazzo floors of their spacious villa, had become Juliana's mentor of late, her arbiter of taste. He gave her unstinting attention, which is what she now craved.

He was young, a bright-eyed elf with the brains of a toad, waiting in the bush for the properly pre-senescent butterfly to snag with his garrulous tongue. He wrapped his carefully tanned but knobby, depilated legs in a pink sarong and was forever shoving furniture here and there, fluffing pillows, and rearranging potted plants; and he ferreted Juliana through chic little shopping malls, where they gobbled down exotic snacks while on the run to nowhere, laughing and stuffing themselves with passion fruit and Mongolian yogurt.

He was what every Palm Beach matron dreamed of, at one time or another, to console her amid the converging infirmities of incipient old age. Pathetic little Gregoire! If that's what she wanted, she was welcome to him. Harry smiled: anyway, the "*affaire*," as only a hopelessly naïve observer would call it, would not last long.

He packed up his antique Rolls-Royce — one of those enormous, black, big-fendered, and glassy coaches that still sported old-fashioned carriage lanterns mounted at the sides of the back doors — with those few things he actually owned in his own name, which wasn't much, depending on the context you put it in. He tossed his expensive wardrobe wherever he found space in the roomy passenger compartment. He scraped together his collection of gold tie pins, diamond cuff links, and absurdly expensive Italian watches into a leather satchel; and, with some care, he carted down from his bedroom the little oak casket with brass fittings that he called his "pirate's chest."

He'd saved it, as a kind of joke really, for a "rainy day," thinking he would never need it. It was filled to the brim with shiny Krugerrand gold coins. He may also have had about five hundred dollars in his wallet at the time.

All of this would be, to say the least, a goodly loot for the average citizen — worth, all told, perhaps, three or four hundred thousand dollars; but in Palm Beach, needless to say, such a sum was paltry, negligible, virtually parsimonious.

With this "sparse" patrimony, Harry was well aware, as he took his place in the chauffeur's niche and navigated the stately vehicle down North County Road and past the Dolphin Beach Club, that the only route for him to take was the one directly out of town. Exclusion from Palm Beach society was as rapid, as inexorable, and as capricious as was its inclusion. If you had money, you were in; if you had none, you were out. Exceptions were made for the ability—well, let's say, the willingness—to provide certain "exceptional" services. Any effort to circumvent these barriers, the slightest hint of deprivation, the slightest vagueness or prevarication in your explanation would lead to immediate branding of social leprosy, however genteel its expression might be. Didn't he know? Hadn't he seen it done more often than he now cared to think of?

Accordingly, reaching the Breakers Hotel and the Royal Poinciana Way, he took a right turn, drove westward toward Lake Worth, and crossed over the bridge into mainland Florida. To those not familiar with the geography whereof I speak, from the perspective of that long, slender, offshore island luxuriously crowned with palm groves and with the crested mausoleums of the rich, mainland Florida is synonymous with disgrace, with destitution, and with despair (unless somewhere, over those shimmering plains, you also own a ranch well stocked with thoroughbreds and polo ponies and the manicured stables to keep them in). And since Palm Beach has no hospitals, it's the mainland where one goes, not just spiritually but also physically, to die.

Yet somehow Harry, in his all-so-endearing phlegmatic way, knew he wouldn't be gone too long. Someone, he knew, would need him. It was just a matter of time.

Harry had one other asset, a little secret he'd closely guarded all these years. It was a remarkable item for a man of his social stature (as ambiguous as that had always been) to possess, and yet nothing in this world could have signified more perfectly who Harry was and where he came from. Harry visited it from time to time, and, like so many who withdraw to mountain or monastic retreats of various kinds to rediscover who they are, there Harry was refreshed and renewed again in precisely that identity that Palm Beach society at heart so delighted to see in him.

The item in question was an old scow moored, among other, not-too-dissimilar craft, in a mangrove swamp about an hour's drive from Palm Beach: a dirty, paint-chipped, utterly disreputable little barge with a small cabin fore and a warped, corroding deck aft — absolutely, I tell you, the best place in the whole world to hang out on a blisteringly hot afternoon, a fishing rod dangling negligently over the side, a chest of cold beer readily accessible, and a lethargic pelican perched on the faded gunwales, waiting patiently for the occasional fish that it knew Harry would eventually toss in its direction.

Rarely, it must be said, did Harry actually spend the night there; but the cabin, outfitted as it was with a cot and stove and dining table, was always ready to receive him in its penurious manner — after a brief inspection for, and consequent dispossession of, big hairy spiders and other unwelcome inhabitants. So Harry had a place to live, a roof over his head after all, a shelter from the ferocious noonday sun and equally ferocious downpours of the evening thunderheads. He was as much at home here, frankly, as in those lushly terraced palaces he normally occupied.

He might, of course, have to explain his altered situation to his neighbors in the surrounding boats. There was Al, the ruined stockbroker, who mumbled incoherent figures all day long; the Prophet Dan, a Seminole half-breed who spent his life reading the book of Daniel over and over again and who had three old hound dogs, one yellow, one black, and one white, named, respectively, Shadrach, Meshach, and Abednego (though collectively he called them the "races of man"); Hiram and Jessy, the elderly black couple who caught and sold enough crayfish and prawns to make a small living from it; and Dillon, the ex-Marine, who kept reliving in his vociferous dreams the assault on Iwo Jima.

But Harry was quite satisfied by all of this — as strange as it was to see his Rolls-Royce drawn up to the old dock and still crammed with his assorted stuff. His impoverished neighbors accepted him graciously as one of their own, without flattery or resentment or interest in his apparent riches.

At this point, no doubt, you're all ablaze with questions: and I don't mean to ingratiate you when I call those questions "philosophical," for they touch, in a way, on those fundamental issues that tell us something about who we are and where we're going as a civilization. But don't worry, I'm not going to—sorry, I amend that—I'm not *yet* going to present you with a philosophical disquisition apposite to our subject. I'm simply alerting you to a significance whose intimations you may already have discerned.

For Harry, you see, is all of us. He's what and who we really want to be. As the old bard of Camden would say, speaking for so many of us: "I lean and loaf at my ease, observing a spear of summer grass." But more about that later.

Life, I should say, was as good for Harry on his impecunious scow as it would have been anywhere else in the world—and that's saying a great deal, for Harry had indeed been many places in the world and had tasted generously of those myriad paradises that the world holds out in such profusion but that so few of us ever have the requisite time or resources to visit. On top of that, every place was a kind of paradise for him, or at least readily adaptable to whatever paradisal longings he may entertain at the moment.

For the passage of time was for Harry a kind of pageant whose every detail he noted and relished to the highest point. Take, for instance, the stillness of a white egret fishing in a nearby lagoon, with the dawn spreading its soft rose and amber hues among the dark-green mangrove. Or the glide of pelicans over the surface of the water, or the circling of buzzards high in the morning light, or the buzz and hum of colossal bees among the palmettos and the scraggy riverbanks. Or the sluff of little waves against the hull of the scow when, half hidden under the brackish waters, an enormous manatee sluices lethargically by on its way to its feeding grounds and the little flotilla rocks up and down, the boats scraping lightly against each other.

The Prophet Dan always rose early to chant, in low mumbly tones, his curious oblations; Shadrach, Meshach, and Abednego would surround him, waiting for breakfast, whimpering, curling around, and pawing and scratching their ears. At midday, Al and Dillon might share the day's news together, talking to each other from across their bows, gesticulating and pointing to the piercing blue of the sky and the sunny cloud banks drifting overhead, as if that was where everything was happening, calling to Harry on occasion, soliciting his opinion on this or that story in the papers. In the evening, Hiram and Jessy would sometimes pay a short visit, bringing with them a pot of steamed rice and shrimp and a spicy creole sauce in a small ceramic dish. Harry would reflect, in such a case, that he'd not eaten better in some of the greatest restaurants of the world. He meant it too; and Hiram and Jessy knew he meant it, as they laughed and clapped their hands.

Harry, then, might stay up until late at night, as he was inclined to do, when the stars blinked large and bold over the tropical marshlands, all of them clinging to the deep, sloe-black skies like summer insects to a windowpane. He would gaze for hours into the tender hollows of the universe, which churned melodiously around him, presumably for the sake of his sole pleasure and delight.

Now, Harry had hardly had much time to "settle" in (I use that term advisedly — there really was nothing to "settle" into, and Harry was always "settled" anyway) when, one day, a large, lividly pale-green automotive monstrosity rolled out of the early wetland mist and up to the dock where Harry's Rolls-Royce was parked. Shadrach, Meshach, and Abednego barked wildly until the Prophet Dan, assuming a magisterial Mosaic prominence, rose up with his staff and stilled the unruly multitude of "the races of man."

Meanwhile, the vehicle sat there for a minute. The door swung out. A pair of thick, hairy legs in yellow pants, but barefoot, also swung out and rested there for about a half minute, the almost round feet with tiny, appended toes suspended in midair. Then a pair of loafers were dropped noisily on the ground, the feet tilted downward and slid heavily into the loafers, and a figure stood up, huge and portentous. He wore a salmon blazer and an open green shirt. A shark tooth was suspended from his ruddy, many-layered neck with a thick golden chain. Harry, alerted by the yapping of the dogs and happening to catch some of this action from down below through a "porthole" in his little cabin, quickly recognized Bartolf Pearson, manager of the Dolphin Beach Club, and emerged from the cabin to greet him.

Harry helped him over the short gangplank and into the scow, which tipped precariously as Pearson sat down on the lid of a bait box. He looked at Harry and nodded with a smile, "Well, old Harry Wiedenhausen! Gone just a few weeks and already we need you back, you old son of a bitch, Harry Wiedenhausen."

Now, you can imagine that this encounter might be a bit awkward—for, in a sense, Bartolf came as an emissary from a higher world, lowering himself to the dregs of this marginal society, a potential bestower of good or evil. But it wasn't like that at all: he came, instead, as a suppliant. He came like an imperial eunuch seeking, in a remote mountain cave, the sole ancient warrior who could save a kingdom from its final dissolution.

Ha! How odd to think of Harry as a warrior! But Harry sat on a gunwale opposite Bartolf, sat as he would sit anywhere, a medium-sized man in every way, not distinguished, an ordinary fellow, after all, with his arms folded, his head tilted, a smile on his face, a sharp, clear look in his eyes, attentive, reposed, utterly and fully confident in his almost illimitable powers—as the old bard of Camden would say: "... looking with side-curved head, curious what will come next."

That Harry could save the kingdom, should the kingdom require saving, was never in doubt for Bartolf, for Harry, or for anyone who knew him.

Bartolf came rapidly to the point. He had, of course, apprised himself of Harry's situation. And now, if you please, hold on to your seat. Bartolf had come to offer him a job. Yes, a job! To put Harry's name and the word "job" into the same sentence seems like a most unnatural thing to do. But this was the fact, although we must give credit to Bartolf that he never used such an opprobrious term; he called it instead simply an "offer." And in this case the "offer"—yes, you guessed it—was for Harry to do nothing, come back to Palm Beach, come back specifically to the club, and begin doing again what he always did anyway: just be who he was.

In his absence, the club had suffered. People had become abrasive; some stopped coming. Without Harry, Bartolf said, the club would go "belly-up"—yes, "belly-up," like a huge dying sailfish in the Gulf Stream offshore. And if it went "belly-up," what else would not go "belly-up" along with it—persons, marriages, families, the whole society?

Harry demurred just a bit. Bartolf took note of that and raised one corpulent hand, spreading his heavily bejeweled fingers as if to dispel objections. "You will have a room at the club—yes, even a small apartment there, if you so wish. We already have such quarters for some of our staff. And a salary..."

"A salary?" Harry interrupted.

Does one offer a fellow like Harry a salary?

Certainly not.

"A stipend," Bartolf corrected himself. "Or call it a 'royalty.' Or a 'remittance.'"

"And its terms?"

"To do what you did."

"Which was . . . ?"

"To do nothing. And, oh yes, to park your Rolls outside the club in its usual place. It's important that people know you're there."

"And what other inducement is to lure me away from these most inimitably luxuriant surroundings?"

"A sense of duty to your old friends. A sense of duty to the world itself. For if you can regard destitution as a luxury, the rest of us know in our hearts that luxury is a destitution—arguably the worst destitution in the world. Anyway, you can come back here whenever you want: a short vacation, as it were, from the demands of not having any demands made on you at all."

The problem was clear enough. Harry, of course, had been a habitué of the Dolphin Beach Club—quite regular, in fact, occupying *his* table in a corner of the cocktail lounge, nursing a drink that never seemed to disappear, engaging in idle chitchat with all comers, telling stories, exchanging gossip, filled with an inexhaustible fund of information about all sectors of the leisured life, from horse tackle to fishing lures, from exquisite beverages to the high cuisine of all times and places and seasons. About fine art and fine music of all kinds, about antiques and cinema and oriental rugs and a dozen other things about which he seemed to know everything there was to know. He could talk about everything—not always as learnedly as a scholar might talk but always well—as long as it touched upon all those good things that eased the human soul and salved its wounds.

Moreover, and most importantly, he liked almost everybody and found them superbly interesting, for some reason or another. Each person was special and different. As the old bard of Camden would say (and pardon me if I'm impelled to cite Walt Whitman once again): "Clear and sweet is my soul, and clear and sweet is all that is not my soul." Now and then, a few unfortunates, unwary of what they were doing and incited by their own aggressiveness, would invade Harry's repose and challenge his gentleness and imperturbability. But they always found him serenely unassailable. Soon enough, the edge of their aggression, and its all-too-apparent discomfort even for themselves, had been blunted, to their own infinite satisfaction.

In short, people came to the Dolphin Beach Club to be there with Harry, even if they didn't actually speak with him. Just to see him at his table made them feel all right with the world, feel it was okay just, for a while, to be — yes, just to be; *to be a being*. How odd to say something so obvious, and so unremarkable: *to be a being*. Just to watch and look and take things in. To witness and to wait.

With a single glance Harry could dispel all regrets, calm all anger, heal all sorrow, resolve all tension. For above all, Harry was, in his own somewhat complicated way, a truly simple man; and he brought out in all those who sought him a kind of simple happiness. To be affixed, if only for a moment, in Harry's invariably appreciative and ingenuous gaze was to bask for that moment in the recognition that one mattered, that your very *being as a being* mattered as much as anything else mattered in this all-too-troubled, all-too-cluttered world. Harry, indeed, was the Dolphin Beach Club's most valued member. He was, indeed, the Dolphin Beach Club itself.

Well, I shall not belabor you with the details of his reinstallation at the club. Saying goodbye to his fellow members of the diminutive swamp flotilla was, as ever, easy to do — he would be back quite regularly. And since he'd never unpacked the old Rolls-Royce, departure presented no particularly strenuous exertions. The spiders and other such creatures could move back into their preferred quarters, and the pelican would have to fend for itself for a while, as it usually did. Soon, the great, black-coached car headed back for Palm Beach and over the Flagler Bridge, spanning Lake Worth. At North County Road, it turned left and arrived withal at the pretentious pink portals of the Dolphin Beach Club itself.

But now it's time to interject, if I may, my long-deferred disquisition. I implore my readers' patience in this matter; please do not shun my words but attend to what I have to say, for it applies to you and yours, no matter how vigorously you deny it.

Fourscore and who knows how many years ago, our forefathers came to this bounteous land so that they could suspend a hammock between two trees and take a long siesta.

Okay, okay, I hear that clamor of voices raised in truculent objection. But I tell you that all those "huddled masses" came, still come, to our shores so that their toil would bear fruit and that, therefore, they would not have to toil anymore—no imperious earl or baron, no angular party functionary, no scrofulous commissar to wrench away their hard-won gains. They would suspend their hammocks from the trees, suspend them from coast to coast across the undulating heartlands, and sway in those hammocks in the soothing breezes of prosperity.

Sure, the dream didn't work out like that for most, and many were denied that dream from the start; many others discovered it was more difficult than they had expected; and many more had not anticipated those who, from boundless private greed or from lofty public aims, had developed a voluminous appetite for harvesting fields that others had planted.

But that was the dream.

That was our dream.

For America is the perennial vision of the Peaceable Kingdom, the vision of still waters and green meadows, "every man under his vine and under his fig tree." America works as ardently as it does so that it doesn't have to work anymore. It's a place where we work in order to "retire"—and the younger that retirement, the better. Who else other than that founding patriarch Thomas Paine could enunciate more succinctly the highest purpose of our polity when he said, "Every man wishes to pursue his occupation and enjoy the fruits of his labors and the produce of his property in peace and safety and with the least possible expense. When these things are accomplished all objects for which governments ought to be established are accomplished."

And where else in the world, one wonders, does the twenty-two-year-old, in applying for that first serious job, make inquiries about the retirement plan? And why, when we retire, do people "congratulate" us as if we have achieved something, when, in fact, we're achieving nothing except the opportunity to reap the harvest of a redolent cornucopia that amounts, finally, to nothing much at all? To sit back—the front porch, the rocking chair, the sunlit street—and to watch the parade of life that thumps and blares, with flags and drums and twirling batons, down Main Street; to bundle up in the hammock in the yard, suspended between two great cool, leafy trees: that's who we are.

Yes, despite our frenzy of making and buying and selling, that's who we really are: the fisherman half-dozing on a sunny wharf, the beachcomber kicking up sprockets of sand into a waggish breeze, the sprinkler of flowers and the watcher of baseball games and the swinger of golf clubs and the browser in old bookstores. Add to this the habitué of the barbershop hypnotized by the black ceiling fan sluggishly stirring a breeze on a hot afternoon, the motorcyclist reclining backward in the wide saddle of his Harley, the inveterate putterer organizing an entire day around hammering a single nail into a shabby barn door, and the elderly tyke finding final consolation amid the bright lights of glitzy casinos and in the cool depths of lush, tropical cocktail lounges.

In that sense, Florida can be construed, in its own distinct way, as the quintessence of America; Palm Beach the quintessence of Florida; the Dolphin Beach Club the quintessence of Palm Beach; and, as we have already noted, Harry the quintessence of the Dolphin Beach Club.

So why do we need old Harry Wiedenhausen?

Because he points the way with a clarity, a sureness, and a resolution we all must envy (though no one in this world would ever really envy Harry himself). No backsliding for Harry, no doubts, no guilt. To do nothing but gaze at things is what it's all about. *To be a being*.

Now there he sits, as he once did, in the bar of the Dolphin Beach Club, sublimely doing nothing, looking out at everything with still, untroubled, lucid eyes—not the sleepy, watery eyes of the dissipated, nor the ingratiating, predatory eyes of the seducer and the confidence man—but with the eyes of the lover beholding his beloved.

He watches and he waits. He lets things happen. He knows that someday Juliana, too, having survived her pre-senescent fling, will join him at his table, as she did in the past, in the early evening—the two of them giving just the right tone to the dinner hour that follows. It's good to be there, because he's there.

The "good-for-nothing lout" turns out to be the one who is, conversely, "good for everything." As the old bard of Camden would say (and I beg the indulgence of my readers if once again I quote Walt Whitman, who knew us all so well): "I'm satisfied—I see, dance, laugh, sing."

What else is there to do?

"Je te veux"

You are a fallow pasture
    Swaying in a summer breeze.
You are an ivory-plaited surf
    Where pelicans trace the seas.

You are a winter sky
    With cordoned stars so bright
The moon must pause to marvel
    In its nocturnal flight.

You are a lake and cove
    Whose waters are never still.
You are those piney woodlands
    You wander at your will.

You are a festive banquet,
    A gate that never closes.
You are a font of laughter
    Wherein all joy reposes.

You are my heart's desire,
    A petal in a nook;
A melody of lovely tone;
    A lily by a brook.

You are a crown of honor
    Imperishable and true.
You are everything I ever sought,
    A paradise in you.

"The Triumph of the Human Spirit"

"Eustacia! Such a pretty name! Don't you think so, Mildred?" Miss Wither-spoon tilted backward in her chair and peered over her shoulder at Mildred. Mildred nodded affirmatively and murmured in her deep, throaty voice, "Indeed, it is so, Miss Witherspoon."

Mildred slid the pupils of her perpetually half-closed eyes to the side and fixed them on me. She had a square, blank face with a thick jaw and a wide, lipless slit of a mouth that slanted downward from right to left. Her brows were a single flat band of shaggy hair that stretched from one side of her face to the other and that contracted back and forth, on occasion and for no discernible reason, like an accordion. She always stood behind and slightly to the side of Miss Witherspoon whenever Miss Witherspoon offici-ated at her headmistress's desk and in her headmistress's high-backed throne.

Mildred was dressed, as ever, in something that looked like a particularly ascetic version of a liturgical chasuble — an oval shaft of coarse woolen cloth, usually brown, folded in half with a circular cutout for the neck and head. Underneath that was a shapeless black garment, a caftan of sorts, sweeping the floor and having a tight turtleneck. On her head was a disorderly flop of gristly hair that seemed to lean, curiously, to one side of her head as if it were about to fall off.

Miss Witherspoon, on the other hand was a bony, petite woman with a sharp little woodpecker's beak for a nose. Her brows, if she had had any, would have bordered the high-arched mother-of-pearl crescents over her eyes that made her look as if she had two oysters on the half shell embedded in the front of her head.

She sat at her spacious desk attired in fluffy white lace and engulfed in a heavy cloud of what smelled like witch hazel. The polished surface of the desk was crowded with porcelain statuettes of birds of all sizes and species—a glittering mute aviary frozen in time and space, though Miss Witherspoon did her best to make up for the fluttering and tweeting that was noticeably absent among her glassy birds.

At least that's how I remember all of it now, almost a half century later.

It happened when I was a student at Foxglove Hall before the war—a private boarding school for young ladies located in eastern Massachusetts. I had been at the school for two years, but this was the first time I had ever entered the headmistress's office alone and under such potentially auspicious conditions.

I had been warned, in some detail by the girls in the dorm, what it would be like. Miss Witherspoon would sit at her desk in her tall-backed chair, erect, nervous, trembling, persistently twittering away and referring every opinion she uttered to Mildred by tilting backward in her chair, peeking coyly over her shoulder, and seeking her approval.

Mildred would stand behind her, half hidden by that chair. She was huge, taciturn, and broad-shouldered, with arms folded and as motionless as a proverbial cigar-store Indian, and muttering her husky approbations from time to time, as was required.

That she always and invariably approved whatever Miss Witherspoon said reinforced the impression that all such opinions had somehow been approved in advance, or even that Miss Witherspoon was simply repeating what she had been told to say and her referral to Mildred was to make sure that she had done that correctly.

It was one of the more delightful, if malicious, rumors among the pupils at Foxglove Hall that Mildred was actually a man in disguise—was, in fact, Miss Witherspoon's husband and the real power "behind the throne," managing Foxglove Hall and making all the important decisions. The speculations upon which these rumors were based, as treasured as they were, didn't attempt to account for the purpose of such an elaborate ruse, except that

Foxglove Hall was known to be, ostensibly at least, devoted to promoting something like an Amazonian ideal in young women, and, accordingly, the board of trustees (Amazonians all, apparently, in spirit if not in fact) insisted on having a single woman for the headmistress.

If any of this were true, it was obviously in Miss Witherspoon's interest that the presumptively duplicitous flop of grisly hair didn't, on some lamentable day, slide off Mildred's presumably balding head and thereby compromise both her and his(?) precarious positions; though if Mildred, as we were all quite convinced, was really the one in control—of the school and of Miss Witherspoon—then he(?) was most likely in control of the board of trustees as well, and there was little to worry about.

I suppose a later and more sophisticated generation of pupils might have expounded a different set of hypotheses, but, in those days, we were just so terribly naïve about everything.

For me, the reason I was summoned to the head office was actually rather embarrassing. I had won the student poetry contest.

First, let me say that I hate poetry. What normal person doesn't? Actually, I don't hate poetry. Sometimes I can tolerate it for a while. I do hate what most people, including most poets, literature teachers, and critics, think poetry is. I hate the abuse to which they systematically subject it.

Secondly, I didn't intend or want to win that contest. I was bored to death in study hall; I didn't want to memorize any more French verb forms; and I was being driven to the brink of lunacy by a fellow student in the music building across the lawn from the study hall who was practicing the first movement of the *Moonlight Sonata* for the thirty-thousandth time, missing notes and then screaming bloody murder and banging the keyboard with her fists every time she did this.

So, inspired as I was by such an inglorious set of circumstances, I decided to write a detestable little poem—you know, just for the fun of it. I tried to make it as overtly self-expressive (or self-obsessive) as I could, shrill with figurative obscurity and with hideously pathological images, arrayed in an incoherent sequence like white worms oozing around in gooey sludge. I tried to make it quite as awful as the creepy dancing of those contortionists whom Miss Witherspoon and her ambivalent consort insisted on enticing up from New York to perform for us and to turn us budding Amazonians forever against all forms of artistic production.

Those lady dancers slithered and rolled all over the gymnasium stage like dying lizards, gasping for breath and moaning and emitting a dreadful odor. Apparently, an aversion to hygiene was taken to be, at that time, a token of protest to whatever needed to be protested.

Consequently, I wrote the poem about just how awful it is to be stuck in study hall, memorizing French verbs, and listening to yet another replay of the *Moonlight Sonata*, accompanied by shrieking and the angry slamming of keys.

In my madness, I submitted the poem.

As a result of that madness, I won.

Hence, the summons to the head office to receive congratulations and my prize. I can't tell you how mortified I was by all of this. I still don't know why I won, but I may have succeeded too well in making my poem like that dancing, and that's why it was chosen.

Well—I guess I don't need to tell you this—Miss Witherspoon just gushed with compliments about my poem. In her high, twittery voice, she said she found it "dark" and "disturbing" and "outrageous." She said I was very brave to follow my impulses into such a "perilous region of the heart" and to pull out of that deep encounter with my "demons" such a resounding "triumph of the human spirit."

She pronounced, religiously and prophetically, that all great poetry was just that, a wresting of affirmation from the forces of chaos, a witness, again and again, to that ever resplendent "triumph of the human spirit." She concluded her kudos by turning to Mildred: "Isn't that so, Mildred?"

In her gruff voice, Mildred responded, "Indeed, it is so, Miss Witherspoon."

I could have died.

I could have died a thousand times over. But I don't know if I would have died of grief or of laughter.

Miss Witherspoon announced my prize (if you really want to call it that). In six days hence, I would be excused from a day of class; and the school chauffeur, Andy, would drive me in the official school limousine to visit a well-known poetess (back in those days they still commonly used that term for a woman poet). It was about a two-hour drive from the school. I would have luncheon with the poetess. We would be able to discuss poetry, and she would be able give me sound counsel about pursuing a career in poetry. Someone as talented as I was should not let such a superb talent go untapped.

Frankly, though I didn't regret the opportunity of getting away from the school for a day, I was horrified by this prospect. The last thing in the world I wanted to do was get trapped with a poetess in who knows what kind of lair and have to discuss poetry with her. I didn't want a career in poetry, and I was quite determined that whatever talents I might have—superb or not—were to go untapped.

Further, there was Andy the chauffeur.

The next to last thing in the world I wanted was to be anywhere nearer than a half mile to him. But I didn't get a chance to express my dual horror. I was dismissed from the head office a bit too quickly for that. As I left the office, Miss Witherspoon looked over her shoulder again and smiled at Mildred, who, in turn, stiffly revolved her head like a self-propelled cork squeaking around in the neck of a musty old wine bottle, and grinned back at her, unmasking, in the process, a maxilla punctuated irregularly by a row of exquisitely tapered tyrannosaurus teeth.

A word or two about Andy. I think every school has an Andy, especially every girl's academy whose function it is to fashion an accomplished, refined, flawless specimen of female humanity, albeit in Amazonian guise. He was the only male around—a scruffy-faced, twisted, dishonest, treacherous, obsequiously arrogant, ill-kempt caricature of a male, but a male nonetheless and, as such, for the students, the perpetual object of fascinated scorn and enchanted disdain.

He was a living model, in adult guise, of the horrifying kid brother every girl would like to have and upon whom shocked contempt and outraged censure can be remorselessly heaped. Every and any new story illustrating something grotesque or perverse about him was received with malevolent rapture. It was widely believed by the younger girls that, for the older girls, he smuggled onto school grounds secret caches of alcoholic beverages and cigarettes; and it was widely believed by the older girls that, for the younger girls, he smuggled onto school grounds copious supplies of the saccharine "romance" comic books so popular back then (you know, the ones with little valentines popping out of the heads of the protagonists as they mutually contemplate the moon and each other). It was supposed, of course, that Andy, pandering to such putative vices, made a small fortune.

I often wonder why such a figure was kept around. Was he meant to be an embodied admonition, a sort of cautionary tale in living flesh, of how awful, generically, men are and that we should assiduously avoid them, now and for the rest of our Amazonian lives?

Was he the only sort of person who would take a job like his — to ferry rich, mainly brainless girls from the train station to the school or back again, as the situation required, each of whom brought so much luggage along with her that, by comparison, the Queen of Sheba and her caravan of a thousand camels would certainly have been put to shame?

Was it that only such a misshapen, surly, groveling caricature of a man would be immune from inspiring the affections of young ladies whose isolation in a heady seraglio of burgeoning femininity could engender all kinds of adverse results? A particularly good-looking, or even just a normal, male might have been intolerable under the circumstances.

I suppose I need not belabor this point; suffice it to say that six days later I was greeted by Andy in person. I was dressed, as I had been commanded to be dressed, in official Foxglovian apparel — a uniform of a sort whose drabness was meant, obviously, to keep me securely in my Amazonian place. Andy stood before me: his wrinkled chauffeur's uniform was olive green with a double row of brass buttons in front (two of which were missing). It reeked of cigarette smoke and some other smell I didn't know yet how to define and was covered with what I took to be dog hair. (Does he sleep in that uniform, and with his dog? — superb debating points for dorm-room pundits!)

The limousine was a LaSalle (a now long defunct relative of the Cadillac, in case you don't remember). It was, of course, filthy, both inside and out; and the dog hair — which was shed all over the interior upholstery — testified that the dog was a frequent passenger in the car and that any other passenger would promptly be garbed in a goodly portion of its furry coat. Why was Andy allowed to maintain himself and the car in this disreputable condition? — another mystery for dorm discussions! In his usual suppliant, yet domineering fashion, doffing his olive-green cap with its torn black visor, he ushered me into the vehicle. I sat in the back seat, as would be expected anyway, but that, at least, was a relief. The farther away from Andy, the better.

The drive took, as Miss Witherspoon had predicted (and Mildred had agreed, naturally), two hours. The weather was nice and the countryside picturesque, though I didn't have the slightest idea at any time where I was or even in what direction I was headed—east, west, north, south? At times I had the odd impression that we were driving around in circles, for either all the towns we were passing through looked remarkably similar or we kept passing through the same town again and again.

Andy seemed to me, at first, to be a cautious, even rather painfully methodical driver, though my initial impressions were altered by the unaccountable swerves and frantic braking that, more and more, interrupted what was otherwise a smooth performance. Being tossed about in that back seat now and then did, I must say, heighten my level of alertness. Back in those days, you must recall, no one had even heard of seat belts.

Also, during the drive I entertained myself with the suspicion that I was being kidnapped. I have to confess that this was not a wholly unattractive suspicion for me, for I dreaded both the luncheon with the poetess as well as returning to the school afterward. I had fun fantasizing about my escape from the kidnapping (which involved galloping on the back of a horse over a "blasted heath," though exactly how I was going to get hold of a horse and where I was going to find a "blasted heath" was, admittedly, rather obscure).

I also held out hope that my ultimate kidnapper, someone at the end of a chain of intermediate kidnappers, would be an amazing buccaneer or someone like that who would whisk me off on his windswept schooner to the dazzling Southern Seas. Moonlight galore but no Moonlight Sonatas down there—of that, one could be reasonably sure!

At the end of two hours, we pulled into a short driveway at the end of which was a church! A church? I wasn't going to church, was I?

It was a morbid Gothic pile in considerable disrepair, more a chapel than a church, made of soiled, orange-red brick and covered with ivy, thorny briars, creepers of various kinds, and other tangled and otherwise uninviting vegetation. The chapel itself bristled with spiny turrets and pinnacles and buttresses and waterspouts and all sorts of other stuff sticking up and out and all over the place, though the overall look was of something crimped and wounded and squashed, like a porcupine run over by a car.

A small legion of tiny gargoyles and wyverns squatted on every cornice and parapet of the edifice and leered at me from above, seemingly waggling their swollen tongues at me in derision. The chapel was ensconced beneath a grove of the biggest, most gnarled, most gloomy oak trees I had ever seen — no sunlight shone through its leafy canopy, and it looked like the kind of place some Druids might be wont to loiter in and sacrifice people or whatever it was they did for fun.

I felt like one of those medieval knights — like one of those female paladins in Spenser, like Britomart or some other ... well, you know, Amazon — arriving at a sinister locale in a dark wood whose baneful inhabitant, having displaced an original but once beneficent presence, now cast a somber, despondent spell over the place.

Andy opened the LaSalle door for me, but I didn't want to get out. Even Andy would be preferable to whatever might reside inside that diabolical chapel. I even began to take some comfort in the dog hair with which, at this point, I was well enrobed. But, true to the Amazonian ideal, I meekly did what I was told. Andy accompanied me to the front door.

The great oaken door creaked open on its massive hinges. A maidservant stood there. She was tall and thin and had a pale, oval, expressionless face that, as I recall, scared the daylights out of me. The memory of it still, after all these years, scares the daylights out of me.

I looked back at Andy and pleaded that he not abandon me. I never thought I could ever be, in any sense, "attached" to Andy and actually desire his company.

In his obsequious sort of way, he promised he wouldn't go. Anyway, I could see he was well supplied with a pack of cigarettes, a newspaper, a sandwich, and a flask of something or other to tide him over. He assured me that he would wait for me right there in the driveway.

I ventured through the gloomy portals and was escorted through the vestibule and into the chapel itself. It was as dark as night inside. It might have been nice-looking once, but now its stained-glass windows were so smudged with dirt and smoke that no color or imagery shone through them. All the pews, altar, pulpit, and railings had been stripped. The apse was hidden by a long velvet curtain draped over a brass pole drawn across it. I later realized that this velvet partition marked off what must have been the sleeping chamber, our poetess's boudoir, no doubt. The sacristy at the side of the apse had been converted into a kitchen or pantry or something like that, and an eerie indigo pallor glowed through the open door that led to it. I couldn't help but think that an assortment of sooty cauldrons was bubbling away in there.

The rest of the chapel was filled with books — thousands, tens of thousands of them, piled unevenly in high, tottering columns. Among the books were bric-a-brac of various kinds; ornate Turkish shawls were draped here and there; and a mangy leopard skin — or was it the shuffled-off coil of some colossal, speckled serpent? — hung from a gothic vault that arched over the center of the chapel.

On the summit of one of the book columns reposed a human skull tipped slightly to the side and wearing a jaunty academic mortarboard cap, its golden tassel drooping over the bony forehead of the skull and disappearing into the left eye socket.

Was I afraid?

Of course I was afraid.

At the center of the chapel was a single floor lamp that shone down over a short coffee table, with a large leather armchair on one side and, on the other, a small seating apparatus of some indefinable sort with an ornate leather cushion perched unsteadily on top of it.

In that leather armchair was enshrined the poetess herself, beckoning me with a thin, long-fingered hand to approach and be seated on the smaller seating apparatus (the deplorable memory and consequent identification of which was triggered, years later on a trip to Egypt, by a camel saddle into which I had scrambled in order to have my photograph taken in front of a pyramid).

But I was glad to be seated on something, whatever it was, because I had feared I might have to spend this interview sitting cross-legged on the floor, facing a similarly cross-legged interlocutor, which, back in those days, was the obligatory ritual form for conducting intense discussions about artful matters between or among intensely artful females.

"Welcome to the Minster," she intoned with a smile as I sat down.

"To the what?" I barked with alarm.

Why a bark? Was I being affected by the dog hair that now covered my school dress? I immediately knew that I had said my first stupid thing.

"To the Minster," she trilled sweetly in her singsong voice. "That is what I call my little sanctuary here amid the darkling woods."

"I thought you said, 'Welcome to the Monster,'" I yelped back, my throat constricted with dread, my voice rising at least an octave, and I being, as I said, still more or less embodied in my canine mode. I immediately knew that I had said my second stupid thing.

"Ah, no, my dear. 'Minster'—a rather old-fashioned word for church— originally understood as a monastic church, as in Westminster Abbey. I find it rather poetic, don't you? There used to be a vicarage here, too, but it burned down many decades ago, and the chapel—a former Episcopalian chapel—was put up for sale. I bought it with my modest funds and have lived here ever since. It's the right sort of place for a recluse such as I am, a sort of modern-day anchoress, you might say." She chuckled. "Yes, I am rather fond of my little minster, under the oak grove, in the dell."

Dell?

Did she say "dell"?

Or did she say "hell"?

I didn't know what an anchoress was, and, at the moment, I didn't particularly want to know. If she was an anchoress, what was she anchored to? Was being an anchoress connected with madness in some way? When she spoke to me, she didn't look directly at me but gazed intently down at the glossy, short-legged table in front of her, as if in eager anticipation of what soon would be there.

"So, your name is Eustacia! Such a pretty name, don't you think, Elly?" she wailed tunefully, turning to consult the tall maidservant with the scary face who stood poised like a narrow, willowy specter near the sacristy door. Elly didn't reply.

My pulse quickened. I now realized that the poetess looked remarkably similar to Miss Witherspoon. She was emaciated and frail, was enfolded in layers of white lace, and smelled like witch hazel.

A sister maybe?

Or Miss Witherspoon herself?

Was I the victim of a particularly demented practical joke?

Yet Mildred wasn't around, and Elly clearly wasn't Mildred, though there were, upon reflection, some uncanny similarities. I relaxed a bit but didn't know why. There was nothing to be relaxed about.

In any event, she must have been able to read my mind, for she began to reminisce a bit about Foxglove Academy, of which she was, I quickly realized, an esteemed alumna. She extolled its lovely campus, its flowers, and "yon sylvan brakes" that bordered its fecund meadows.

Meanwhile, Elly had disappeared into the sacristy and emerged a few minutes later carrying a black-lacquered tray. It had a little railing around it, embossed with gold leaf patterns. This she brought over to the table, on which she deposited two teapots, two teacups, a platter with some diminutive sandwiches stacked in a little circle around a tuft of watercress, and another plate with five or six petit fours adorned with pink and yellow icing, each sporting a little chocolate flower on top. This was the "luncheon."

The poetess wasted no time, rather indelicately pouncing upon her teapot with her tenacious talons, pouring herself what looked like tea, and gulping down the contents of her teacup somewhat vigorously for a lady of her age and condition. She refilled the teacup at once. I should say that I found comfort in the fact that, during our entire session together, she focused a great deal more attention on that teacup than on me.

It's perhaps fair for me to say at this juncture that the poetess in question, whose identity a modicum of compunction forbids me from disclosing, was once rather well known in the American literary scene, though even by the time of my visit her poems were rapidly disappearing from the anthologies and her name from the roster of literary societies, collegiate readings, public library lectures, learned symposia, and the like.

In later decades, I never heard her name mentioned again, except by a doddering nonagenarian gentleman who insisted that we invite her to give a lecture about poetry at our local historical society, being unaware, apparently, that the Minster, and the world at large, had become bereft of its esteemed anchoress a good thirty years earlier.

It's also fair for me to say that my interview with the poetess went reasonably well and didn't last very long. She was a pleasant lady, after all, and the more she drank of that tea, the more pleasant she became. There were a number of long silences, of course—we really didn't have much to say to each other. I nibbled now and then at one of the sandwiches—a salty meat spread of indefinable provenance had been wiped thinly on spongy slivers of white bread and garnished with a bit of mayonnaise and some parsley.

When it occurred to me that the meat spread might conceivably be tinned dog food, a not altogether inappropriate comestible for the occasion, given my disposition and accouterments, I immediately desisted from my nibbling.

I subsequently popped an entire petit four into my mouth but discovered a hardened, stale, quite possibly archaeological piece of cake, which my teeth got stuck in and which I had to loosen up and wash down with the hot tea. I had the rather strong temptation thereafter to lick the chocolate flowers off the top of each petit four, having no further interest in what lay beneath, but my scruples, as well as my fear of the maidservant, got the best of me.

The poetess didn't touch any of the food. My tea, I must say, was very good: steamy and aromatic. Its fragrance blended harmoniously with the witch hazel emanating from the other side of the table and with the scent of the poetess's tea, which I recognized was not too dissimilar from what was exuded now and then from Andy's uniform and the little flask he carried around with him.

Toward the conclusion of our interview, we did finally—and briefly—broach the subject of poetry. As if on cue, she began to warble, in a quavering but somewhat slurred plainchant, the litany of encomia, which in her prime, I was sure, she would recite to inspire and captivate audiences at high-literary revival meetings all across the United States.

She extolled the lonely but prophetic role of poets as they confront the vast forces of darkness and chaos that threaten human destiny. With their imagination, poets create the face of the earth and the meaning of life. They show to the rest of mankind that the human soul is the origin of all things, the maker of its own conditions, the font of all that is vital and significant.

With their genius for figurative thinking, poets trace the mysterious lineaments of eternal consciousness. A poem confers order upon the howling and brutal whorl of insensate reality. A poem is the ultimate victory that humanity can achieve over disorder and meaninglessness. It consoles, it comforts, it reveals the splendiferous and emergent life force that is in all of us.

I interrupted, "But … I mean … what if the poem is a bad poem?"

She glared at me, a little unsteadily. It was the first time she actually looked at me with her small, watery eyes.

I continued, "What if the poem itself is disordered and meaningless?" I immediately knew that I had said my third stupid thing.

Her head wobbled just a bit. Meeting my objection, she declaimed slowly, shakily, but solemnly: "A poem, my dear Eustacia, can never be bad. A poem, my dear Eustacia, is always and ever, nothing less than … nothing less than … a triumph … yes, a triumph of the human spirit."

Her head tilted abruptly to one side, her eyes closed, her mouth gaped. A tiny rivulet of spittle glittered its way down through the wrinkles and folds on one side of her chin. Almost at once the tall maidservant was standing at my side, as if she had been able to predict the precise moment at which this untimely cessation of our dialogue would occur. She informed me that it would now be best to leave.

I have to say that, at the time, I felt intensely sorry for my poetess, partially mummified and precociously immured in this defrocked and desecrated sepulcher, alone, wasted, disconsolate in her declining years, except for the illusory warmth induced by her surreptitious tea and by a coverlet of platitudes that I regarded then — and still do now — as tragically inane.

But I was also glad to go.

Believe it or not, it was a relief to see Andy. He was drooped over the front fender of the car, one leg up on the running board and newspapers spread out over the engine hood. He was smoking and reading the sports news. He was startled and probably upset to see me emerge so soon, for I was interrupting one of those long, lethargic intervals of inactivity that made his job so palatable.

He jumped up from his languorous pose. In his pale green uniform with the row of brass buttons, he looked like a garter snake wiggling spasmodically when suddenly exposed to light. I opened the door and crept into the back seat of the car without waiting for him to go through his chauffeur's routine with its simulated obeisance.

He had just climbed into the driver's seat when I cried out, "Andy!"

"Yes, ma'am," he grunted. (I didn't know what this thus-far-unprecedented "ma'am" business was, but no matter.)

"We can't — we just can't — go back to the school so early. I'll end up in study hall, having to listen to that harridan virtuoso blasting her way through the *Moonlight Sonata*!"

I don't think he understood the allusion, but he was in no hurry to return to the school either. "Comin' to think of it, ma'am, there's a county fair goin' on not far from here. Maybe we could go there. There's some great boxin' matches planned for this afternoon in the main tent."

"Whatever you want," I shouted back. "Just get me out of this damned 'dell' and keep me as far away as possible from 'yon sylvan brakes' of Foxglove Hall."

The car lurched into action with a stupendous roar, bolted forward — practically hurling me through the back window — and screeched to a dead stop — catapulting me forward so that I was about to collide with the front seat when another sudden acceleration flung me rearward again. Did he treat his dog this way when it occupied this seat? Had he misunderstood my reference to "brakes"? With a few more equally enthralling stops and goes, we were on our way.

But to boxing matches!

I'm not really sure why I consented to go along with this. I had never been interested in boxing before, nor have I been interested in boxing since. And I can tell you, even with my limited experience of the sport, that the sort of boxing that went on at county fairs in those gilded ages of yesteryear — so celebrated in Christmas cards and Norman Rockwell prints and other assorted cozy illustrations — was nothing like what anyone thinks boxing is nowadays. Those were punching orgies: no rules, no decorum, no scoring, no defense, attack only, no judges, no refereeing of any sort. Whoever was still standing in the end, whoever was more or less still alive in the end, won. Of course, I didn't know that yet, sitting there in back of the LaSalle covered with dog hair.

We arrived at the county fair. It was the first time I'd ever been to a county fair. As you probably know, one visit to a county fair in New England is enough to question seriously the authenticity of claims made about the so-called Puritan foundations of New England culture. I won't go into the details of this, but just imagine a county fair as — I hate to say this — Andy written large, Andy written on a cosmological scale, the apotheosis of all that Andy is and does.

I soon found myself hurried through a maze of rancid cooking stalls, garish game booths, and grotesque inducements to sordid entertainments of various kinds.

The main tent reeked of cigarettes, cigars, beer, leather, and sweat. A thousand noisy and disheveled men in shirtsleeves and a handful of women capped by mounds of what was called back then "peroxide" hair milled around the boxing ring. As attendants hosed off the surface of the ring, pink, slimy streams slid off its side and into the sawdust below. Other attendants moved through the crowd, selling leaflet programs, hot dogs, pretzels, and beer. Small circles of men clustered here and there, and what to my eyes in those days looked like a lot of money was passing back and forth among them.

Andy was in heaven; he informed me that we were fortunate to arrive just in time for the big fight of the afternoon. A local favorite named Buckthorn was about to square off against a contender from Quebec with the unlikely name of Pierre Le Doux. Andy grabbed hold of my right arm, and after a frenzy of shoving, burrowing, bending, swearing, elbowing, twisting, and squeezing, we found ourselves sitting on a front bench, right next to the boxing ring. What would Miss Witherspoon think if she saw me here! Or, more pertinently, what would Mildred think! (Somehow, I didn't think Mildred would mind at all!)

The match commenced. Buckthorn was introduced, to the cheers of the crowd. He bounced around the ring, waving his hands over his head and basking in the hysterical applause he evoked. He was physically massive with curly auburn hair. Pierre, by contrast, was greeted with boos and catcalls. He was clearly the villain of the match. He was a smaller man, very dark and slightly stooped, with a black moustache. He didn't parade around the ring but went directly to his corner, glowered at Buckthorn, and waited for the match to begin. The bell rang.

In a way, there's nothing much to report about what happened initially. The two went at each other, savagely slugging away, though at first I didn't look. The sounds were quite enough — the smacking and slamming that was going on, the biffs and puffs and gasps, the splat of sweat and spit, the growling and moaning. The crowd was bellowing for what I presumed to be the expeditious and irreversible dismemberment of Pierre, the "Frenchie," as he was being called, whom Buckthorn was urged to "tear to pieces," "rip to shreds," and "smash into smithereens" (among sundry other colorful expressions that common decency constrains me from mentioning).

I must admit, however, that the crowd did indeed wax poetical with its abundance of rich culinary metaphors — a few I recall are "slice," "chop," "grind," "mash," "cream," "scald," "dice," "fry," "crunch," "hash," and "skewer." One patron apparently desired to see Pierre delivered up to him as a platter of French fries, while another called for — albeit unseasonably — the reduction of Pierre into mincemeat.

When, finally, I began to watch, Pierre did seem to be getting the worst of it. Buckthorn was relentlessly hounding him around the ring, pounding him against the ropes, pummeling his head so hard that it looked like, indeed, it could come flying off at any moment. If you can imagine — to continue the culinary metaphors — an electric eggbeater having its accustomed way with an egg, you might get an idea of what was going on.

Was this "the howling and brutal whorl of insensate reality" of which the poetess of the Minster had so magisterially spoken?

Or was this an inimitable conference of poets glorying in their metaphorical acclamations?

The crowd was ecstatic, clamoring for blood. And blood is what it got, or at least it's what I got, for Buckthorn sunk a thunderous blow into Pierre's nose that sent a spray of blood flying out of the ring. It landed all over me, over my face, my school uniform, my dog hair, everything. I pulled a handkerchief out of my pocket and wiped some of it out of my eyes. The handkerchief was streaked with blood.

I looked up at the ring again. Pierre was down, his head (still attached, as I noted thankfully, to his body) lay right in front of me on the floor of the ring, his face bleeding, his swollen eyes looking shocked and anxiously into my eyes. The crowd shrieked and clapped and stomped its feet.

What happened then I shall never understand, and I shall not try to explain. Suddenly Pierre was me, and I was Pierre. Suddenly Buckthorn and his cacophonous retinue of supporters were Foxglove Hall, were Miss Witherspoon and Mildred, were the poetess and her spectral maidservant, were the study hall and the cantankerous pianist and everything else that made, and was making, my life disagreeable.

Suddenly I discovered my authentic poetic voice—yes, I became poet and Amazon all rolled into one. Suddenly it was my sacred task to achieve victory over disorder and meaninglessness in the universe.

I jumped to my feet, pressed the handkerchief into Pierre's face, and peeled it off again. An imprint of blood and sweat was left behind on the white fabric.

I cried, "Go get 'im, Pierre. Make … make … make *pâté* out of him!" (I was speaking figuratively here, of course, and hence speaking just like a poet, though it was a pretty poor effort, I acknowledge; but, trying to be poetic at the moment while simultaneously perpetuating the gastronomical expostulations of the crowd, it was the best I could do. I also thought Pierre might, in any case, appreciate the ethnic twist I gave it.) Then I added, "Remember above all, Pierre … remember the triumph of the human spirit!"

Andy whispered sharply at me from the side, "He don't get none of that, ma'am! He's a Frenchie! He don't know no English!"

I hadn't considered that technicality; nor did I have time, at the moment, to reflect on Andy's string of double negatives. But I had to communicate with Pierre. For the first time in my life, I actually wanted to communicate in French. In French! Yes … even after all those horrible verb forms! "Pierre … Pierre," I shouted in stumbling, hesitant words, "remember … *souviens-toi* … (did I get that right? no matter) … *souviens-toi surtout du triomphe de l'esprit humaine!*"

A second later Pierre bounded back on his feet. He plunged at Buckthorn, head lowered like a bull, driving in at him from beneath, bludgeoning him with left and right hooks and uppercuts. Fifteen seconds later a stunned Buckthorn crumpled to the mat, permanently, as far as that match was concerned.

I hate to say it, of course (it sounds so callous), but he did look somewhat like an uneven clump of a most unappetizing *pâté de campagne*, pockmarked here and there by a swollen bruise that resembled a dark black truffle.

The crowd broke into a riot; members of the audience scrambled up into the ring, trampling the inert body of Buckthorn and attacking Pierre. They soon found themselves punched over the ropes and into the swirling throng, their heads limp and limbs floundering as Pierre engaged in combat with what seemed like the entire audience.

One suitably walloped patron (or poltroon?) was entangled momentarily in the ropes, where he quivered like a fly freshly caught in a web, then flipped over and plopped down into the sawdust right next to me. I took that opportunity, being in high poetical dudgeon, as I was (to say nothing of my newly invigorated Amazonian need for decisive action), to deliver a sharp little figurative kick to his ribs.

"Figure that!" I shouted at him. (Actually, the kick wasn't so figurative, and it wasn't so little either, but one tries to contribute whatever one can). At this point, seeing me gearing up for another not-quite-so-figurative act of self-expression, Andy must have considered it judicious to haul me out of there.

Meanwhile a police escort had thrust its way through the crowd and was helping to rescue Pierre from his besieged redoubt on the ring. As he climbed over the ropes, Pierre turned to me, smiled as best he could through that battered face, and waved. I felt happy about that—immensely happy, to tell you the truth.

Andy managed to snake me out safely through the thick crowd, though some fans were blaming me for what had happened and were becoming hostile to me. Many in the crowd had lost a lot of money on that match, and a few lucky ones were cleaning up quite royally indeed. But the few who dared to confront me were quickly intimidated by the blood and dog hair, as well they might be—I would have been scared of me, too, under those circumstances.

In any event, we escaped from the main tent but had time to stop along the fairway on the way back to the parking lot and to purchase hot dogs, dripping with mustard and sauerkraut, a bag of pretzels, and orangeade. I was famished. Andy diluted (diluted?) his orangeade with whatever was left in that flask of his. He also bought a hot dog to take home to his real dog. It was a wonderful drive back to the school, full of sudden lurches and screeching, inexplicable stops.

We returned to Foxglove Hall by the dining hour. Andy garaged the LaSalle and scuttled back, in his own distinctly inelegant way, to whatever scraggy den at the edge of the campus it was that sequestered his mutt, jug, and cot. He had had a good afternoon of it and was content, and I think I had acquired a small amount—a very small amount, I assure you—of respect for him. At least I wouldn't be so ready, in future dorm discussions, to belittle him as much as I had done in the past. After all, we now shared a secret together—a secret I had no intention to divulge until … well, not until now (forty years later, is it?).

I hurried back to the dorm to change out of my ruined apparel before anyone noticed the curious red splotches and the copious dog hair all over it. I didn't succeed, as I'll shortly inform you, in my purpose. In any event, it wasn't easy to get rid of that clothing without anyone discovering it, but I did manage to do that finally. As for the handkerchief—you may find this a bit morbid, I'm afraid to say—I have it tucked away somewhere, with the dried-up imprint of Pierre's blood still appealing for sympathy and support.

I must report, however, that, on my way back to the dorm, it was my ill luck to run into Miss Witherspoon and Mildred as they took their usual early evening constitutional around the campus. I should have been more wary than I was, being familiar with this routine of theirs, and I did consider sprinting for refuge into a patch of "yon sylvan brakes," but it was too late. They came to a stop and stood there, arm-in-arm, staring at me and being as welcome and endearing to me as would the sight of a gorilla and a baboon out for a promenade together.

"O, Eustacia, my dear, how lovely to see you. I do hope your visit was all you had hoped it to be," Miss Witherspoon piped. Then, squinting through the mellow twilight glow, she noticed my attire. "But it looks as if there's been some mishap—your school dress, it's all …"

"… besprinkled with the blushing roses of life and love," I chanted — figuratively, of course, poet that I was. "I have had the most wonderful day."

"Did you hear that, Mildred? She has had the most wonderful day. Isn't that delightful?" She glanced sweetly up at Mildred, who grumbled in return, "Indeed, it is so, Miss Witherspoon; it is most delightful, indeed."

Mildred slid her cadaverous eyes through their narrow slits and peered at me suspiciously. Mildred knew blood when she saw it.

"It was just … Oh, Miss Witherspoon," I cried as I turned to run off to the dorm, "it was … just as you said … it was a triumph of the human spirit after all."

Old Gander's Weeping

Spring melt-back,
    Maples in red bud,
April woods
    Still sharp as winter in the notches,
Mud on fields and sunny snow —
    That's when we buried her
Down at Burrow's Corner.
    Her folks from Wonalancet came to help;
Anyhow, we got the sugarin' done.
    Barn needs mending, too, 'fore autumn.
'Ought to buck the pine behind the saphouse —
    It fell last January in the storm.
Pine's not like oak, not like ash:
    Pine won't bear grief.

I still can see her, though,
    On the high-deck of that old paddlewheeler,
Steaming its way up Winnipesaukee.
    She saw me; we got married.
She came like she went:
    Pert, and hale, and sudden,
As a hummingbird in a woodland clearing.
    She liked Christmas best of all:
Corn-roasts, dancing at the grange,
    Sledding on the frosty hills
About the verge of evening.
    But the birds are sad this summer.
No raking blueberries either;
    They tumble, ungathered, to the ground.
The flowers wilt among the ragweed.
    No herbs hang from the rafters of the porch.
At high-mowing,
    She'd bring the rig up from the valley,
Fetching fresh johnnycake and cider—
    The boys loved that, resting by the brook.
I was so proud:
    She had more living in her
Than fifty acres put to corn.
    Someday I'd bring my rig down, too,
Down to Burrow's Corner.
    I think she needs me now.
The nights grow colder.
    We'd sleep together as we did,
Beneath the lid of earthen days,
    Beneath the winter moon.

Berceuse

Aged rafters bend and sigh
    Beneath the frosty hush of winter.
Cinnamon and chestnuts,
   Apples, wheels of cheddar cheese,
Repose within the larder.
    The latchkey has been turned.
An earthen crock of warm molasses,
   The kneaded bread beside the hearth
Lend fragrance to the midnight hour.
    The household sleeps.
I wedge a block of knarry wood
    into the flames;
Sparks brighten the darkness.
    Ruddy frets of firelight
Burnish an old brass ewer,
   A pewter pot, and ladle in the corner.
On the gnarled-oak bedstead,
   The eiderdown stirs softly.
I reflect upon the heft of seasons,
   Voices in long twilights by the fire,
Infants bedded down then,
   Like seeds in the warm, fertile earth.
They sleep soundly.
   I would have them prosper . . .
    . . . ripen into the fullness of all things.

The lantern shall burn late tonight;
    A blackened inkhorn rests upon the table.
Outside the cabin windows
    Spruce boughs shimmer in the icy moonlight.
Reindeer herds are moving now
    Over silent tundra and arctic forests.
And dark-cloven fiords,
      snowy spurs of wintry oceans,
Slumber in the starlit robe of night.

Leander Baxter
and the Foxtowne Races

Leander Baxter, all my sports-car-racing friends would be quick to agree, was possibly the ugliest man who has ever lived. His head was shaped like a clothes hanger held up vertically and on its side: it was narrow and was flat in the back, and, in front, both a receding forehead and a nonexistent chin slanted backward from an immense arched beak of a nose. The top of his head rose to something about as close to a point as you can get, and there a single tuft of hair stuck obliquely out of a mass of hardened furrows and sclerotic veins.

The rest of his body was a short, scrawny bag of bones dangled loosely from that head. No belt ever designed could be so meager as to fasten anything around that waist of his, so his baggy pants were supported by a set of suspenders that hung from the tiny spurs of his shoulders — though, to be sure, his pants were sometimes also secured by what looked like the snippet of a worn-out automotive fan belt tied into a knot at his waist.

For all this, however, Leander was not without a certain charm, if I may be permitted to stretch the meaning of that term a bit: he was a cheerful, good-humored, gentle sort of fellow. And though his smile revealed little more than a mouthful of long, yellow, rodent-like teeth, he had two little emerald eyes that glittered and bulged when he spoke in that twangy cockney accent of his, and that gave him a certain curious animation, especially when, as he was so often prone to do, he stretched out his suspenders with his spidery fingers and allowed them to snap back against his shrunken chest.

One other feature of his commanded attention, and not infrequently solicited a respect well beyond what anyone was, at least initially, ready to offer: his forearms, usually visible because Leander always wore his shirts rolled up to the elbow, were built like Italian salamis — just as thick, just as mottled and ruddy, just as, I should add, peppery and sharp for anyone willing to risk the force of their thrust. For his fingers could contract into bony hammers of unbelievable hardness, and, at the end of those powerful forearms, they became weapons that many regretted having ever provoked.

That scene, I'm sorry to say, was a familiar one — or at least it was familiar to drivers, mechanics, team owners, sundry camp followers, and other riffraff who frequented the racing-car hangouts along the East Coast, especially in Florida. I said I was sorry about this, and I'm sorry that there was something about Leander Baxter that made him the target of any bellicose stranger who happened to be passing through and who happened to cross Leander's path at an inopportune moment — inopportune, I might add, in the final analysis, for the stranger and not for Leander.

But I'm not sorry about the inevitable outcome, for it was invariably amusing, invariably welcome to all those who had the good fortune to observe it. In fact, there was no small amount of jealousy among the habitués of the aforementioned hangouts as to who had been privileged to see what and when and how.

Imagine, for a moment, our bellicose stranger wandering into a bar and becoming gradually soused beyond what's prudent for anyone, in such circumstances, to become. Imagine him fixing his hostile glare on the diminutive, warped figure of Leander Baxter and getting annoyed that such a disfigured exemplar of the hominid species could get away with existing and could, moreover, under such obviously adverse circumstances, dare to exhibit some traces of relative contentment, especially when things are not going too well in the stranger's own hopelessly and undeservedly befuddled life. He approaches this unlikely creature and proceeds to rough him up a bit — you know, just shake him around a little, call him a revolting little creep, or whatever befits the more or less insidious predilections of our bully-boy gentleman at the time.

What follows needs to be seen — or rather, needs to be heard — to be believed (one rarely sees it, for it occurs rapidly and without warning). The relative serenity of the hangout is shattered by an unearthly, high-pitched sound—a snapping sound of the most extraordinary intensity and precision, so sharp indeed that it makes your own head involuntarily whip backward. It sounds as if someone has slapped a bamboo shaft violently against a table. Then our hapless stranger either turns around and walks out of the bar, or else, without waiting for that particular formality, sinks in a heap to the floor, right then and there. In any case, he doesn't get far before collapsing. He's lucky if the tip of his chin hasn't been broken clear off the end of his jaw and is not sagging loosely in the flap of skin just beneath it.

Leander's aim is just that precise and just that powerful. His bony hammer of a fist rises in a lightning-fast uppercut, like the piston of a Formula One car, with the palm of his hand upward, as in a softball pitch. It's not the knuckles but the part of the fingers below the knuckles that makes contact with the tip of the chin. It's a blow that maximizes all the leverage and all the strength of his right forearm. Needless to say, there's never any further contact. Leander meanwhile, unperturbed and imperturbable as ever, returns to whatever gin concoction he's been nursing for the last half hour or so and gives the incident no further thought.

I guess we all regard it as something of a favor to have seen this sort of occurrence at least once in our lives—it gives us status; it places us within a particularly noble niche in the sports-car hierarchy to have been a witness to one of Leander's notorious knockdowns; but the greatest privilege of all was to have seen it happen at the banquet dinner that followed the Foxtowne races, and the observers of that event constitute, quite frankly, a kind of aristocracy to this day among their less-favored peers.

There Leander Baxter knocked down his man, as he was accustomed to do; but in doing so, he succeeded—unintentionally, of course—in knocking down the pretensions of an entire city. The supremely pompous and parvenu municipality of Foxtowne fell at the edge of Leander's bony fist. It was a marvel to see, and the aforesaid municipality has never, at least to my knowledge, recovered.

Leander was famous in quite another way as well. He could, if given sufficient time, a good place to work, plenty of solitude, and several cases of a good-quality British gin, transform any automotive wreck you gave him into a reasonably well-functioning racing car, if not into a contraption of demonic speed and dexterity—and I use the term "contraption" quite deliberately here, for such creations, however capable of the most stunning feats, were as deformed and ungainly as their unfortunate creator.

Some people—people prominent in the world of sports-car racing—thought Leander was perhaps the best automotive mechanic they'd ever known; but this was a difficult hypothesis to test. He didn't like to work with new cars, he detested any kind of team organization, and the whole commercial side of racing was, for some reason, anathema to him. As a result, he was never connected, at least officially, with any of the spectacularly successful teams and car firms, and efforts to recruit him into a position commensurate with his abilities were always tenaciously resisted.

Consequently, it was difficult to assess the extent of his skills. He was more interested in turning junk into speed.

Rumor has it that when he lived in Coventry, England, during the war, he was given the job of taking variously damaged military aircraft and making them fly again. It's said that he was very good at this. It's said that he was the only one who was good at this. After the war, when he became a racing-car mechanic, this sort of perverse talent was transferred to automobiles. But, as good as he was, no major racing team could ever interest him, and no brand-name car attracted his attention ... unless it already had the status of scrap metal conferred officiously upon it by someone who should, presumably, know what he was talking about. This is where Leander came into his own; he was the master of desperate cases. And yes, he could make them work—work beautifully—for a while.

In the early 1950s, he immigrated to the United States.

Rumor had it that he suffered some tragedy early in the war, especially as the result of the great bombing raid on Coventry during the Battle of Britain. He kept his former life a secret, however, though on rare occasions, when deep in his cups, his face suddenly drawn and haggard and his glittering emerald eyes momentarily dulled by some inscrutable suffering, he might, quite unexpectedly, be heard to mumble, half to himself, half to his ill-prepared listeners, "In Coventry, durin' the war ..." But that's as far as he ever got. He would slosh the remains of his gin around the bottom of his glass and mumble again, "In Coventry, durin' the war ..." There was never anything more than that.

No one presumed to press him on the matter, to ask him to continue, to plead for an explanation. We all supposed that perhaps a once reasonably presentable young man was dragged from the smoking ruins of an exploded hanger, transformed into the gnarled and broken human corpus we all could identify to this day as poor Leander.

Whatever military hospital he'd ended up in for a while had not been able to do for him what he'd been able to do for those wrecked aircraft he'd so gallantly and skillfully put into service once more. Or maybe it had. No one had ever claimed that Leander's salvaging operations looked very good, but they certainly worked. The situation with Leander himself was, unfortunately, all too analogous.

Now, I should point out that Leander's arrangement with Bill Hennessy, Palm Beach multimillionaire and international *bon vivant*, was ideal. Bill was a tall, portly, barrel-chested man with wide, roundish cheeks that curled up into large apples when he smiled his cherubic grin. Hennessy was interested in racing cars — that is, in both the cars themselves and in ferreting them, at very high speeds, around racetracks in the fellowship of like-minded colleagues; but though he was enormously wealthy, he wasn't interested in paying exorbitant sums to buy expensive equipment. Furthermore, he fancied that he had a certain ability to design cars and was always dreaming of making some sort of hybrid automobile that would stun the world by combining, in some extraordinary way, the parts of many different well-known racing breeds.

This suited Leander perfectly: he could collect the parts, most of them bent and burnt from whatever catastrophe had put them out of commission; work on them at leisure in the roomy Spanish hacienda-style garage in Palm Beach that Hennessy let him use and that had a small apartment attached where Leander could live; submit to the verbose, but luckily infrequent, discourses delivered by Hennessy on his hybrid dream car of the future while limitless bottles of gin were opened, emptied, and tossed into a mound of hollow motor-oil cans and rusty auto parts; and, several times a year, roll out of the garage some patchwork monstrosity that was bound to outrun anything that you wanted to put up against it, at least until Hennessy, in his inimitable way, had destroyed it — a feat usually accomplished by the fifth lap of any race he entered.

For Hennessy, if I may be permitted the liberty of passing on gossip that everybody knows already, destroyed everything he touched: the theatrical shows he sponsored always closed a day or two after opening night; his marriages foundered, one after another, leaving behind a costly wake of alimonies; his multitudinous hunting and fishing expeditions had a singular way of never producing the desired quarry (it always got away, for some, usually absurd, reason); his harebrained schemes to increase his already enormous inheritance generally resulted in its sizable, if momentary, reduction, even as it enriched every high-level confidence man (and woman) operating within the New York–Palm Beach axis; and his car racing was a series of disasters.

Yet he found all of this very amusing.

Hennessy reveled in failure with an enthusiasm and a *joie de vivre* as intense as his equally bedeviled and now deceased father had reveled in success. In fact, every failure was the source of some hilarious joke that Hennessy could tell at a dinner party. He had lots and lots of these jokes. And when he guided the smoking remains of a racing car into its first and final pit stop, its clutch ground to powder, its gears stripped, and its brakes practically red hot, he laughed deliriously with triumph as he yanked off his goggles, revealing an island of crinkled white skin and jocular blue eyes in a face besmirched with oily fumes.

After all, who did lead the pack — I mean really lead the pack — until the car came apart?

Hennessy was one of those men who love machines but don't understand them, don't understand that they can endure only so much stress and no more, and consequently are excessively brutal with them, quickly pushing them to a premature demise.

Leander, I think, was probably always just a bit depressed by this outcome, even though he knew in advance that it would happen. But that's when he would really go to work — no longer on Bill Hennessy's car, but on everybody else's, wandering up and down along the pit-stops of the racing teams and pitching in to help them out, often solving problems with a speed they couldn't match and putting their own cars back on the course in crack running order. Oddly, this skill was never envied or resented by other mechanics. He intervened only when he was asked to, he carried out the task with humility, and he walked away without expecting anything in return. Least of all was he looking for someone's job. Hence, his arrangement with Hennessy was ideal. There was nothing else he wanted.

Now, all of this brings me back to Foxtowne.

Some cities, like some people, grow faster than they should, and it gives them odd ideas about themselves. The municipal elders of Foxtowne, at the pinnacle of its glory—which is to say, before it was brought down by Leander—decided it was time for the city to make a name for itself; after all, it was, of late, no longer a mid-Florida shantytown surrounded by vast snake-infested swamps and inhabited by a few dozen contentious, tobacco-chewing alligator hunters.

In its own perception, it had grown, it had blossomed—if I might here be allowed to invoke a florid rhetoric befitting the object of hypothetical praise—into ever the most exquisitely burg-like of all burgs in this burgish world, with boulevards and highways, fast-food strips and shopping malls (though without the best stores, to be sure—a problem certain to remedied, however), and acres of tiny houses and patterned driveways stretching endlessly over the Floridian savannas and baking like little tin pastry trays under the remorseless Florida sun.

To celebrate its transformation into a major municipality, the Foxtowne elders decided to add an "e" to its original name of Foxtown and to build a gigantic, and utterly pretentious, recreational center with a cheaply constructed banquet hall as its crown of glory. But the city elders, having achieved the erection of what was, after all, a monument to themselves, conceded that there was one final problem that needed to be solved. No one used the banquet hall, because no one came to Foxtowne. Somehow the town needed to become justly celebrated throughout the world.

Well, like some other Floridian townships, Foxtowne had nearby a series of landing strips used as Air Force supply dumps in the past and now abandoned to clumps of swamp grass, scorpions, and waddling possum families. Like these other townships, it conceived the idea that it could convert these strips to some novel purpose: Why not use them as the basis for what might turn eventually into an international racing track? After all, world-famous Sebring, not too far to the north of Foxtowne, had originally done something of the kind and had made of itself an astounding success. Certainly, Foxtowne could do the same.

But it would start off modestly—that is to say, with minimum investment of either city money or city intelligence, both of which, it may be said, were in short supply—and invite the Palmetto Sports Car Association of Southern Florida to hold its annual weekend convocation at what would be touted as a new and exciting racing facility. The two days of events would be highlighted by a grand banquet on Saturday evening specifically for the racing teams in the magnificent new banquet hall.

Frankly, I don't know what made the governing board of the Palmetto Sports Car Association accept this proposal without looking into it more carefully than it did. That it holds its biannual meetings in the cocktail lounge of the Sunny Vistas Hotel in Miami didn't help matters too much. Anyway, whatever firm the Foxtowne elders hired to do the public relations pitch did a great job; I understand that no one from the firm had ever actually been to Foxtowne or ever planned to go there; but they sold it as heaven on earth, and the gradually more and more inebriated members of the governing board believed every word of it.

As a result, in late spring of that year—an inauspicious time, for that's when Florida begins to get too hot for an event of this kind (or, arguably, for an event of any kind)—hundreds of racing cars on trailers and thousands of sports-car devotees descended on the hitherto obscure little city of Foxtowne. Hennessy was among them, driving a large, well-equipped RV camper and towing behind him a trailer with Leander's most recent fabrication—a bashed-up version of a Lotus with a dozen parts borrowed from other cars packed variously into it. Hennessy had hoped to enter it at Sebring, but it was finished too late for that, and the Foxtowne event, though largely an amateur affair, would be a good testing ground. Leander was somewhere in the back of the camper, taking a nap because, as he often did, he slept during the day and worked at night.

In one sense, the details of Hennessy's race were largely unexceptional. As usual, he took off like a rocket but destroyed the car before the third lap by running into a cinder block that had been carelessly left by the side of the track and that others were swerving to avoid and that Hennessy, for some odd reason, was convinced he could clear if he was going fast enough, though his Lotus hybrid was the lowest-slung car he'd ever driven. The block ripped out the bottom of the car, and it returned, sputtering and bleeding oil, to its pit stop with its entrails dragging along the ground like some wounded and savagely gored picador's horse in a Spanish arena.

Hennessy was bellowing with laughter, as if he'd just had the funniest experience of his life. Apparently, he thought somehow that the car would jump over the block as if the car actually were a horse and he was racing it in a steeplechase event. Leander was noticeably disconcerted by such idiocy, as he always was; but that was the price he paid for the freedom he wanted. He muttered something and walked away to see what he could do for other drivers and their cars.

The cinder block was, in its own way, merely an exemplary case, if I may use such a lofty expression to describe such a paltry thing, of what the whole weekend was like. The racetrack was a horror. Failure to consult the right people, coupled with the determination to spend the minimum of money, had left behind a clumsily demarcated obstacle course, filled with dangerous potholes, bumps in the corroded concrete surface, right-angle turns almost impossible to negotiate at any speed, bad visibility, and sections of slippery molds and fungi where the original landing strip had become partially immersed in the surrounding swamps.

Animals wandered onto the track at will: one old hound dog was killed early in the race, and an entire possum family was reduced into a furry blood slick upon which cars skidded and swung out of control. One car avoided hitting a miniature Key deer by leaving the track and swerving off like a swamp craft over an adjacent wetland until it sank finally into the muck and fronds, leaving no trace behind except for intermittent bubbles popping up through the mud and a swearing driver jumping up and down and frantically pulling leeches off his drenched racing jacket. He was lucky; he didn't have to deal with the deadly water moccasin that yet another driver noted coiled up sleepily in his bucket seat just as he was about to hoist himself into the cockpit.

Needless to say, accident followed accident, and fortunately none of them were too serious because the good city fathers had provided almost nothing in the way of emergency fire or medical equipment. Further, tickets to watch the race were expensive, and this expense was compounded by additional fees that spectators had to pay to move from one section of the track to another, which fees were again charged if they retraced their steps. Getting to and from the limited and utterly lamentable toilet facilities under these circumstances could turn out to be a costly venture, so much so that gradually even the most obsessively modest among the day's sports-car aficionados found themselves drifting off to nearby clumps of mangrove or other barely adequate cover in order to heed the call of nature.

Off the track, things were even worse. Foxtowne wasn't prepared for the huge influx of people who planned to spend at least one or two nights there. Camping areas had been set up, but they were situated on such poorly drained land that countless cars and campers sank into the wet ground and had to be pulled out by the curiously abundant tow trucks available around the perimeters of the campgrounds. Pegging tents in such marshy terrain was out of the question; sanitary facilities were absent; and at night clouds of mosquitoes arose from the swamps, making the barbecues and other traditional festivities of the racing weekend utterly impracticable.

In town, businesses raised their prices to the highest level they thought they could get without causing a riot. Meanwhile, the local police force, reinforced for the weekend by droves of officers brought in from surrounding towns and by a group of not altogether reputable citizens deputized especially for the event, managed to post No Parking signs in every location it was necessary to park, as well as to create on every road leading to the racecourse special speed limits that were impossible not to violate unless you were piloting a three-year-old's tricycle along such a road with at least one of your legs in a cast.

The result of these measures, added to a traffic-control system as chaotic as it was rigidly enforced, was a level of police harassment that quite defied anyone's memory of an occasion that could equal it. Furthermore, the ramshackle and as yet unrenovated Foxtowne courthouse, an unsavory relic of a juridical past better left unremembered, remained open throughout the weekend and late into the night, staffed by a succession of magistrates, each more surly and imperious than the one who just vacated it. Local authorities wanted to be sure that no one left town without paying their parking and speeding tickets. Accordingly, throughout the weekend a parade of racing fans was dragooned through the unpainted hallways of the sweltering building, often made to wait for hours, threatened with being clapped into a crowded cell if the charges were contested, and forced to pay an inevitably hefty fine before having their impounded cars returned to them.

On the racetrack, matters were not helped by a violent thunderstorm that passed over the region in the late afternoon. In the steamy aftermath of the storm, the first day's final race was conducted by a few dispirited drivers who no longer cared what was happening. When the checkered flag was brought down on the final race, a young, unknown driver in a Jaguar glided into victory, his car and his energies, much to his own surprise, being among the few that survived the day. He apparently didn't mind spinning and sliding around huge palm fronds, plastic trash bags, and Styrofoam food receptacles scattered all over the track by the storm and left there by the negligent maintenance crew (who, in fact, had already gone home).

In a damp, scarcely noticed little ceremony, he was awarded a monstrous, gold-painted plastic trophy for his pains, presented along with a wet, lip-sticky smooch from a local beauty who sported possibly the loftiest bouffant of peroxide-blonde hair the world has ever seen and who represented the Foxtowne Chamber of Commerce.

He also was forced to listen to a long harangue from the mayor of Foxtowne extolling the virtues of his municipality in setting up such a public-spirited event, while a photographer from the *Foxtowne Bugle* snapped several photographs and took down some notes. He asked the victor if he was deeply grateful to the good people of Foxtowne for all that they had done for him (this gratitude obviously having not been volunteered); the victor mumbled something that neither the reporter nor anyone else heard, but the reporter wrote down a gushing reply of his own invention to flatter the readers of Sunday's newspaper. During all of this, the spectators drifted back to their soggy encampments and prepared to settle down for the night.

The next day, the rally, the gymkhana, and the acceleration tests were supposed to take place.

None of this happened. It couldn't happen, not after Leander had done his … his job, or whatever you want to call it.

The paramount event for the weekend, of course, was to be the banquet on Saturday evening. It had been heralded as a black-tie affair, and wet, exhausted, soiled drivers and their mechanics found themselves in the awkward situation of struggling into rented white dinner jackets and the accompanying apparel without showers or appropriate places to change. Gradually they began to converge on the banquet hall itself, mainly on foot.

The facility was only about a mile away from the track, and they realized that to drive might take an hour or more as they were marshaled by traffic control along some circuitous route that would wind inexplicably through the entire city, as well as possibly incur an infraction of some draconian traffic rule that could land them in the courthouse for hours. As it turned out, the decision to walk there had benefits later on, which no one could have anticipated.

The banquet hall was a curious combination of something contemporary in style with something traditionally Southern. Its front entrance was set off by a colonnade of ornate classical pillars molded out of plastic. Behind them, glass doors led into a large, gymnasium-like area where exposed girders and cooling ducts laced back and forth high over the dining area and supported garish chandeliers that dangled below. At one end of this cavernous edifice was a stage. A twenty-member dance band, dressed in a pale-pink livery, had set up their equally pale-pink music stands and their brassy instruments and made ready to entertain the honored guests.

In front of the stage was a large buffet table covered by a floor-length tablecloth and by that sort of display of food—of pineapples and frosted hams and spiny Florida lobsters and other items—that is familiar to anyone who has had the nauseating experience of viewing such gustatory outlays on cruise ships and in gambling casinos and that, for some reason, despite the smiling chefs who stand behind these exhibits, never gets eaten by anybody. In this case, an attendant with a white tunic and slicked-back hair hovered unctuously over the display. His job was to keep people away from it.

On the left side of the stage and buffet was a long bar where several bartenders awaited what they figured, and correctly so, would be a heavy demand for drinks. Between that bar and the stage were two sets of swinging double doors that led into the kitchen. On the right side of the stage and buffet were two doors, quite close together, one labeled "Ladies" and the other "Gentlemen."

If you looked toward the opposite end of the banquet hall, you saw a colossal mural in chalklike pastels, covering the entire wall, of Ponce de Leon discovering the Fountain of Youth, backed up by his band of astonished conquistadors. They had good reason to be astonished, for squirming around in the fountain was a bevy of the most lascivious-looking nymphs, or mermaids, or whatever, that have ever been painted in the history of the world. I've never known what the word "fleshpot" actually means, but in this painting the Fountain of Youth was certainly depicted as a pot of flesh.

The banquet hall wasn't, however, without a touch of elegance, for on the far side of the hall was a series of tall French windows with delicately fashioned fans over their doors. These doors, however incongruent with the décor of the hall, were wide open and led out to a spacious and manicured lawn behind the building. The lawn itself was bordered by a dense woodland of cypress and tamarind, all hung dramatically with long swaths of Spanish moss.

The banquet commenced.

The band, known as the Baying Hounds, began to play a kind of swing music from the thirties in a whiny "country-western" style—just the sort of the thing intended to regale an over-eighties crowd, if such a crowd happened to be there and could stand to listen to it. The sports-car teams filed in and looked for places among the garishly decorated tables.

The banquet was free, supposedly, the tab being picked up by the Foxtowne Chamber of Commerce, but hidden costs began to emerge. For example, the drinks were not free, nor were, as people found out too late, the bowls of chips and pretzels and other comestibles served up with them. Since dinner was intentionally delayed for as long as possible, and, since the price of everything was astronomical, the teams found themselves paying lots of money out of pocket.

Naturally, a great deal of drinking went on. The long bar near the kitchen doors was kept busy for a full hour or more as waiters rushed trays of glasses back and forth, delivering well-diluted but still, over time, potent drinks to the impatient customers. The sight of the food on the buffet table, counteracted by the rancid smell of its preservatives, served only to exacerbate their appetite with a mix of attraction and repulsion.

The arrangements for the banquet were presided over by a short, rotund *maître d'* in a pink dinner jacket, a white ruffled shirt, and a little black bow tie. He had a remarkable resemblance to one of Walt Disney's three little pigs — the industrious one who made the brick house — and he kept, not quite appropriately, given the characters in the original tale, huffing and puffing up and down the lanes between the tables, giving orders and rebuffing the complaints of the sports-car teams with comments both contemptuous of them and self-pitying of himself. The waitstaff was a strange lot. Were they migrant waiters on loan from the toughest seafood joints from higher up on the East Coast: from Atlantic City or Asbury Park or Coney Island or wherever unpredictable and dangerous customers might be expected to convene?

The *maître d'* had also presumed to hire a staff of bouncers in case anyone became too boisterous. This staff was provided by an assembly of thugs, about fifteen of them, enlisted from the local motorcycle club and stuffed into ill-fitting evening clothes. They sat in a special room reserved for them behind the kitchen, read magazines, pulled up their sorely strained cummerbunds and dress shirts so that they could display and study each others' belly tattoos, and waited to be called into action, if such action were ever, at any point, deemed necessary.

The great repast was finally served: canned fruit cocktail with a splotch of melted lime sherbet as a garnish, followed by a plate of prime rib au jus, so fat and so overtenderized that it looked like a clump of whale blubber floating in puddle of greasy beet juice. It was accompanied by a white slippery mound of whipped something or other, presumably potatoes. And carrots diced up with peas — you know, I'm sure, that mutually incompatible concoction, especially when the carrots are undercooked and the peas are overcooked. The meal was eaten in silence as the "hounds" of the band "bayed" on and on with relentless monotony.

Dessert? There never was dessert. Maybe dessert was that chocolate cake and the other confections that ended up all over the place. Who knows?

Now listen. Here it comes.

It was never, under any circumstances, a pleasant thing to eat close by Bill Hennessy. Yes, in the proper setting, Hennessy was something of a gourmet. Indeed, he'd partaken of much of the finest cuisine that the world can offer in its finest restaurants; but he was also something of a gourmand, and vile food, somehow, induced him into what resembled a consumptively maniacal state. The viler the food, the viler became the barbarian relish with which he slurped it up. He attacked his roast beef and whipped potatoes with unbridled passion. Indeed, I think that the entire slab of roast beef went down in one piece. It's amazing he didn't choke to death on it.

Leander, having finished God only knows how much gin and needing to put a little distance between himself and the monster of consumption at his side, decides to make the perilous journey to the men's room. Why perilous? Because he's in no condition to go anywhere.

He gets up and starts his walk. He seems to be lost. He swerves back and forth, bumping into tables, chairs, people, even a waiter or two. Several accommodating gents, figuring out where he's headed to, give him a little shove to get him turned back in the right direction.

Everyone begins to watch. They laugh.

The waiters and the *maître d'* begin to watch. They scowl.

The band stops its baying. They watch, too.

The attention of the entire banquet is now focused on Leander as he maneuvers his way to the front of the hall. He gets himself poised about twenty yards from the men's room door, squints to make out the word "Gentlemen" on it, aims himself accordingly, backs up a bit and then plunges forward. His trajectory veers off course. In he goes through the door marked "Ladies."

The banquet hall erupts into applause—clapping, shouting, hollering anything and everything you can think of—which breaks the gloomy demeanor of the sports-car teams.

But the unctuous and decorative attendant behind the buffet table doesn't have the same reaction and is no longer quite so unctuous and decorative anymore. He dives through the ladies' room door a moment or two after Leander and reemerges, holding Leander practically suspended in the air by the back of his collar and shaking him, so that Leander looks not altogether unlike a freshly snagged pompano flapping back and forth as it's lifted up on a line out of the Gulf Stream and into someone's fishing net. The attendant then lowers Leander to the floor and, still grappling him by the neck, begins shouting obscenities at him.

Leander has his footing again. That's a bad thing (for the attendant, that is).

Leander has his footing again. And that's a good thing (for Leander, that is).

He's anchored.

The entire banquet hall falls into silence—a silence of breathless anticipation. They know what's going to happen.

Suddenly it comes—the sound of a bullwhip snapping, or a tree cracking violently in a hurricane hitting the Bahamas, or a bat hitting a baseball with unspeakable force.

The quondam warden of inedible frosted hams and plumed pineapples rocks back and forth for a few seconds, his eyes glazed and his tongue lolling out of this mouth, sits down on the floor, rolls his head around once or twice, and, with one shoulder and hip propped up in most awkward way, pitches over and lies motionless.

The audience is almost as stunned. In a stupor, Leander gazes down at his most recent victim, as if he doesn't quite know what's happened.

A waiter bolts out from behind a nearby table and lunges at him. He never gets close. From somewhere in that banquet hall a plate filled with prime rib au jus and whipped potatoes rises up to meet the attack. The waiter falls back, wiping gravy and slippery potatoes from his jacket and threatening to "kill" the guy who did that. The *maître d'* quickly motions together a squad of tuxedo-clad shock troops and advances on Leander. He snorts as he struts, huffing and puffing his way toward Leander. "Ah knew it, ah jus' knew there'd be trouble, ah knew …" He's cut off by a martini glass that whizzes past his nose. More plates rise up to block his squad. Bellowing and booing and hurling plates come from every direction in the banquet hall as the squad, hunched down and with arms over heads, retreats to the kitchen doors under a shower of flying utensils.

Leander, meanwhile, disappears.

After this, there's a short respite. The drivers and mechanics, roused at last from their dispirited torpor, joke with one another, stand up and make impromptu speeches, offer toasts and challenges, and call out noisily to friends at the other end of the hall. Seeing Leander pull off one of his famous knockdowns in such a particularly spectacular setting is a cause of no little celebration. They're elated. They jump up on their chairs and whoop and shout and dance, turning around in little circles and wrapping bunches of plastic flowers on their heads. Leander has just enacted for them a kind of collective revenge for everything that has gone wrong in Foxtowne. Meanwhile, all the banquet personnel evacuate the scene while the Baying Hounds creep down behind their music stands and instrument boxes and keep out of sight.

But trouble's brewing, and the more perspicacious members of the crowd begin alerting their fellows to what's about to happen and to get prepared. For when the kitchen doors swing open again, discharging a wild mob of waiters, cooks, busboys, dishwashers, and the gang of thugs hired as bouncers, the attack is met by a solid wall of flying plates, silverware, ice cubes, bread baskets, vases with plastic flowers in them, glasses, beer bottles, and chairs.

The noise of the first onslaught thunders and reverberates through the dining hall, as its impact pins the opposing army to the walls by the kitchen doors and drives many into the kitchen again, while others scramble over and hunker down behind the long bar. The *maître d'* makes a rather late entrance, comes huffing and puffing through the doors, and tries to stop his own people from counterattack. To no avail. He's hit in the face with a slab of roast beef and sent reeling and gagging back through the kitchen doors.

The counterattack takes place. Banquet hall personnel explode out of the kitchen again, now armed with pots and pans, ladles, mixing bowls, brushes, brooms, sponges, scouring pads, and other projectiles that they fling through the air, while their comrades, pinned against the wall or behind the bar, begin picking up and throwing back the things that had initially been tossed at them, contending all the while with the bottles of booze whose short careers have come to an end as broken glass in alcohol-reeking puddles.

The sports-car teams immediately flip their tables over to use as barriers facing the enemy and then return the fire. Soon enough, by linking table to table, they create a series of trenches and cross trenches in which individual combatants can move back and forth into different positions as the battle demands.

Meanwhile, a group of waiters manage to take possession of the stage and, with the now eager participation of the Baying Hounds, is able to use it as an ideal spotting position to fire downward at the drivers below. Several waiters even drop into the space between the stage and the buffet table and shower the drivers with the food display. One driver is hit full in the face with a frosted ham, while another is gashed on his wrist by the claw of a careening lobster.

It's then that one of the more notable acts of martial bravery takes place, one that is especially fortunate, as it turned out later, for Leander. A gaunt figure, probably six foot five with immense shoulders, rears up from among the tipped-over tables, and, in the full force of the flying objects that filled the air, begins to chant the Marine hymn as he leads an assault on the stage. He's followed by ten or so young stalwarts.

Accompanied by the cheers of the entire assembly, they drive off the waiters posted behind the buffet tables and mount the stage, where a furious battle ensues. The Baying Hounds retreat in frantic disorder, leaving their instruments behind. The waiters are tougher and hold out to the last before they're driven off. The victorious Marine snatches up a trumpet that had been stashed under one of the chairs and blows a series of harsh, loud blasts over the hall. Everyone hollers their approval, while in a far corner of the hall several voices are lifted in a Notre Dame football chant.

Bill Hennessy, meanwhile, kept looking for Leander. He figured Leander must be under that buffet table and hidden from sight by its floor-length covers. He knew that Leander could be in serious trouble and that he should get him out of there as soon as possible. It would be only a matter of minutes before the police would show up. He began to crawl through the network of trenches, encouraging the pockets of combatants as he went, until he reached the front line, where the exchange of projectiles was most intense. The space between the front line and the buffet table would be perilous to cross, but now at least he had cover provided by his colleagues on the stage. The floor was littered with broken glass and slippery with food. He eyed the stained and battered buffet table and took the plunge. A moment later he was underneath the table and surrounded on all sides by the heavy table coverings.

It was dark there, and curiously silent as well, as if the coverings filtered out most of the noise, even though there were regular thuds and muted explosions, as an object hit the top of the tables or the nearby floor and shattered into little pieces. It was like … It was like being in a kind of bunker or in some kind of bomb shelter.

In the darkness at the far end of the table he saw Leander, sitting, his back stooped, his head just barely touching the bottom of the table, legs folded, his hands in his lap. His face was drawn and haggard. The light had gone out in his eyes. He gazed emptily into the darkness.

"You all right, Leander?" Hennessy asked.

He nodded. His body rocked just a little bit back and forth.

He mumbled something Hennessy could not hear. He moved closer.

"In Coventry …" Leander began.

He hesitated.

"In Coventry, durin' the war …" he said again.

"Yes," said Hennessy, crawling up to Leander and sitting down in front of him, though he had to stoop his head low to be in a sitting position. "Tell me what happened in Coventry during the war, Leander. Tell me about it."

There was a long silence. The thuds, the breakage, the uproar outside continued in full force around them, though muffled by the heavy tablecloths. One large piece of pottery smashed on the table right over their heads.

"Yuh know, boss," Leander mumbled. "I'm 'earin' some blokes say I got ta look the way I do 'cause a' somethin' that 'appened ta me durin' the war."

"Yes, Leander, I've heard people say that."

"Well, fact is, I was born this way. Me dad neva saw me 'cause I was born aftah 'e went away to Flanders in the first big row, and 'e did'na survive that. Me mum used ta say 'e was a lucky man for all a' that. 'E would'a found 'is grave any'ow the first moment 'e seen me, says she. Better lookin' down the snout a' one a 'em Hun machine guns than at me, says she. That's me own mum who says that. That's how bad it was, Mr. 'Ennessy — when yuh own mum makes a point, now and again, a tellin' yuh how ugly yuh are."

"I think I understand — maybe just a little bit."

A series of shrieks and cheers reached them from beyond the tablecloths. Some major attack had begun, but it died down quickly. The attack had obviously been repulsed.

In the darkness, Leander still stared down at his hands in his lap. "But there's anotha thin' that's even more difficult to understand, boss. Yuh see, one day I be meetin' this girl, and 'er name is Alice. Alice ain't no ordinary girl; she's a real beauty, I mean she's a real special girl. And she goes for me. I mean she luvs me. Can yuh figure that, she actually luvs me? And I luv 'er."

Leander looked up and gazed at Hennessy through the shadows of the tablecloth.

"Yuh know, if yuh're born lookin' like some kinda bloomin' mistake, and the prettiest girl in Coventry takes a fancy to yuh, that's no small thin'. I mean, no small thin'. Course, the otha' blokes in town, what with all their preenin' and all their charmin' ways, dunna take to this all that well. That's 'ow I learned to knock a fella down — it was for 'er sake. They gave me a lot a' trouble for 'er sake. And they gave 'er trouble too."

A heavy crash on the tabletop above them suggested that someone had jumped from the stage onto the buffet table. Footsteps slammed along the tabletop, followed by another loud thump as the bounder leapt off to the floor and ran away.

"What happened to Alice?" Hennessy asked.

Leander looked down again at his hands in his lap for a moment before he answered.

"It was'na me, boss; it was she got dragged out from a buildin' afta' the big raid on Coventry. They could'na save 'er."

Leander shook his head slowly, resignedly.

He explained, "Yuh know, a fella like me does'na get a second chance, even if 'e be wantin' it. Aftah Alice, I did'na even want it. Nothin' could be the same as 'er. It's been a lonely life evah since."

They sat together in the darkness, sat in each other's presence, ignoring the riot going on around them. Hennessy, perhaps for the first time in his life, was able to join seriously, if but momentarily, in another's grief. Then he shook himself, as from a stupor. The sounds of the battle had taken an ominous turn.

Hennessy said, "Leander, we need to get out of here. The fun-and-games part of this situation is pretty much over. Now the serious part will begin, and you'll be in big trouble if the police get hold of you. They'll blame you for the entire thing."

Life flickered back into Leander's eyes. He looked up. "Then we'd bettah be on our way, had'na we?"

Hennessy lifted the tablecloth and peered out. "We could wait for a lull, if it ever came, but we should go right now. At least we know we're protected from the back."

The situation in the banquet hall was worse than ever. A new sortie from the kitchen doors, led entirely by the motorcycle gang, armed with fire extinguishers and spraying foam wildly all over the place, was repulsed by a thunderous salvo of dessert plates, each with a piece of chocolate cake or some other pastry on it. These desserts, hundreds of them, stacked up on dollies, had been discovered by some of the more enterprising drivers reconnoitering for fresh ammunition. They'd been distributed just in time for the new onslaught from the kitchen.

Of course, they're picked up and returned with equal force, many of the pieces of cake ending up as black splotches on the great mural of the Fountain of Youth. The fleshpot of squirming nymphs no longer looks all that enticing, and Ponce de Leon's beaming visage has been effaced by a splatter of key lime pie.

In the meantime, a number of chandeliers either had gone out or been torn down from their roosts, leaving behind intimidating gaggles of live electrical wires and plunging the banquet hall into an eerie twilight darkness.

Hennessy and Leander scrambled out from underneath the table, jumped to their feet, and, accompanied by the whoops and cries of their confreres, ran across the debris on the floor to the first line of tables, leapt over the first table, and stooped down just as a barrage of cooking items clattered against it. The surrounding combatants promptly returned a volley of dinnerware.

Crouched behind the same table was a rather jovial man, stout, wearing a captain's hat and sporting a thick mustache, who had collected a copious supply of glass ashtrays, which he'd stacked up in a column. Ceremoniously he lifted one ashtray after the other from the column, lobbed it in a high arc over the no-man's land, and whistled in imitation of a mortar shell as the ashtray disappeared with a soft thud behind the bar, usually followed by a flood of obscenities and a raised fist or two shaking above the bar.

Leander and Hennessy realized they had no time to linger over this curiosity. From table to table they crawled, getting pounded on the back or having their hands shaken by the combatants as they went. They had just reached the French windows with their wide-open doors when sirens were heard in the distance. They were the first ones to escape from the hall and to run across the adjoining lawns to the woodlands beyond.

A stampede followed. In one great surge, the entire banquet hall was evacuated. Drivers and mechanics bolted over the network of tables, tripping and falling, and just as quickly springing to their feet again. Banquet personnel squirmed out of their hiding places and raced across the room in pursuit, though they didn't anticipate the terrain they would have to cover and began to slip, stumble, and collide with each other. Realizing how difficult it would be to go beyond the first line of tables, they stopped and began to mill around angrily in the front of the hall.

The police, significantly delayed by their own system of traffic control, arrived. They burst through the front doors as an armed phalanx, swinging their billy clubs, mistaking, in the dim light of the hall, the waiters and cooks and bouncers for the diners. The police lit into them with their clubs; the banquet personnel fought back; and it took a minute or more of savage clubbing and screaming to clarify the mistake.

Then the police tried to run through the hall. The turned-over tables, slippery food, fire-extinguisher foam, and mounds of eating and cooking utensils littering the place were difficult for them to traverse. They had scarcely reached the windows as the last few men vanished over the far lawns and into the woods. One policeman actually drew his revolver and fired several shots into the woods before another officer stopped him. It was lucky the drivers and mechanics had walked to the banquet: now they didn't have cars to retrieve from the parking lot and were able to melt into the crowds of campers and fans that jammed the town and the outlying fields in every direction.

Nobody, frankly, knows how the fire got started.

Yes, that was next.

Theories abound to this day. Some attribute it to the torn electrical connections of the chandeliers, others to something that may have happened in the kitchen with stoves left burning during the melee, and yet others to the sudden appearance of a flaming acetylene torch in the hands of a rabid motorcyclist bound on revenge for having received the full impact of a heavy glass ashtray directly on top of his head. In any case, the depletion, at this point, of usable fire extinguishers and the traffic tie-up in town preventing rapid access of the fire department, resulted in one final and lamentable outcome.

By morning, nothing was left of the banquet hall, or the recreational center, except a smoking heap of tangled ducts and girders and the remains of the plastic columns, which had melted down into grotesque caricatures of classical architecture of the sort you would see in a surrealistic painting. The glory of Foxtowne was gone.

Further, a nighttime ensued of policemen frantically tramping through the soggy camps of the sports-car fans, shining flashlights into the faces of sleeping campers, hustling hundreds of unsuspecting victims out of their cots and sleeping bags and through the paint-cracked halls of the courthouse and submitting them to threats and interrogations. The search narrowed down to one individual whose name could not, quite oddly, be remembered by anybody but who could be easily identified as a scrawny little fellow with a huge, hooked nose and pointed head whose equal in ugliness the world had never known.

Just before dawn, Hennessy awoke in his camper with a start. Where was Leander? he thought. What was he doing? He looked out the window. The fields were still dark, although a slight glow of red stretched along the eastern horizon and a heavy mist hung over the cars and trailers and encampments spread over the wet grass. A few people here and there had risen and were preparing pots of coffee and toasting bacon over campfires and small portable stoves. Slowly, the camp, which resembled a nomadic army, was coming to life in the early dawn. Hennessy doubted that the events scheduled for the day would take place, especially after the previous evening. There would be a massive exodus. It would take place soon.

He exited the camper and walked around to the back, where the trailer was attached. He and Leander had already loaded up the Lotus on the previous afternoon, soon after the race. And there was Leander, standing on the trailer with his body already bent over into the car's engine cavity. He was rapping gently on some engine part. The car's hood was propped open and stood up against the ruddy eastern skies. Leander looked up momentarily. "Mornin' ta yuh, boss. There's fresh tea on the stove," he said.

"Thanks anyway," Hennessy replied, "but I think we need to go. Right now."

"One or two more details ta attend ta, and I be finished." He kept tapping into place whatever it was he was tapping. Hennessy clambered up onto the trailer and looked down into the engine compartment.

"I think that can wait. We don't have a moment to … Good God, Leander, hide yourself! Get under the car! Something!"

Out of the roseate mist of the heavy dawn emerged two state police officers not more than forty paces away. They squished slowly through the marshy ground with high boots. They wore wide-brimmed hats, thick leather belted holsters with immense forty-five-caliber revolvers tucked into them, and, despite the low light, huge round sunglasses. Hennessy heaved Leander up by the back of his suspenders, turned him over, and squashed him down into the engine compartment, slamming the engine hood on top of him.

"Uh! Did yuh 'ave ta …?"

"Shut up!" Hennessy whispered loudly. He rubbed his hands as if he was finishing off some little job and turned to face the officers.

They stood about ten paces from him.

"Good morning, officers!" Hennessy said cheerfully.

They eyed him silently, hands cupped over the glossy hilts of their revolvers.

"Mechanic, huh?" one of them asked.

"Me? A mechanic? Oh no, I don't think so. But I could use a good one. Do you know any?"

"Smart-ass!"

"We're looking for one too — a fella, they say, who looks like someone put him through a wringer on one of those old-fashioned washing machines. You seen him around?" the other officer inquired.

"Yeah, a shrimp with a nose like a fishhook and with forearms, they say, that look like Popeye's," the first officer added.

Hennessy appeared to think for a while. "The description's familiar. There's a guy like that around. I've seen him. But I don't know what his name is or where he is at the moment."

The officers had heard this story before, again and again, throughout the night. They smiled sarcastically at Hennessy. They demanded that he step down from the trailer, examined his driver's license, and took down his name and number. One of the officers took a rather strong interest in the peculiar looking car on the trailer. He mounted the trailer.

"What a mess!" he exclaimed. "How could anyone race in a broken-down rig like this?"

"I told you I needed a good mechanic," Hennessy clucked nervously.

"Let's take a look under the hood," the officer demanded. "I want to see what makes this thing run."

"Really, there's nothing there to …"

"Open the hood! I want to see what's in there!"

Hennessy leaned over the trailer, reached into the cockpit of the car and released a catch. The hood sprang slightly open. The officer grabbed it and swung it all the way open. He looked down into the engine cavity, at one point bending over and moving his head close to the machinery. He stood up straight again and laughed. "I guess you have your problems, all right, mister. That engine is the ugliest mess I've ever seen."

"I hit an obstacle on the track, a cinder block …"

"I guess so. And I've seen some pretty smashed up cars in my time." He slammed the engine hood down. He didn't hear the muted "ouch" that accompanied it. He clambered down from the trailer. "You let us know if you see that fella we're looking for."

The two officers ambled slowly off into the misty plain, their boots pressing bubbly footprints into the soggy grass.

"Lemme outa 'ere," Leander moaned.

"When we're ten miles down the road," Hennessy answered. He climbed into the RV, started up the engine, and slowly guided it over the field, avoiding the scattered encampments and the especially wet patches of ground, and onto the road. He turned toward the sun, which was now a glowing orange ball in the east, suspended in a thick gray fog.

Fifteen minutes later, he pulled over to the side of the road, went back to the trailer, and released the hood. Leander popped out of the engine cavity and stretched himself. He snapped his suspenders against his chest and smiled.

"What the hell happened back there?" Hennessy asked.

Leander shook his head slowly. "Got me, boss. That bloke was lookin' right in me face. In fact, he lowered 'is big mug inta strikin' distance. I was ready to let 'm 'ave it, ta tell the truth. But then 'e draws back and laughs the way 'e did. I guess there are times in life when lookin' like a piece of bloody machinery 'as its advantages. Course, I was 'alf wrapped around that engine, so maybe ..."

Hennessy let out a roar of laughter. "Leander, get into the RV. Let's go home. You know I can't stand being this far away from the ocean, and that sun is promising to turn this place into a frying pan by midmorning."

They got into the RV. Leander went into the back to catch up on his sleep. Hennessy drove home, a big smile on his face. He rehearsed in his mind how he would tell this story at the next big dinner party, chuckling to himself as he reviewed one incident after another.

And that's how I heard about much of this story, though I actually saw some of it —witnessed it myself— especially what happened at the Foxtowne banquet hall. I'm the one who got his wrist slashed by the flying lobster claw. I can show you the scar if you'd like to see it. And I share the privilege of having been present at Leander's greatest knockdown ever, along with a few hundred other guys. I'm proud of that. It's a story to tell my grandchildren.

The rest of it, as I said, I heard from Bill Hennessy, who dominated an entire luncheon party at the Belle and Bauble Club in Palm Beach with his account of what happened—of what happened under that table, of what went on afterward. Hennessy laughed his way all through that story, except for the part about the conversation he had with Leander under the table. That he took seriously—which was rare for Bill Hennessy, who couldn't take very much too seriously.

All of this happened quite some time ago. Foxtowne, I understand, after recovering as much as it did—which took a while—turned its attention to becoming a center for an annual national quilting convention. But it never rebuilt its banquet hall, and the landing strips have been returned to permanent occupation by their rightful inhabitants: the possums and egrets and water snakes and whatever else.

Leander Baxter has departed for a habitat somewhere that none of us know about. Maybe he went back to England, back to Coventry, back to where he'd plucked from a ravaged life the few real moments of happiness he'd ever known. He's only a memory for us now. If he was the ugliest man we ever knew, as ugly as those high-tuned contraptions he patched together, he, like them, had the soul of a sleek Ferrari blasting through a turn at Monte Carlo at two hundred plus. That's what we saw in him.

Maybe that's what Alice—Alice, the prettiest girl in Coventry—maybe that's what she saw in him too.

The Story of My Life

Sure, there's room. I'll squeeze over a bit. There's plenty of room. Sit down. Make yourself comfortable. Where are you getting off? How's that? Fifty-Seventh Street? Great place to get off — Tiffany's, Bonwit Teller, Carnegie Hall, Russian Tea Room! So, which one are you going to? A dentist? Yeah, I bet you are! Really? Well, that's no great place to be going, is it? Can't you just feel that drill already boring down into your teeth! I can feel it, even though I'm not going.

Me? I'm getting off at Thirty-Fourth. Empire State Building. I'm just going to look at the view. For about the hundredth time, I think. I like looking at the view. I love New York, and I love just looking at it.

So, what's in the paper this morning? I don't read the *Times*. It's got too many ads.

I'm not being a pest, am I? I guess if you buy a newspaper, you buy it to read it. Never mind me. I run on a bit now and then. But I'm not like one of those guys who sits down next to you on a bus and insists on telling you the story of his life. Heck no, I'm not like that. I can't stand that kind of thing.

Eighty-Fourth Street. Museum! I spend a lot of time there. What a great collection! Still got a long way to go, don't we? You see that fat guy in that seat over there? He's taking up two seats, isn't he? Why doesn't he have to pay two fares? Now you answer me that.

Sorry! Didn't mean to interrupt you. Hey, that looks interesting about the D.A.'s office. Excuse me, I'm just trying to catch that one word in the crease. Yeah! Got it. Thanks.

But don't let me disturb you; I mean, don't put away the paper on account of me. Well, if you must. Excuse me again, if I stand up and look for Cleopatra's Needle as we pass. Yeah, okay, it's great. Cleopatra's Needle is great. But you can't really see it well from here anymore, now that they built that big extension on the museum. That's too bad. But I still look for it anyway. Just a habit. I love those ancient Egyptians. Do you love them? Ancient Egyptians—they're my kind of guys. Excuse me, I'll just squeeze down again.

I love this time of year in New York. Early March. Pretty soon they'll be painting the green stripe down the street for the St. Patrick's Day parade. I love that—all those crazy things, those people carrying along Fifth Avenue banners saying, "England, get out of Ireland." We all need a cause, don't we? Makes life more fun.

Me? No, I'm not Irish. Come on, now: do I look Irish? I mean it, do I look Irish? Who ever saw an Irishman who looked even remotely like me? What Irishman has a nose even half as long as mine?

No, I'm ... Well, I'm not going to tell you. No, I'm not telling. No, sorry, I'm not. Well ... maybe I will. People always get such screwy looks on their faces when I say it. So here it comes. Ready? Sure you're ready?

I'm Montenegrin.

I knew you would get a screwy look on your face. Everybody does. They're positively embarrassed. Montenegrin? Montenegro? What is it with this guy? Is that some place in a comic strip—the kind of place the Phantom would hang out in? Or Mandrake the Magician? Or a vampire of some sort? There's no such place. Maybe he's talking about Monte Casino, or the Count of Monte Cristo, or something like that?

Of course, some people know, I mean, like there actually is such a place, and then they act even more screwy. Montenegro! No one comes from Montenegro! I mean, it's impossible. Where the heck is it, anyway? You surely know it's tucked away in a corner of Yugoslavia—the former Yugoslavia, to be exact, right next to Albania. Don't you? You don't. Well, now you do.

And, if you do know, isn't that the place that has been cut off from the rest of the world for the last hundred years — provided, of course, that it ever was connected with the rest of the world anyway, ever in its history? Isn't that the place where people run around in crazy robes and hit each over the head with glinty sabers all the time and discharge long-barreled flintlocks with fancy carvings right between their neighbors' eyes? You get the picture? It's no great picture.

Seventy-Ninth. Hey, that fat fella got off. The bus feels like it rose up three inches, doesn't it? I'm not pestering you, am I? I know I run on.

Now about this Montenegrin stuff, I always like to say that Montenegrins are one of the most ancient peoples of Europe. But I don't say that. I mean, I said it, but I don't usually say that. I figure someone might say, "Ancient? Yeah, and they stayed that way!"

So, I don't say it, even though I said it. You understand. You would never come back with a dumb crack like that, would you?

I knew you wouldn't.

Now, what do you think it was like for me as a kid? I grew up in a small college town in New England. It was one of those real preppy places — no place for a Montenegrin, let me tell you.

My father ran a grocery store where the college kids bought all their beer. It did a great business. So, of course, I was, in addition to being Montenegrin, a "townie." You know what a "townie" is? A "townie" is just about the worst thing you can be — a kid who grows up and lives in a college town.

But everything got even worse. I did really well in high school, and they gave the best student in the high school each year a free tuition to the college. Now don't get the impression that, because I did so well, I'm smart or anything like that. Immigrant kids always do well, because they're too stupid to know yet that goof-offs are the ones who really get ahead in life. Gee, mister, you must have done really well, what with that expensive suit and reading the *Times* and all, but I bet you were no goof-off, were you?

The college was rolling in money, so this business of giving a scholarship was its little gesture of goodwill to the local people. Goodwill? What goodwill? After being a "townie," the next worst thing is to be a "townie" enrolled in a college in whose town you're a "townie." I mean, that makes you Mr.

Jerk from Dorkville, even though all these students are paying astronomical bucks to spend four years of their lives in that town too. Do you get that?

And heaven forbid you should ever get a good grade in a college course. "His father sells under-the-counter booze to the prof's perpetually crocked wife; that's why he got the A."

Of course, I didn't want to go there. No luck! My father tells me, "Here, or nowhere!" Little did he realize that "here" and "nowhere" were the same place in a situation like that. But Montenegrins do what their fathers tell them to do. The saber. The flintlock. You get the picture? It's not always a pretty picture. Anyway, kids whose fathers run grocery stores don't turn down free tuition, even if it's from the University of West Hell.

Seventy-Second Street! The model boat pond is not far away. You know, Conservatory Water. And the statue of Hans Christian Andersen. I love Hans Christian Andersen. I love those stories. Do you love those stories? Hans Christian Andersen — my kind of guy!

College was as bad as it could have been. It may have had a fancy name and reputation and all that, but it *was,* for all purposes, the University of West Hell. One day I tried, Mr. Jerk that I am, to invite a pretty co-ed from out of town to my house for a special family occasion. Why did I forget? How did I forget? When Montenegrins have dinner on special family occasions, the women eat in the kitchen and the men eat in the dining room. "Hey, honey, you in there with the women, me in here with the men! Of course, none of them speak English. But you'll get by. They'll keep smiling these big smiles at you and pushing big slices of spinach pie in your face. By the way, don't expect their teeth to look like American teeth. And don't spill your spinach pie!" That went over like something else! She never spoke to me again. A Montenegrin and a "townie" all at once — it was too much.

I'm not boring you, am I? This bus sure is crowded.

But one day something really bad happened. Maybe it wasn't so bad, but it was bad. Well, there was this fraternity. Maybe you don't know what a fraternity is. Maybe you do. Maybe you belonged to one? Well, don't answer that.

A fraternity is a house where lots of kids crowd together in some murky basement room outfitted like a tavern or whatever and hang out all day — kind of like bats that like to hang upside down, all jammed together in a dark, drippy cave.

Now, this fraternity had all these kids who must have been kings or something because they all had "the Second" or "the Fourth" behind their names. They decided to throw a party—I think it must have been some charity idea, to have a party for people whom they would never dream of inviting to a party—people, in other words, who didn't belong to some fraternity or other or who were social misfits of some kind. People, in other words, like me.

It was a big college weekend, so they were putting themselves out to let their place be used like this. It was supposed to be a costume party. You come in some kind of crazy get-up—you know the kind of thing—pirates, ghosts, whatever.

Well, I'm up to this, and I accept the invitation. What an idiot!

I go home and tell my parents. What an even greater idiot!

And what do you think? Well, they go clear out of their minds. They'll get me into a costume like no one ever saw before. People's mouths will drop. I say "no"—I'll just go as a tramp, or something simple. I heard that everybody goes as something simple. Some of the people might not even be in costume at all—that's the rumor that was going around. But my parents won't accept that: kids at a big-deal school like this being so unimaginative!

"You just don't know them, Poppa! Being unimaginative is the name of the game. Why else do you think they tank up on so much beer?"

But, as I told you, you don't argue. I mean, not much. A musket ball right between the eyes if you argue. You get the picture? As I said, it's not always a pretty picture.

The next thing, I know I'm dragged up into the attic, and big trunks are opened up that I never knew were up there. And what's in these trunks? You got it. *Montenegrin stuff!*

The stuff is pretty musty—who knows how long it's lain there? But it's gorgeous. I mean, I've never seen such gorgeous things. It would make your Montenegrin blood dance to see such things—if you had any Montenegrin blood, and, mind you, I'm not trying to suggest that you do.

Pretty soon I'm outfitted in a get-up that makes me look like a Montenegrin warlord fresh out of his fortress on top of some great marble mountain.

And that's not all. Over a gold-embroidered coat of flaming red my father straps an immense, clanging saber, and a thin, long-barreled flintlock whose stock is inlaid with ivory and walnut and is embossed with silver and brass. Then he puts this crazy turban on my head.

I never saw such a smile on my father's face. I never saw such a smile on any man's face. And my mother — she's beside herself. She immediately goes down to the kitchen and makes some spinach pies — you know, in order to celebrate or something like that.

Well, that's just an initial test. Many other things are tried on, aired out, cleaned, mended, polished. On the day of the party, my parents work all day on the costume. By evening, I'm arrayed in something like I'm sure no college town in all of New England has ever seen or will ever see again. My mother even cuts off a lock of her own hair (her hair matches mine), which my father fashions into a huge curving mustache and affixes to me somehow with great skill.

My parents are so proud. My father even photographs me in the costume. When I look at myself in the mirror, all I can think is, "I sure wouldn't want to be someone who runs into me in the dark of the night."

Unfortunately, that's how some other people feel, too, later on.

Sixty-Seventh Street! Look at all the traffic!

Maybe I'm boring you. Maybe I should stop. Go back to the paper.

Well, well.

Hmm. Hmm.

So, you know what happens? I knew you'd be interested. I knew it when you didn't pick up the paper. Right?

Okay. I go to the party. I don't want to startle anyone, so I take a shortcut through the woods to the fraternity house. Well, that's a typical "townie" thing to do, anyway — take shortcuts through the woods. "Townies" always know everything there is to know about shortcuts through woods. Then I approach the brightly lit windows of the frat house and take a peek in.

Somehow, I suspected it, but I never believed it: there they all are, guys and girls, some solitary with hunched shoulders and haunted eyes searching for the nearest corner to squeeze into and disappear, others clustered nervously into tight little intimidated groups. Misfits all, just like me. Everyone socially paralyzed. No one having any fun. And *no one* in costume.

Then it dawns on me. The frat boys wanted to see who would be so dumb as to show up in a costume. I guess they would parade in at just the right moment and get a big laugh out of it. At least the others got that much figured out.

Well, there was one guy dressed up sort of like a clown — either that or that's the way he normally dresses. Anyway, he edges closer and closer to a door, embarrassed, as clownish as indeed he looks, waiting for an opportunity to make his escape.

I'm mad. Mad at myself. I want to draw my saber. I want to load and fire my flintlock. Actually, I couldn't. I don't have any ammunition. The ramrod is broken. And my saber is blunt.

I know I can't go home because my parents would be so disappointed. I can see them, sitting together at the kitchen table, nodding their heads, stupendous smiles on their faces, imagining me moving like the prince of the mountaineers though the admiring faces of the pale flatlanders, however titled and kingly they might be.

And here I am, a great big idiot, peering through the windows, with tears coming down my face and gradually washing away my mother's mustache — I mean, the mustache made of my mother's hair. But I stick it back on again, so that no one will recognize me.

I slip through a back door of the fraternity, just so that I can say I actually went in, grab a bottle of something or other from a table in the cocktail pantry — I think it was scotch — and go out into the orchard behind the row of frat houses. I know I can't go home for at least several hours. I climb up into an apple tree, drink that scotch, and get drunk. Then, laying myself out on a broad, flat bough, tucking my saber underneath my leg, and bracing the musket against my shoulder, I fall asleep.

Sixty-Fourth Street! The zoo! Hooray for the zoo! I like to visit the orangutans. I love them! Do you love them? You do? You don't? No opinion on the matter? Well, it's not important. I'll try to remember not to ask you again.

Orangutans are my kind of guys! Did you know that an orangutan is seven times stronger than even the strongest human being? Isn't that something! Someone told me that. You should know that, just in case you ever get it into your mind to push an orangutan around. Sometimes I even wish

I were an orangutan, though I wouldn't want to be in a zoo with all kinds of crazy people gaping at me. I mean, I wouldn't even want me looking at me.

Which brings me back, incidentally, to sleeping up in tree boughs—you know, like orangutans do. Anyway, I was asleep for a while, right up there in the tree bough. Later on, I'm awakened by some kind of quarrel going on underneath me. It's really late now, and there are these three couples directly beneath me and illuminated by an automobile's headlights aimed across the lawn and through the orchard. They're all arguing with one another. Sometimes it's the three guys against the three girls, and sometimes it's one guy and two girls against the two guys and one girl, and sometimes it breaks up into little separate arguments. Eventually, it's every combination you can imagine. Have you ever known these groups of couples that always hang around together and act like one big couple? I don't know why. I always figure one couple is enough of a problem.

So, on goes this argument. I think it's about cars or something. Who drove whose car and where and why and should they have and so on. They must have been psychology majors or something like that, because the argument is full of psychological words and accusations. I guess there are many different kinds of nuts in the world, and these people know all the names for them and how to apply them in a situation like this.

Now, one fabulously cute girl, or so it seems from where I'm perched, is wearing this really low-cut evening dress. Remember, I'm seeing this all from above, craning my neck as much as I can to get a view. Of course, now the view is rather a bit more interesting, so I crane my neck even more, and ... I fall.

Yes, I fall.

I fall from the bough right into the middle of them. What's worse, I land upright on my feet, my mustache bristling, my saber clanging in its scabbard, and my musket following me down and, almost magically, slapping into my open palms.

There's this horrible shriek and jostling and pushing. One girl faints and falls to the ground, and two guys and two girls rush toward the nearest frat house—to get the "posse" or the "vigilantes" or something like that—while the other guy, who must have been some kind of football player, grips my neck with one hand while he bends over the fainted girl and shakes her with his other hand.

I didn't know what to do. I meant no harm. But I have to get away from there. So, twisting myself around somehow in the iron grip of that guy, I grasp the musket by its barrel and slam his gigantic crupper so hard with the flat of the walnut and ivory stock that he loses his grip on my neck. He dives down over the poor girl, and his head practically digs into the ground.

Then I see a crowd streaming out of the frat house like … like … well, just like a swarm of bats fluttering out of a cave, you know, the way they do when it gets dark. I make a quick check to see if the girl is still alive under that enormous, bulging hulk. She is. In fact, she's regained consciousness, stares at me for a second from below that colossus, and begins screaming.

Satisfied that she's okay, I take off though the woods, running like hell and holding on to the musket with my right hand and the scabbard of my saber with my left hand so it won't clatter at my side and give me away.

As I told you, I knew all the shortcuts through the woods and neighborhood backyards and was soon safely home, creeping into the cellar through a low window so that my parents wouldn't know I'd returned. I could just imagine them still sitting upstairs at the kitchen table, dreaming about what a dashing figure I was making at that party.

By the way, I have to confess that there were moments early in my escape when I thought of turning around, taking a stand, and engaging in combat, single-handedly, with the whole pack of my pursuers. It's just the sort of thing a Montenegrin mountaineer would have done, which is why, I understand, there aren't all that many Montenegrin mountaineers still left around to do it anymore. But I didn't do that. The craven townie in me prevailed over the valiant mountaineer.

I never told my parents what happened.

My father wanted to hang that photograph, immensely enlarged, of me, fully costumed, and surrounded by an enormous and ornate brass frame, in a place of honor in the grocery store where acres of six-packs are stacked ten feet high — you know, exactly the place where everyone in the college always goes and would be sure to see it.

It took a lot of work to dissuade him from that. I actually had to argue with him — not a safe thing to do, as I've told you. Anyway, it would have been curtains for me, if he'd done what he wanted to do, because talk of what happened spread throughout the campus and the frat guys were busy sniffing out the guilty culprit, whoever he should turn out to be. They never did recognize me. Luckily, I'd kept my mother's mustache on at the time. And the turban helped too.

So why do I tell you all this? Because this *is* the story of my life. I mean, my whole life has been like this. I'm not complaining or anything like that. I love my life. I love who I am. I love what I am. I love being Montenegrin, and I revere my ancestors. They were noble people. But I just have a way of always being — you know, as they say — "overdressed for the occasion." Of dropping out of nowhere into the middle of someplace or something where I should not be. Of being in the wrong place at the wrong time. Of putting myself out for something or some people I shouldn't be putting myself out for. Of talking to the wrong guy about the wrong ...

Fifty-Ninth Street! I love looking at the horse carriages with the Plaza in the background. It looks like something you might see in — well, in Montenegro. You know — a royal palace or something like that, with horse carriages in front because they don't have automobiles yet or whatever. Just kidding! But I don't really know because I've never actually been there.

Hey, where are you going? This isn't Fifty-Seventh yet. This isn't your stop. What are you doing? You forgot your paper! What's the hurry? Hey ...!

Hey!

I've done it again.

I've done it again.

Hmm.

Sure, sit down. I'll squeeze over a bit. There's plenty of room. Make yourself comfortable. Where are you getting off?

"Good Night, Sweet Prince"

A cat? Yes, a cat! A simple household cat;
    Felis domesticus. For you de\part this day
To sleep beneath the pine boughs on the hill.
    How shall we presume to praise
Your brindled vest of brown and gray;
    Your face and feet as shimmering white
As snow upon a sunny field;
    Your black-ringed, magisterial tail?
We shall miss you,
    Lithe stair-climber, dweller in lofts,
Imbiber of new-fallen rain,
    Stalker through the lilies in the dawn.
You were our hearth-companion
    In long winter evenings by the fire—
Old wanderer, old wayfarer, old friend.
    We thank you now and ever
For the peace and solace of your ways.
    In your dreams of Paradise,
We ask you to remember our devotion.
    Good night, glad comforter of our days.
"Good night, sweet Prince."

Canso d'Amor

Vermilion-saddled destriers
Pounce and paw the dusty square;
Studded hauberks gleam afire;
Torches on dark ramparts flare.
    Yet I would tarry in her bower.
For I would be the fruit she eats.
I would be the locks she pleats.
God, what hands, what savory lips!
God, what taut and supple tips
Of orchid and of honeycomb!
Turrets of Carcassonne shall bloom
Like viols beneath a spandrel moon.

    Let the wide world see and hear,
    Unicorns consort with deer.

Shaggy hilltops' coppiced brims
Like quills of arrows, flint and tart,
Hedge the quaggy battle plains.
Harlèd heralds stand athwart.
    Yet I would linger in her loft.
For I would be the air she breathes.
I would be the braids she wreathes.
God, what long and ardent kiss!
God, what sap profuse with bliss
Of vineyards and sunflowers!
Scimitars and broadswords bare
Shall be cusped in poppies fair.

    Let the wide world see and hear,
    Unicorns consort with deer.

Mounted escorts ford the streams;
Surcoats embossed with vair and gold
Trounce and sparkle in the fray.
Visors rattle gruff and bold.
    Yet I would dally in her tower.
For I would be the shift she wears,
I would be the pearls she bears.
God, what eyes in rapture meet!
God, what dulcet marguerite
Of spade in dewy spathe enclosed!
Moor and Christian as one may breed
Where wolf and wolfhound together feed.

    Let the wide world see and hear,
    Unicorns consort with deer.

    Envoi
Valiant song, hail thee apace
To where the Rhine and Rhone embrace.

    Let the wide world see and hear,
    Unicorns consort with deer.

Maura Briscoe

If life was anything for the girls at St. Mary of Cleophas Academy, it was one of eager anticipations, a solemn and joyous procession of sacred festivals and complex ritual activities of all kinds. Not only were the high holy days of the ancient Church preserved with all due ceremony; a multitude of others were likewise celebrated: Candlemas, St. Joseph's feast day, the feast of the Annunciation, and rogation days, to name but a few. (If school was in session on Gaudete Sunday in Advent and Laetare Sunday in Lent, these feasts, too, were honored in ways truly worthy of their names.)

In addition, this girl's boarding school in rural New Hampshire could boast a full roster of those celebrations common to all schools: the usual sporting events, Christmas and Spring proms, drama performances, parents' days, homecoming weekends, and assorted field trips. Some events were reserved for particular classes: there was, for example, the freshman ascent of Mount Cardigan every fall and the canoe trip along the Contoocook River for sophomores in the late spring (a trip more renowned for its encounter with the burgeoning population of blackflies than anything else) and the junior trip to Quebec to visit, among other places, the shrine of St. Anne of Beaupré and to mourn, yet again, the British occupation of French Canada.

For the girls of St. Mary of Cleophas, there was no lack of exciting events to look forward to, adventures to have, entertainments to share — from week to week, season to season, and year to year. But as delightful as were all of these great occasions, the grandest, the most wonderful, the most eminent was the annual journey to Rome conducted by the Latin teacher, Maura Briscoe.

Of course, this excursion was restricted to seniors and, moreover, only to those seniors who had survived the truly demanding rigors of a four-year Latin curriculum—which meant, in effect, only the very cream of the student body found themselves sufficiently privileged to go. Yet the effort to survive that program, and the competition to keep up with the other students in the program, was positively fierce—if for no other reason than that the journey to Rome was seen as the consummate experience that St. Mary of Cleophas could provide.

Even the excluded multitudes could participate in this experience in a surrogate way, if only as those who eagerly anticipated what would assuredly be breathless accounts of what had occurred—stories that never disappointed and that quickly accrued to the vast repository of legend about the trip in school history.

And, if that journey to Rome itself were not marvelous enough, the most marvelous of all was the excursion, traditionally taken on the penultimate day of the trip, a hundred or so miles to the south of Rome, to the ancient, once buried city of Pompeii.

Even this excursion itself had its summary moment—its "moment of moments," if we can use such an expression—though a curious kind of silence reigned about what exactly went on in that "moment of moments," as if what happened there was too esoteric, too special, too sacrosanct for anyone to discuss except in the most vague and allusive terms.

It took place during the visit to a roofless ruin of a house at the edge of the city. Here, after a tour of the house, replete with intimate details of the busy life that had once ensued there, Maura would astonish and terrify her Latin students by standing before the hearth of that ancient house and offering up a sacrifice before the apse of the sacred Lar, the household god. For, claimed Maura, this very place was her ancestral domicile, the house where she was living in A.D. 79, when, as a little girl of eight years old named Egeria, Vesuvius erupted and buried Pompeii, and her, and all that was most dear to her, in burning cinders.

Is the story I'm about to tell you a happy story or a sad story, a story of birth or a story of death, a story of regeneration or a story of unspeakable loss? I wish I knew.

But let me tell you a bit more about Maura Briscoe. When I knew her — during those few years I spent as a fellow teacher at St. Mary of Cleophas — she was in her mid-forties, unmarried, living by herself in a small cottage that overlooked a small, solitary lake close to the school. She was about mid-height, slender, vigorous but by no means muscular, an ardent walker, with bushy brown hair and a pert, small-featured face. She was always cheerful, always alert, and always laughed at little things.

She had a master's degree in Latin from Columbia University and had — certainly an unusual gift in modern times — a curious ability to speak it, though what she spoke was not the Ciceronian Latin one studied in the classroom but more the language of characters in the plays of Plautus and Terence. (She claimed, of course, that it was her "native" language.)

She also grew lovely flowers around her little cottage, went for hikes, often alone, in the White Mountains, traveled a great deal in Europe and was familiar with most of the great sites of classical antiquity spread from Asia Minor and across Europe and northern Africa to the coasts of Spain and Britain.

In the schoolroom she was a devoted teacher; she loved her pupils to distraction and yet demanded everything from them (and got it). She was a colorful and animated figure on campus, in the library, at school events, and in the dining hall.

Most fascinating of all, she was a pagan.

I mean a real pagan. You know — Jupiter, Diana, Mars, Minerva, Apollo — that kind of pagan.

Or so she said.

Now, granted, that seems odd in a school such as St. Mary of Cleophas. In a way, yes; in another way, no. The positive reason should be obvious enough — after all, this was a Catholic school that took itself very seriously; the negative reason may be a bit more abstruse.

For Maura Briscoe gave a different version, in its own way more intense for youthful minds, of what was imparted to them day by day in the glowing liturgy that St. Mary of Cleophas made of life itself — and here the pagan and the Christian could vaguely converge and resonate with one another. "All things," as Herakleitos would and did say, are "full of gods"; and St. Thomas Aquinas could add, "God is in all things, and intimately so." But what the students learned at St. Mary of Cleophas, they learned primarily as a sacred ambience imparted by stained-glass color and Eucharistic candles and cheerful bouquets laid at the feet of smiling saints.

Here, by contrast, in Maura's world was something infinitely chiaroscuro — a bronze and verdigris world with darkness and somber golden light and the heavy shadows of the numinous and sad beyond all words. You could say, certainly, that Maura Briscoe was a religious woman — filled with *pietas* for the ancient divinities of earth and sky, of tree and pond and sacred well and mountain. Beyond that, you could speak of her ancestral worship, of her devotion to the household gods who inhabit hearth and bedchamber, of her attachment to the sacral precincts of a homeland and of those hallowed enclaves that lead ever downward to the dusky underworlds of the spirit-voices and the venerable dead.

To listen to her speak, enwrapped as she could become in some ancient text, was to feel a chill in your bones, the hair bristling on your skin, the inexplicable awe at the unfathomable mysteries deployed so palpably around her.

She was also a scholar and led her students assiduously through the tangled mazes of Latin grammar, drilling them in the high exercises of translation and composition, verse scansion and oral recitation and memorization of sometimes lengthy passages from Cicero and Virgil. She taught them to walk in Latin, talk in Latin, play in Latin, and dream in Latin. She unfolded, day by day, the richness of the Latin in the English language and enjoyed illustrating for them how French and Spanish and Italian (in all of which she was fluent and one of which most of her students were pursuing as a second language) were developments of what she called "provincial street Latin." She also regaled them with her displays of classical Greek and her occasional evocation of ancient Sanskrit or Old Irish or Proto-Germanic cognate words and forms. And she taught them to love the ancient past — its architecture and literature, its philosophy and its technology, its sense of law and its reverence for the spiritual in life.

All of this was, in a general way, preparation for the senior trip to Rome. In a more specific way, Maura began to prime her students a year in advance for exploring the city itself. Each girl who would go on the trip was given the responsibility to research extensively a particular ancient site and to act as a guide and a resource for that site when the group was in Rome.

The students also became acquainted with the general layout of Rome, its history in the post-classical period, and with much of Renaissance and of modern Rome as well. A quick crash course in modern Italian, beginning a few months before departure, prepared the girls for an interesting and exciting engagement with the modern city.

Moreover, they studied sites outside Rome itself, such as Ostia and Hadrian's Villa and the Etruscan cities to the north, and would be able to visit them if time permitted. Occasionally, a student group might even seek out Horace's farm in the Alban Hills. And, of course, they studied Pompeii, studied it in detail from someone who, it appeared, knew it as thoroughly and intimately as you could know it.

It was only in my third year of teaching at St. Mary of Cleophas that I was invited, by Maura, to act as one of several chaperones who normally accompanied the students on the trip. It was an honor, of course, to do this; no one who had ever taken the trip came back without having been thrilled by it. It was a marvelous opportunity to see Rome in a way that you could rarely see it.

Maura made the most of it too. Though she managed, in her own way, to have her wards do everything that tourists in Rome usually do, she also managed to have them do it in a way that other tourists never do it. She would enter the usual places and, after the designated student had given her presentation, would then focus attention on some curious nook or cranny ignored by everybody else and give some marvelous account of something that had happened there. The student in question always loved this special reinforcement of what she had presented, and the others were thrilled by the intimate narratives Maura could supply in such a spontaneous and lively way. In many locations, she would, in a sense, "strip away" time, descending to ever and ever lower and older layers of what was in front of them.

Moreover, she saw a Rome no one else saw, a Rome not just of antique buildings and jumbled ruins but of action and interaction. She could point to the spot where and when this and that happened, and who was there and what they said or didn't say. She could show the roost where the sacred geese were kept who warned the guards on the Capitoline Hill of the stealthy approach of the Gallic "commandos" (as she called them); she would stand at the base of the great staircase leading up to the Ara Coeli and relate how Cola di Rienzo, in the Middle Ages, was finally cut down there by the angry Roman crowd; she could lead her charges among the somber pines and tombs of the Via Appia and conjure up for them a Roman legion, standard-bearers garbed in grim wolfskins, marching through an early morning mist and accompanied by the dull thud of drums and the flat blare of enormous tubas.

All of this, of course, added immeasurably to the students' morale since they became so aware that their thoroughness of preparation and intimacy of knowledge so expressly differentiated them from the hordes of other tourists who were carted brainlessly about the city in buses, rather a bit like sides of meat suspended from hooks in grocery vans, rocking them back and forth passively as the buses hurtled through narrow streets.

And all of this is to say nothing of the sites they somehow surreptitiously entered. Such escapades gave an aura of secrecy and danger to the activities that, if sometimes jolting to the adult chaperones on the trip, were invariably wonderful to the girls. They always seemed to be sneaking into places where they were not supposed to go. One year, apparently, they infiltrated the Domus Aurea of Nero in the dark after visiting hours were over; the students, it was said, clambered about with tiny flashlights purchased for this purpose and some even got lost (so they thought) in the great labyrinth of halls and chambers.

I surmised, eventually, that Maura probably knew many of the custodians of these places, had prearranged the visits at unusual times (e.g., gates were left curiously unlocked), and had even prearranged the chase that would cause the group to scamper out of a site with a supposedly enraged guardian hot on its heels. Such an episode inevitably made for a lively dinner discussion at some restaurant off the Campo de' Fiori afterward.

Then, as I was told, there always was a run-in with the Roman police, a tumultuous event in a police station, and the sudden appearance of a short, heavy, balding attorney who looked like Bacchus fresh in from the vineyard (or from the tavern, whichever was most relevant at the time). After a few waves of his arms and a few summary expostulations with the authorities, Maura kissed him on the head and shepherded the group out on the street again to face whatever new adventure might await it.

The year I was there, we stayed in a fairly roomy hotel tucked in between the Palatine Hill and the Circus Maximus. Since there were a number of other student groups from different nations at the same hotel, Maura got the idea of organizing a foot race around the Circus, among teams of four from each nation (the evocation of four chariot horses was all too clear). The point of the race, however, was to win not simply by the fastest running but, by the reinstating of an ancient practice, preventing the other teams from winning. The result among the five "national" teams that raced, to say nothing of their supporters—who at least for a while were patiently cheering on their teams while sitting on the grassy banks around the racecourse—was enough to undo fifty years of work by the United Nations, the European Union, and whatever other organizations exist to promote international peace and goodwill. In any event, the Roman police were soon careening through the streets of Rome, sirens quavering and batons frantically brandished from the windows of diminutive Fiat police cars. Bacchus made his compulsory appearance at the police station, and Maura, her students, and everyone else involved were loosed on the world again, all quite certain, despite a few bruises, that it had been great fun.

But the journey to Pompeii was, as it was meant to be, the climax. Here we did, as was usual, lease a bus and were driven southward toward Naples through the Liri Valley—with a brief stop at Monte Cassino, where Maura gave a brief but impassioned account of its monastic history, focusing on St. Benedict's founding and concluding with the massive bombardment of the monastery during the Second World War. Not long afterward we arrived at the outskirts of the ancient city of Pompeii itself.

It would be fruitless for me to try to explain most of what would and did happen in that visit. Maura made the city alive for us: its origins in the old Sabine and Oscan country folk; its newer Roman, Latin-speaking population; its vibrant textile industries; its rebuilding from the great earthquake of 62; its markets and Odeon and forum and games in the amphitheater;

its busy commerce with the huge Roman naval base at Misenum, not far away — right down to the details of where its bookies and gamblers would cluster, downing goblets of the local wine while waiting for the race results from the Circus Maximus in Rome to arrive by carrier pigeons.

Toward midafternoon we finally converged upon the ruins of a house in one of the far quarters of the city. It was Maura's ancestral home. We entered it and learned of the intricacies of daily life and familial deportment that once went on in those old cubicles and atria, the loggia and gardens, which bore, in their present state, such a heavy witness to the swift and tragic demise of that household. This is where that eight-year-old girl, bearing that quintessential Roman name Egeria, had lived and played by the fishpond in the center of the house. This is where her family had practiced the sacred rites that made them a family and made them proper citizens of a city and of a great world empire. Maura was unusually somber as she explored those chambers with us, and the students listened intently and solemnly.

And then …!

What I — what we — saw would demand the eloquence of a Sophocles to do it justice — and it's upon that eloquence that I shall draw. For we were all abruptly herded into a dark, cavernous alcove, where we were suddenly blinded by a dozen parallel shafts of dazzling sunlight slanting downward at a steep angle through jagged crevices in the fractured masonry. We stumbled and tripped and jostled one another.

When we recovered our sight and our footing, we saw Maura standing in the midst of those blazing shafts as if transfixed by a phalanx of luminous spears. Her hands were lifted and bent backward in some kind of ritual gesture before the apse of the sacred Lar, her fingers splayed and crooked upward like thin, naked talons and her palms filled with a fine ash that now whirled about her in a storm of cloud and sunlight.

She stood there amid that whirlwind, like the ancient Antigone herself, emitting the piercing shrill cries "of a disconsolate bird, its nest despoiled, its kindred robbed and vanquished." Three times in rapid succession she swung her lustral offering of ashes over the shrine and remembered all those unmourned and unmarked dead, whom the chthonic depths of the underworld itself had risen to inter with its fiery deluge and whom the

Roman world itself left immured in its ashy entombment and so rapidly forgot.

The students recoiled with terror, clutching one another, trembling, speechless, eyes riveted on the almost violent rite that unfolded before them and which, for all that they had been led to expect, exceeded anything they had ever imagined.

And I, too, was astonished. I could hardly recognize Maura as the one who stood before me and enacted what I was witnessing. I also, for just that moment, saw, or thought I saw, revealed in front of me—with an immediacy I never considered possible—the loss and suffering, the fathomless and inconsolable despondency, the *lacrimae rerum*, that permeated the consciousness of the ancient world and all its cultic visions.

I envisaged then too, envisage even now, the terrified child, Egeria, groping for the hands of her parents in the panicked crowds as they tried to protect her while holding pillows on their heads against the torrents of pumice and sharp little stones pouring down from the skies; the shoving and pushing through the thick ash, the crying and choking, the impact of human bodies against each other, the collisions with frantic dogs and goats and donkeys, the flapping of geese and squawking hens; the impenetrable blackness brindled by jagged strips of flame crackling through sulfurous clouds; houses and roofs collapsing; the sea off the Porta Marina boiling and retracting from the land like gums from crumbling, blackened teeth; thick, poisonous gases, clothes and hair on fire, eyes burning and clotted by dust, mouth and lungs filling with thick, hot cinders; tears and gasping and blood and fright; incandescent fire waves of enormous temperatures surging at immense speeds down hillsides and roads and vaporizing instantly everything in their path; and the untellable passage of the great rivers of agony and death converging and parting through the dark arsenals of the underworld, of icy Styx and toxic Acheron, of fiery Phlegethon and tearful Cocytus and soporific Lethe (and yet, for this person, this Egeria alone, the memory-effacing submergence in Lethe only partially completed)—and then a scream, an arching, heart-wrenching scream, a scream ripping through the fullness of her flesh, the scream of an awakened life, the deep flush of fresh, invigorating air suddenly sluicing downward and flooding her lungs, hands holding her up, suspended like a jewel in the bright, cool sunlight of a New Hampshire morning: "It's a girl!" a voice exclaimed—a girl has been born.

Or so one could imagine in just that moment, somehow, somewhere, in the depths of one's heart.

Everything was over as suddenly as it began. Within minutes we had left the house, and Maura and I soon were walking briskly along one of the old streets well ahead of the students, who hovered in a tremulous group behind us, trying, as best they could, to calm themselves and to stammer to one another what little they were able about the scene that they had just witnessed.

They knew already that for the rest of their lives the most important part of this story was sealed up in their memories as a secret too frightening—maybe too serious—to tell; and they wouldn't add it to the lore they would transmit on to others, making it as much a shock yet again when a new group would see it.

Maura, meanwhile, hooked her arm in mine, as she sometimes did with anyone she walked alongside of, and glanced up at me as we walked, her face smiling and her eyes cheerful but a bit strained in the glare of the intense Mediterranean sun. All traces of the ferociously tragic Antigone were gone. She seemed somewhat pleased with herself, as we all do when we feel that we have accomplished what we set out to do and can savor yet another job well done.

She looked at me and then away, tugging at my arm, and then looked at me again and said: "Well, how did I do?" She smiled. Obviously, she didn't expect me to answer her question. She had done very well indeed, and she knew that. She was happy, yet she still seemed so oddly pensive and sad.

I was puzzled, of course, by all of this; she must have noted the puzzled expression on my face, for she added, "How else can I help them make the connection and take it all seriously, as serious as it really is, as serious as it really was?"

At the end of the street, in the far distance, I could see the tall gray cone of Vesuvius, ominously silhouetted against the late afternoon sky. We all had a delightful dinner later that evening, at Sorrento, in a restaurant surrounded by an orange grove and overlooking the Bay of Naples, which was golden and darkly glowing in the fading light.

The following morning, we returned to Rome. The final day of the trip was always traditionally reserved for shopping. The girls had the liberty to wander among the boutiques of the Corso and purchase the fashionable accessories that abound in modern Italy with such finesse and elegance, as well as to collect their souvenirs and gifts for the people back home. Maura was not part of this, however, and went off by herself. The final day of the trip was always her own, her very private day. One wondered where she went and what she did.

Well, you know, it's difficult not to speculate from time to time about a person like Maura Briscoe, and I certainly will not try to do so now; but I knew then in an odd sort of way, and my knowledge was only confirmed again and again in those brief years that I enjoyed her company, that the destination of her final, private foray into Rome was the *sanctum sanctorum*, the holy place of the holy ones, the household of the sanctified — no, not the Pantheon, as you might have presumed, or the remnant of some other pagan shrine but the domicile of that old Pontifex Maximus himself, Builder of Bridges, of the bridge that spanned the ages, that linked an old to a new dispensation, that spoke to the eternal longings of antiquity and that assuaged its immeasurable sorrow.

Previously I posed the question whether the story I was about to tell was a happy story or a sad story, a story of birth or a story of death, a story of regeneration or a story of unspeakable loss. I think, in retrospect, it is all of these things.

I don't know, and I highly doubt, that an eight-year-old girl named Egeria ran along the darkening streets of a doomed Pompeii; and if she did, she was not the same person whom I had the privilege of knowing. She was a fiction after all, a fiction like Sophocles' stalwart Antigone herself, who served a purpose sublime and magnanimous and grave.

But the person I did know was someone who was able, or perhaps to whom it was given to be able, to gather into herself all the pain of that event, and perhaps of all such events that had happened innumerable times before and would happen innumerable times again, whenever a child would find herself suddenly abandoned in a fiery city, her brief life soon to be cut short by the peremptory eruptions of nature or man; and this person could let the rest of us know, through her, about some small portion of all of that, and about the grandeur of life itself that, in other ways, served only to underscore the poignancy of its all-too-precocious and unspeakable extinction.

The Egeria she invented was her way of doing precisely this.

And it worked.

How could any of us who observed that "moment of moments" not harbor in our hearts, for the rest of our lives, that piercing cry of a noble soul face-to-face with the boundless and inexplicable suffering of the entire animate creation, with the sacrificial loaves of the universe itself, with the blood of every sacred vessel that has ever mattered, lifted in lustral offering?

I should say, in addition, that such cognizance gave an ever-new meaning to Maura Briscoe's presence at a school named after a personage, St. Mary of Cleophas, about whom nothing is known except that she stood, a mute witness, at the foot of the Cross. And, if life at St. Mary of Cleophas Academy featured its flowered feasts and sparkling windows and smiling saints, it also displayed at its center the bleeding visage of the figure whom St. Mary of Cleophas gazed upon.

We embarked at the airport early the next day and returned to the academy. Its eager students awaited our triumphal entry, and its repository of Roman lore would again be enriched by a multitude of stories, as it always was and always would be. It's many years now since I've been a colleague of Maura Briscoe. Our ways parted long ago, as I drifted off into the ever-illusory opportunities afforded by the world of schools and education, wondering why I had left my original appointment in the first place, wondering why I had left the company of one of the most genuine persons I've ever known.

But still, after all this time, I can't imagine her being anyone other than the person I knew back then, *nunc et semper eadem, nunc et semper nova*: now and forever the same, now and forever new.

Maître Renart's Shrovetide Confession

Confiteor, my goodly *père*,
With contrite heart I do declare
All my misdeeds, both great and small,
My lies, my theft, my sly cabal.
De Polognie à Portyngal
No greater sinner therewithal
Than I, who sought the rich to bleed
(Relieving them of excess greed),
The powerful to bring to heel
(Curbing their all too boastful zeal),
And many a good wife to enjoy
(They were neither shy nor coy.
Such things, *bon père*, could make you blush,
To your *belle maîtresse* quickly rush
By my adventures aptly spurred.
So do forget what you've just heard!)
I beg reprieve of those I've hurt:
I chomped Dame *Dinde* for dessert;
Tybert *le chat*, I cracked his pate;
Loup Isengrin, I raped his mate;
Duke *Sanglier*, his brood I ate;
Bruin, *l'ours,* I fleeced his skin;
In barnyards near I raised a din,
In barnyards far my mayhem reigned,
Rumpus, disorder unrestrained.
Goose and gander flapped and flailed;
Ducks their ducklings sore bewailed.
(What joy it was to hear them quack,
Those succulent darlings in my sack!)
Oh, how they all would hoot and sigh

As I escaped their hue and cry!
Count Écureuil I felled his trees;
Tierclin, *corbeau*, I conned his cheese.
Firepel, *leopard*, strong and lithe,
I snared and made him yowl and writhe.
Seigneur Lion, majestic king,
I stole his royal signet ring.
Chauntecleer, may he pardon me
And forgive my flagrant flattery.
(Next time I ask him home to dine
He'll trust me then and won't decline.
Though *coq au vin* will be our fare,
Steeped in that wine he'll hardly care.)
To Sire Grimbert I was unfair,
Inviting him to my distant lair,
Making his stay *chez Maupertuis*
So crude poor badger had to flee.
Blancart, *le cerf*, I scorched with fire,
His doe *Courtiose* I splotched with mire.
How many masquerades I've worn!
Abbot, bishop, monk well shorn,
Philosopher, crusader, knight,
Guildsman, peasant, anchorite;
As troubadour I roam at large,
A penny a poem is what I charge.
(The same old poem I sell anew,
The same old doggerel, tried and true.)
Certes, I'm what you want to see
(If you ignore my perjury).
All of this I've vowed to change,
All bad habits I will estrange.
Never more will I blaspheme;
Pious deeds will be my theme.
From taverns, brothels, I'll recoil

To grievous penance and hard toil.
Extortion, blackmail, forgery,
Sedition, bribes, dark calumny
Will no longer spur my stride,
No longer be my source of pride.
Alchemy will be justly spurned,
No longer swindling what you earned.
Salaciousness I will uproot,
Smudging my face with ash and soot.
With staff and badge and hooded head,
With bare and bleeding feet I'll tread
The path to holiness instead.
De Polognie à Portyngal
At palmers' shrines I'll make my call.
From life of crime I shall forbear.
When shriven pure, I shall forswear
My violent ways, my earthly lusts.
I'll live on pods and old, stale crusts.
No more *lapin* in sauces creamy;
No more *agneau* in ragouts steamy;
No more *foie gras* in clay terrines
Or partridge stuffed with herbs and beans;
No casks of sweet and mellow wine
To soothe my palate when I dine.
No crocks of ale, no *brie*, no cake.
Dear friends, now for Our Lady's sake,
Open your gates, discard your locks.
You need no longer guard your flocks,
Or hide your jewelry in your socks.
I AM A MOST REPENTANT FOX.
From you, *bon père, proficiscor,*
I venture forth to sin no more.
Cleanse me as when my life began.
(If this won't fob them, nothing can!)

Aunt Jennie's Christmas Pie

It's generally held that every family has its secrets—little mysteries of one sort or another that it discloses to the rest of the world, if ever, only with the most obstinate resistance or in a language intended, by virtue of its recondite phraseology, to confuse and obfuscate, as much as to illuminate, any potential auditor.

In one sense, certainly, I intend—and flagrantly so—to violate such a generally held principle, for the revelation of family secrets will be my stock-in-trade. In another sense, I'm bound to the principle in spite of myself, for the deepest mystery of all is as mysterious to the family members themselves as it would be to anyone from the outside who endeavored to plumb its shadowy depths.

That's why it would be futile for me to attempt any description of that sumptuous pastry so notable in my family's history—futile and possibly self-defeating as well, for the enigma of Aunt Jennie's Christmas pie itself has, assuredly, been part of its charm and part of the reason why the Ballankirk clan has treasured its memory so deeply, even as it has tried to fathom its inscrutable contents.

Suffice it to say, in the present context, that Aunt Jennie's Christmas pie is a curious combination of candied fruits steeped for several days in the appropriate spirits and covered with a thick cream, or possibly custard, flavored with nutmeg and other spices, and chilled in a rich pastry crust. That much is known; what is unknown are all the specific choices and measurements of these various ingredients. What, for example, are the "appropriate spirits"? — a subject which, in any event, is dear to the Ballankirk heart regardless of its relationship to the confection under discussion.

Endless attempts over the last century and a half have been expended in the effort to determine what the original ingredients of the pie might have been — on the supposition that Aunt Jennie's prototype had a flavor whose sublimity couldn't be surpassed; and a traditional feature of the great Ballankirk Christmas gatherings is the submission of at least a dozen variants of the pie for the discrimination and judgment of the clan members. Needless to say, none of these submissions ever passes muster, and all are ultimately — though politely — rejected as not being "quite the real thing," though I've never really understood what standards are being applied in rendering such a judgment, since no one, for the last century and a half, has, to my knowledge, ever tasted "quite the real thing," though there is one candidate for this honor, and he, a complete stranger to the family and of unknown provenance, has disappeared altogether from the annals of gods and men. To this fortunate one, though profoundly unfortunate in another sense, I shall return later on in my tale.

Indeed, the quest for the pie's ingredients might be thought of as having assumed a role, within the hermetically enclosed (though soon to be disclosed) world of the Ballankirk clan, analogous to the search for the Universal Elixir among alchemists of old, or for the restorative waters of the Fountain of Youth among enterprising conquistadors of all stripes.

These analogies are more than capricious; the quest for the recipe is driven not only by a gastronomic hunger but also by a distinctly spiritual desire that no Ballankirk would ever confess to having and yet which all of them have in one way or another: a deep-seated though rarely articulated longing for something we might vaguely call "reconciliation." I know that such a claim is apt to appear a bit odd at the moment, but that's what, finally, the pie is really all about, as I shall endeavor to explain, though my explanations require precisely the sort of family secrets I will purport to divulge.

As a final note, in all deference to whom I hope will be my patient reader, if I did know the actual recipe of the pie, I certainly wouldn't tell it. I'm prepared to tell a great deal, much of a deeply personal nature about my family, but of such a monumental betrayal of family confidences, I am not, and, God forbid, never would be, capable.

Aunt Jennie is a person whose stature in family history is almost as remote and as mythical as the pie itself. She lived her brief but memorable life sometime in the early to middle part of the nineteenth century—that is, about five or six generations ago. The Ballankirks had recently resettled from Canada to the hills of northern Vermont, and Aunt Jennie, a younger member of the clan at the time, was a sprightly girl who married a young farmer not far from the parental household and who died at the age of twenty-two when giving birth to twin boys in the middle of a particularly bitter winter. Within a day or so, her two sons followed her to the grave, and all three were buried in the same coffin together, Aunt's Jennie's arms tenderly wrapped around each of her deceased children.

Aunt Jennie was noted for, among other attractive features of her personality, her cheerful and generous disposition—a quality of character not especially prevalent among Ballankirks but prized by them nevertheless; for in every generation since the demise of Aunt Jennie, Ballankirks have eagerly sought out the traces of Aunt Jennie's character in fellow family members, a quest that's not, I must confess, easily rewarded. Yet every generation or two, an Aunt Jennie does seem to appear, though such a solitary figure tends to be acknowledged as such only in retrospect—that is, after he or she has ceased to be of any possible living challenge to the complex play of hostilities that animates the mutual life of the Ballankirks and gives such infinite, if transitory, joy to their hearts.

Aunt Jennie was also noted for her culinary skills. Once again, this made her unusual for Ballankirks whose tastes in food and drink can best be described as execrable, though they like to talk a great deal about such matters; and, if talk were a guide to what is real, you'd imagine that all Ballankirks were gourmet chefs and connoisseurs of fine cuisine with the most impeccable credentials. Nothing could be further from the truth; all Ballankirk cooking, even if it's spaghetti with tomato sauce or lobster bisque or roast duck, ends up tasting like some version or another of burnt oatmeal.

But Aunt Jennie was different, so it's said.

Her greatest contribution to family history, however, was her invention, or rediscovery, of a pie recipe especially designed for the festive Christmas season. You must recall, at this juncture, that for people like the Ballankirks, even into the first half of the nineteenth century, Christmas was a time of year to be rigorously shunned as tainted with the vestiges of medieval idolatry and papist superstition.

Aunt Jennie must have been quite a rebel in this regard; or perhaps living in the proximity of the French inhabitants of Canada had exerted all too subtle an influence in bringing the Ballankirks back to at least some of the customs of their own ancestors many centuries before, so that they were, by Aunt Jennie's time, receptive to her startling innovations. For Aunt Jennie's pie was redolent of something sweetly and succulently medieval — as rich and full as an illuminated manuscript, as light and gracious as Gothic tracery, as joyous and colorful as a stained-glass window. Aunt Jennie restored Christmas for the Ballankirks, and her pie succeeded in giving the tone (or I should say, more properly, the final tone) to the season.

If, as we shall see, a Ballankirk Christmas is not always as merry an affair as it might be, it's precisely Aunt Jennie's pie that brings such a festive occasion back to what Aunt Jennie, in the goodness of her heart, had seen as its proper purpose. I might add, incidentally, that the endemic culinary handicaps of the Ballankirks, mentioned above, are surmounted only in relation to this pie, for the multiform efforts at reconstruction, though inevitably off the mark, are nevertheless tasty enough concoctions to satisfy the most exacting gourmands.

The central fact is that, as I've intimated several times already, the Ballankirks are not, by any standards, a peaceable folk: and, though they spend much of their lives fighting anybody, at any time and at any place, for any reason whatsoever, they mainly fight among themselves. I've little doubt that, when some Roman legionnaire, fresh from the fragrant hills of the Campagna, looked northward from Hadrian's Wall in horror at bands of naked, blue-painted warriors (of both sexes, incidentally), twirling axes in their hands and shaking spears tipped with venom, he was viewing the remote ancestors of my illustrious clan. Both extra- and infra-clan warfare kept them happily occupied for the centuries that followed, to say nothing of holding back the "Saxons" from the south, as well as raiding Saxon cattle herds and burning down their granges, whose burgeoning storage bins argued for all too unseemly a devotion to industry and skill.

It's no accident that the first Ballankirks showed up on the North American continent in the mid-eighteenth century to fulfill any number of variously combative roles: to take on Indian tribes as warlike as they were, to ambush French explorers and settlers, and to march southward from Lake Champlain with General Burgoyne's British army against the rebellious thirteen colonies, though the Ballankirks were no more loyal to the English crown than the insurgents against whom they fought. If poor old General Washington had had more ready cash on hand, the Ballankirks would have traded sides in an instant.

As it was, their English paymasters didn't have much ready cash on hand either, but the Ballankirks were amply rewarded for their service, even despite the defeat, with substantial land grants in Canada. As soon as real estate prices had peaked (and Ballankirks always know when prices of any kind have peaked), these lands were sold, and the Ballankirks moved to Vermont and later spread throughout New England, where they mostly reside today.

To be sure, things have become somewhat more genteel with time. The verbal challenge, the insult, the stinging reproach have always been uppermost in the arsenal of the Ballankirk character; but the days of the accompanying claymores, dirks, poisoned goblets, studded war clubs, and burning strongholds are over; a later age of canes, broken whiskey bottles, hairpins, darning needles, and other instruments of assault have also been replaced with more ostensibly civilized methods. For example, no truly serious hair-pulling incident has taken place since Great-Aunt Bertha's wedding, eighty-five years ago (by "truly serious" I mean a situation in which the hair-puller successfully uproots a substantial fistful of hair from the hair-pullee). I should mention that kicking, scratching, and biting are reserved for interspousal conflicts and enter into larger family rows only when a husband and a wife happen to find themselves on opposite sides in a major clan split—which is rare but is likewise fruitful in providing some fascinating, if delightfully vicious, ancillary skirmishes and ambushes.

Even the language of reproach has undergone subtle alterations through the years. For example, it's reported that a great-great-grandfather went to the Pacific Northwest in his early years as a trapper and "mountain man" and returned to eastern Canada fifteen years later with two girls said to be his daughters by an Indian woman whom he had married in the west and who later succumbed to smallpox. The two daughters became the progenitors of the so-called western division in the Ballankirk clan structure, which could claim Amerind ancestry and which adopted a strange propensity to resort to a kind of "westernese" in its linguistic habits, especially when tempers were blazing hot, as they frequently were.

Thus, expressions such as "warpath," "firewater," "wampum," and "bad hombre" (applied to both sexes) gave vent to outrage and provocation. Referring to a fellow family member as a "paleface" was generally regarded as an especially opprobrious charge—a curious enough reproach given that all Ballankirk visages are as blanched, if not bleached, as the most proverbial linen sheet ever was, since they all scrupulously avoid any direct contact with sunlight (for a variety of sinister reasons, no doubt; though some have to do with superstitions regarding the notorious "noonday devil," but we'd better not get into this matter). That such "westernese" phrases were actually picked up from dime-store novels and early western films (and that everyone seemed to know pretty well that they were) didn't deter either their forcefulness or their usage.

Another example of linguistic change can be illustrated by the ability that all Ballankirks in the past claimed to have: an ability, that is, to discern with spiritual acuity who is, and who is not, a member of the "elect" in quite a theological sense. To be able to make such a discernment was itself obviously a sign of being "elect," and it just so happened that anyone with whom one was in conflict at the moment was one of the "reprobates" and needed to be rather urgently and persistently reminded of this fact.

We don't need to worry about the inconsistencies that may have arisen in this discernment, given that one's antagonists shifted from time to time and hence membership among the predestined "damned" was subject to correlative revisions as well.

Nor do we need to worry about the sources of this extraordinary charism, nor the mode of its characteristic expression as derived from the lore of many a learned divine; but I think that even John Calvin himself would have trembled in his grave if he could have heard the earth being rocked by some Ballankirk pronouncement of eternal damnation. For in every Ballankirk, male and female, there lurked a fire-and-brimstone preacher poised perpetually to leap out, even if the setting was in a playpen and the protagonist was a four-year-old Ballankirk girl precociously declaring that her antagonist, in this case her three-year-old sister, was a "daughter of Jezebel" and a "whore of Babylon."

But those days are over.

Freud has replaced Calvin as the arbiter of salvation. The "loony bin" and "the funny farm" have replaced Hell as the place where one definitely, as well as indefinitely, deserves to be. And the language of theology has been replaced by the language of "fixations" and "complexes": "neurosis" and "schizoid" and "obsessive behavior" and "bipolar" and other psychological terms whose implications are taken to be as deadly and their effects as permanent, incurable, and irredeemable as adverse theological predestination ever was.

Of course, no Ballankirks have ever had training in scientific psychological observation, but this doesn't in any way impede the certainty with which they make their diagnoses of other family members, nor the authority with which they enunciate them.

It's not uncommon, for instance, for one Ballankirk to accuse another of having an "inferiority complex." Such an accusation is an absurdity to begin with, because whatever gene in the human chromosomal makeup allows people to have inferiority complexes, such a gene is utterly lacking in a Ballankirk. It's as impossible for a Ballankirk to have an inferiority complex as it is for an elephant to be a giraffe.

But the charge itself is guaranteed to put its receptor into a towering rage, for the mere suggestion that one would think oneself somehow inferior to others is enough to put one's sense of inexorable superiority to a most severe test. This set of facts holds true even despite the not infrequent practice among Ballankirks, especially the females, of engaging in prolonged bouts of verbal self-flagellation and accusation. The function of these bouts is purportedly to elicit compassionate denials from its audience, but such denials are not, and never will be, forthcoming, and the self-flagellator knows this full well from the start. Hence, the silence of the audience is taken to mean its tacit consent to the self-accusations, which therefore now become *its* accusations, for which it will be held, for the next century or so, to be responsible.

Since I'm speaking of linguistic usage here, I should conclude by mentioning that no Ballankirk ever uses obscenity in verbal engagements; such a practice would be regarded as intolerably beneath a Ballankirk's ability to score a hit with a more precise and wounding locution than the hopeless vacuity of obscene language could ever hope to accomplish. "Obscenity is stupidity": that's the Ballankirk view, and the case is closed.

And no Ballankirk, unfortunately, is stupid; in fact, they just about all have what are called genius IQs. If they could ever learn to use intelligence for constructive purposes, they would be a formidable force in this world. But don't worry. That will never happen.

At this point the inquisitive observer might be prompted to ask: "What, after all, are they fighting about?" Everything and anything is the answer, except for the two things that most other people tend to fight about: money and politics.

Ballankirks never fight about money because they all have much more than they need. The proceeds from the original sales of the Canadian land grants have proliferated over the last two centuries into multitudes of bulging investment portfolios that support virtually all the Ballankirks very handsomely without their having to work, except at the management of their own accounts—a task for which all Ballankirks seem to be particularly well-suited. An inexhaustible ingenuity for buying and selling, for hoarding and evading and hiding, has resulted in an enormous accumulation of wealth over the years.

This talent is compounded by a stinginess so profound that no one, except a Ballankirk, can understand either its boundless range or its abysmal depth. For example, Ballankirks live in old, simple if spacious houses, passed down through the generations and sparsely furnished in the interiors with monumentally fashioned porch furniture which is as indestructible as it is grotesque and uncomfortable. They drive shabby cars, twenty to thirty years old, whose mufflers sometimes drag along the ground and send up showers of sparks, even though the typical adult Ballankirk could afford, if he or she wanted, to buy out the entire inventory of a local car dealership by writing a check on the spot. They never go to hotels or restaurants and never travel, except to visit one another—and they do a great deal of this, if for no other purpose than to nurture their feuds. Occasionally, a Ballankirk indulges in an eccentric hobby that might engage some infinitesimal percentage of his or her total assets, but no other extravagances are evident. Hence, concerns about money are rarely at the focus of quarrels.

Ballankirks never fight about politics, either. It's true that college-age Ballankirks sometimes go through a brief Marxist-Leninist phase when they think that their allowances are insufficient to ferret aside enough cash to start their own stock portfolios.

But that phase, usually terminated at the age of twenty-one, never outlasts the first, and inevitable, dividend remittance (which, of course, is immediately reinvested).

Beyond that point, Ballankirks share one political conviction: that is, once the legal age is reached and whatever perpetual trust targeted at a certain individual kicks in, all thoughts of a social utopia pop like a bubble blown out of a child's little wire hoop; and whatever it is that, long ago, made them want to keep the Roman legions out of their viper-ridden fens, the "Saxons" away from their wind-blasted moors and dales, and everybody else as far away as possible, unifies them into a cohesive group vis-à-vis the outside world.

"Hands off my stuff!" says it all.

Then what do they fight about?

They fight about "making sacrifices" and "being slighted." First, about "sacrifices": no Ballankirk ever makes a sacrifice. It's just not in their nature. But for some reason they think they're constantly making them. In fact, what they're doing is making fairly risk-free investments of time or energy in others, for which they expect to receive about a 200 percent return—a return that they always get, by the way, but not with gestures of the appropriate gratitude and the groveling flattery that all Ballankirks feel is due to them but which they would never confer upon each other.

Even though what would constitute an adequate response is subject to the most capricious standards, it always follows that the "sacrifice" has been unappreciated. If you were to believe what you'd hear during one of those massive, multifaceted family confrontations, you'd imagine that such a den of snarling lions represented the highest concentration of sacrificial lambs in the world.

Second, about "slights": such slights can take an infinity of forms, and that they be unintentional, of course, is utterly irrelevant to their being slights. Even more important is the memory of slights. All Ballankirks have prodigious memories; and the capacity to produce, at a moment's notice, an exhaustive litany of slights received from a given adversary over the years is one of the most treasured, if not indispensable, accoutrements of any successful combatant. There is a certain irony here, of course. To remind an adversary of his or her insults over the years is both to flatter their pride and imagination as well as to instigate aspirations for even higher levels of achievement. It's also to invite a rejoinder such as, "Well, I was right about that, wasn't I?"

Ballankirk slights arise from many factors. One important source is pets; Ballankirks have some of their most ferocious quarrels about pets. A sacred Ballankirk rule, for example, is that all pets, whether dogs, cats, horses, parrots, fish, lizards, turtles, boa constrictors, or tarantulas, may do whatever they want to do, wherever, whenever, and to whomever they want to do it, without the risk of incurring even the mildest complaint, either explicit or implicit, by anyone other than their personal masters. Any infraction of this rule will be taken as one of the worst of slights to the personal master of the pet in question, even when, and especially when, that pet has long since departed to its Happy Hunting Ground.

I should mention in this regard that even the suspicion of complaint, though never validated, can count as a serious slight. Every Ballankirk has some animal or another that he or she worships and expects the rest of the world to worship with at least equal devotion. Sometimes — yes, I hesitate to mention this — these animals are not domesticated. Ferocious and long-lasting wars have been fought over any number of bears, chipmunks, birds of all kinds, mice, otters, raccoons, foxes, deer, moose, frogs, bees, possums, woodchucks, daddy longlegs, skunks, dragonflies, butterflies, porcupines, coyotes (also known as "feral canines" or "coydogs" in our neck of the woods, depending on your social status), and other creatures that have won a place of endearment in some Ballankirk heart.

My mother even had a third cousin, once removed, who dedicated her life to doting upon spiders — creatures with which she obviously identified because she was always crocheting long, thin, woolen afghans that she drooped like spider webs all over her house. Molesting an actual spider web, or a spider, in her presence could provoke a dreadful retaliation.

In any event, such quarrels extend, I regret to say, even to plants, a cardinal Ballankirk principle being that any plant over which you can claim proprietary rights is to be regarded as an irreplaceable miracle of natural beauty (no matter how loathsome it may actually be).

Further, any plant over which *someone else* can claim proprietary rights is to be regarded as a horrifying weed (no matter how lovely it may be) and should be, according to all reasonable protocols of man and nature, summarily stomped upon or uprooted, or both. Such stompings and uprootings have borne consequences that have lasted for decades.

Another important source of slights, real and otherwise, is the giving of gifts — but we will put off our somewhat detailed account of that until a bit later because that will bring us back to Christmas and to Aunt Jennie's Christmas pie, for Christmas is the proper setting of this marvelous pie, and the role it plays in the life of the Ballankirk clan is so utterly different from anything that I've been thus far describing. It's the one thing that manages to dampen fury and, miraculously, to bring out the more positive side of the Ballankirk temperament — and that's no small accomplishment, given that there is close to nothing about the Ballankirk character that's positive.

But before we advance to explicating this rather "miraculous" phenomenon, we must switch our attention to an incident remarkable in family history for its specific violation of the connection between Aunt Jennie's pie and the Christmas season. This violation was perpetrated by Great-Aunt Gwendolyn, who was perhaps her generation's candidate for the most Aunt Jennie–like person in goodness of character and kindness of heart. It's she who probably came closest of anyone in Ballankirk history to rediscovering the actual recipe of the original pie.

But she didn't make the pie at Christmas; she never submitted it to the judgment of the clan; and she destroyed the recipe soon after the pie was made, without even having tasted it herself. It's a deeply, deeply tragic story, and I warn my thus far (presumably) indulgent readers that they shall shed many a tear before it's over.

If it's true that Great-Aunt Gwendolyn was the recipient of the rare and gracious Aunt Jennie strain in her character, it's likewise true that she gave birth to a son in whom all the most surly and contentious traits ingrained in the Ballankirk heritage were distilled to the point of—shall we call it?—perfection. His name was Ossborough. He was also known as Ossborough the Terrible and, somewhat more affectionately, as Ossy of the Baleful Eye.

Ossy was, to use the expression commonly applied by Ballankirks to any child other than their own, "not a particularly lovely child," except that in this case the description, even if a gross understatement, had a certain veracity about it.

Indeed, Ossy was a very ugly child.

Except for a head quite a bit too large for his body, no particular feature could be pointed out as being especially repellent. But a protracted, malevolent, venomous glare emanated from his eyes with such power that it somehow gave the impression that Ossy had three, rather than two, eyes in his head, all of which were lined up in one straight row beneath a single, shaggy, menacing eyebrow that stretched across the entire width of his face. It was as if nature, frustrated in its ability to provide a sufficient outlet for such reserves of boundless animosity in a single soul, had endowed him with three vehicles with which to express what couldn't have been otherwise expressed with two.

Ossy's father was one of the many innocents who married into the clan but who, unlike most of those innocents, was not instantaneously transformed into a 100 percent, full-blooded Ballankirk. Testimony to this is the fact that he continued to perform productive labor even after his marriage to Great-Aunt Gwendolyn. The nature of his work as a sea captain, of course, and its entailment of long absences, may have assisted in maintaining his purity. Then there was Great-Aunt Gwendolyn, who was so unlike a Ballankirk and who would have exerted little pressure on him to conform to family standards.

As a result, Great-Aunt Gwendolyn and her husband, contrary to Ballankirk tradition, lived a somewhat luxurious life consonant with their fortune, occupying one of those stately mansions that surround Louisburg

Square on Beacon Hill in Boston and furnishing it with fine antiques and a small collection of old master paintings. They exercised, within prudent limits, that ancient virtue of "munificence," sharing resources generously with others and patronizing judiciously the practices of elegant craftsmanship and studious service. The only difficulty in this arrangement was Ossy, whose horrifying manners began to occupy more and more of Great-Aunt Gwendolyn's time and devotion.

Anyway, his father had noted with some vague alarm the peculiar three-eyed effect while Ossy was still of "tender" age (though the epithet here is merely conventional, I can assure you). But he had not found it especially troubling until a second cousin of Gwendolyn was invited over for tea and rather pointedly called it to his attention.

The second cousin began by referring to Ossy as "such a cute little thing" —again, another standard Ballankirk expression intended to mean its opposite and followed inevitably by a wide, teeth-baring grimace known to exist only among Ballankirks and among certain breeds of East Tanzanian mountain baboons. The relative continued to praise that "marvelous third-eye effect" which gave such "distinction" and "character" to Ossy's visage. The poor father and sea captain spent several sleepless nights thereafter, as he wrestled with the memory of a grotesque three-eyed idol he had once seen in Malaysia, and which had haunted him during a long bout of malarial fever while riding at anchor off the steamy coast of East Timor. Now, whenever he gazed upon his own son, he saw that idol, and his physique was once again racked by malarial tremors.

Not long afterward, on a bright, sunny day, with sails flapping merrily in the wind and the ocean raising joyous white-capped waves on Massachusetts Bay, Ossy's father piloted the last great clipper ship out of Boston Harbor, bound for the far reaches of the earth, the "Antipodes" of song and legend. Neither he, nor the ship, nor the ship's crew were ever seen again, though it's said that a derelict seaman, presumably a member of the vanished crew, appeared many years later among the waterfront taverns and boarding houses of Boston Harbor and spoke of some earthly paradise where the crew had settled down to live in the South Pacific. Nobody believed the foolish old man—except for those who had ever had a run-in with Ossy and who knew that half the watery earth was scarcely enough space to put between him and his distraught father.

Meanwhile, good-hearted Great-Aunt Gwendolyn settled down to a life of pampering her son. She came to the conclusion, as many parents do, that the way to a child's heart is through desserts—the richer and more sumptuous, the better. Accordingly, she devoted herself to preparing a dessert that Ossy would finally appreciate and that would, consequently, temper the burning fury in his youthful heart. The only problem was that Ossy abhorred all desserts, with the sole exception of chocolate ice-cream cones, and all his mother's efforts were in vain. Even more, she failed to grasp, through all those years, that her efforts had precisely the reverse effect they were intended to have—the more refined, the more exquisite a dessert was, the more Ossy was provoked by it into an unspeakable rage.

Every afternoon, the same scene was enacted in the dining room of the old mansion in Louisburg Square. The room itself was ornate in a simple and tasteful manner. Oak paneling, tall, sunny windows, and a great glistening mahogany table surrounded by high-backed chairs gave it a tone of mellowness and serenity. On the side of the room facing the windows was a fireplace with a mantelpiece of carved ivory upon which graceful nymphs and satyrs danced as they held up bunches of grapes and sheaves of wheat. Over the mantelpiece was hung a large Van Dyck portrait. It depicted the sixth Duke of Hallingforth standing in a regal pose, with one gloved hand on his hip and wearing a gilded cuirass embossed with a picture of Mars. Between the painting and the mantelpiece was a sizable scar on the wall, where the oak paneling was bruised and splintered. This is where Ossy, with deadly accuracy, always threw his desserts.

When lunch was over, Great-Aunt Gwendolyn would bring in the dessert that she had spent most of the morning preparing for Ossy. She would place it in front of him and watch anxiously, but with ever indefatigable optimism, to see how he would react. He would prod the dessert with his spoon, pushing it down against the surface of the mixture to explore, with all three eyes, what suspicious fluids might ooze out of the concoction. After turning the spoon and scooping up a small amount of the dessert, he would lift it slowly to his lips.

But before it even touched his lips, he would let out a great yell, spit violently, start choking and gasping and clutching his neck as if being strangled, grab his dessert, dish and all, and pitch it clear across the room, where it would smash into the accustomed place on the wall, showering the dancing nymphs and satyrs with broken pottery and sticky clumps of whatever dessert it was that day.

Ossy would leap from the table, screaming that he was going to run down to the pharmacy on Charles Street to get a chocolate ice-cream cone. He would exit the house with an enormous slam of the front door. The domestic staff would enter the dining room to clean up, and Great-Aunt Gwendolyn would return to her cookbooks.

She tried everything.

She scoured every cookbook of every nationality and every age to discover a delicacy that would finally appease Ossy's taste. She tried Austrian strudels and French crepes and Russian tarts and Sicilian marzipan and honey cakes from Tehran.

Nothing worked; and, of course, Great-Aunt Gwendolyn, who never could and never would doubt Ossy's judgment, always concluded that the dessert must indeed have been just as bad as it seemed to be to merit Ossy's treatment of it.

Then, one bright day, she remembered Aunt Jennie's Christmas pie. Of course, at the time, the Christmas season was still far off, but she was impatient for results. She was also determined that this pie, with all its succulent memories and promises, would be the thing that finally worked.

For a period of time, her regular parade of desserts went down in quality somewhat — not that it would make much difference to Ossy anyway — as she devoted most of her energy to a vast research effort to recover the original recipe. Under her tireless supervision, hundreds of old cases were opened, attics and closets from Maine to Connecticut were ransacked, thousands of old letters were read, and interviews with all living Ballankirks were conducted. Finally, by putting together hundreds of clues and scraps of information, she was able to estimate, with a relatively high degree of certainty (so she thought), how the pie should be made. She even managed to unearth the original pie pan that Aunt Jennie had used so long ago.

The fateful day arrived.

Great-Aunt Gwendolyn woke her staff at 4:00 a.m. so that the pie might be ready for lunch at 12:30. At 11:00, the pie had been completed and was prepared for serving. Great-Aunt Gwendolyn forbade her servants even to lick the spoons or bowls that had been used in making the pie, though several servants ventured to sniff the precious mixture, and they simply ululated with pleasure; never had they sniffed anything so good. It inspired in them momentary hallucinations of gastronomic paradises. The elixir had been found; the magic key had been discovered. Even Great-Aunt Gwendolyn didn't taste the pie. That joy of discovery was to be Ossy's and Ossy's alone.

As usual, she brought in the dessert and placed it on the table. Ceremoniously she cut a slice of the pie and placed it on Ossy's plate. Then she put the plate in front of him. The servants all peeked from the pantry door to see what would happen.

Ossy lifted his spoon. He bent low over the dessert. His lips curled. Three rays of cold, bitter light seemed to emanate from his eyes at different angles and to fix the dessert in their crossbeams. Even he couldn't help but notice that there was something very special about this dessert. His mother clasped her hands in delight as he prodded the surface of the pie with his spoon. No suspicious juices oozed out. The first test had been passed.

Great-Aunt Gwendolyn beamed with pleasure. Ossy scooped a tiny bit of the creamy yellow filling with his spoon and lifted it cautiously to his lips. Great-Aunt Gwendolyn held her breath. Suddenly an ear-splitting scream tore the serenity of the dining room from top to bottom, causing the servants at the pantry door to fall violently backward into the pantry.

It was followed by the most ghastly swish as the plate flew toward its accustomed place, and the entire pie hurtled after it. The plate smashed home, the pie dish clattered directly behind it, but not before its contents had risen from the dish and ended up as a bright yellow swath across the Duke of Hallingforth's cuirass.

Ossy scuttled out of the dining room at full speed, screeching for a chocolate ice-cream cone and slamming the front door with more than usual ferocity as his mother collapsed in shame and horror.

Part of the tragedy of this story is that Great-Aunt Gwendolyn came to her usual conclusion: the pie must indeed be detestable, even despite her servants' intimations to the contrary. The consequence was that she destroyed the recipe, as well as many of the clues she had found—so deep was her humiliation at the failure of the pie. Later generations would mourn, quite aptly, this loss to family tradition, though by now much of their attention had shifted to what she had discovered—a mystery in itself as inexplicable as the one her investigation set out to solve.

There was one person who did taste the pie prepared that day, but, as I've already indicated, he has passed into ignominious oblivion. His story is noteworthy for the international controversy it aroused at the time. First, we must give an account of the events that led to such an extraordinary occasion as that of a complete stranger partaking of the joys of Aunt Jennie's pie.

As we have been at some pains to illustrate, Ossy was an unpleasant enough fellow, and several decades later, his unpleasantness went to the point, as it does unlaudably in some Ballankirks, of conspiring to remove from this lamentable vale of tears any elderly personage whom one might finally construe as being an obstacle to the rightful and timely passage of a bountiful legacy. In this case, it was his own mother, who, even if Ossy had been able to forgive her for all those unwanted desserts pressed daily upon him, was considered to have lived quite long enough.

Now, there was a standard procedure for this kind of thing in the family: it was to take your intended victim out for a drive (formerly in a horse carriage and, of more recent vintage, in an automobile) that turned out to be so harrowing that only the sturdiest could survive it.

If you were really serious about this procedure, you loaded your victim into the back seat of a drafty convertible and set off for Florida in the dead of winter. As we all know, Florida is warm and balmy in the winter months, but the twelve or so states you must traverse in order to get there are locked in a vast North Atlantic chill that gets a bit milder, if not a lot damper and clammier, the farther south you go.

Remember, we are speaking of the days before superhighways, glossy motels, and restaurant chains laced together the regions of the country in their dreadful monotony: but the local color of bumpy roads looking like endless back alleys extending through miles of piney hills and plains and little corroding towns was scarcely more attractive; and what could a pair of tired New England eyes think when confronted by plate after plate of that old Southern roadside food with its pale, leprous mound of grits inexorably simmering in a puddle of hot, pungent grease?

The outcome of all of this is too clear to need mention. After a week of hard travel, the corpse is returned to Boston by way of railroad car and lugubrious cortege and is laid to rest in the family grave in Mount Auburn Cemetery in Cambridge.

So it happened to Great-Aunt Gwendolyn.

I've seen the actual farewell photograph. Ossy hugs the wheel of his monstrous Pierce-Arrow, with all three eyes burning holes in the photographic paper. A glint of satisfaction plays about his mouth as if he were anticipating the biggest, and indubitably the best, chocolate ice-cream cone in his life. Great-Aunt Gwendolyn sits in the back seat, optimally placed for catching the worst drafts, despite the masses of fur in which she's bundled and which makes her look vaguely like an Eskimo about to be led forth to her demise on the icy tundra of the north.

Three weeks later the funeral was held in Boston. It was a typical Ballankirk funeral replete with wailing, gnashing of teeth, quarreling, blaming, confessions of guilt (not to be believed, by the way), and the dreadful Ballankirk custom of the entire clan following the casket up the church aisle while walking on their knees, keening and ululating, the whole penguin-like procession wobbling and bumping into each other — a practice that it's thought (though in vain) will placate the assuredly angry spirit of the deceased.

After the funeral, Ossy collected his spoils and did a most unlikely Ballankirk thing: he detached himself for good from the clan, moved to California, and never, to the contentment of everybody, was seen again. The house on Louisburg Square was sold and all its furnishings and adornments auctioned off at Sotheby's to sundry art collectors of the world.

The Van Dyck portrait eventually found its way to the Fogg Art Museum at Harvard, where it became the object of a long and bitter academic controversy. Papers were written, scholarly symposia were held, and heated arguments conducted—all of which were to explain the glowing yellow band that stretched across the Duke of Hallingforth's cuirass.

Two major schools of thought evolved in regard to this question.

Prof. Eselkopf of Yale contended that the band was a golden ribbon added by Van Dyck to commemorate the duke's participation in the great battle at Tumble-Up-and-Down-on-Tweed between the Cavaliers and the Roundheads.

Dr. Gerhard Schwarmer, however, firing his scholarly salvos from his well-fortified bastion in Princeton, argued against this position, claiming that the duke's participation in that notable battle was one of unmitigated cowardice and that the yellow band had been added by an unknown, though hostile, painter and was intended to underscore the duke's headlong flight from the thick of the fray.

Both schools of thought conceded that the band indeed was a later addition to the painting.

The progenitors of these positions, and their rabid followers, fought out the question for years, doing everything in their power to block academic appointments, deny tenures, and destroy both the reputations and careers of their adversaries.

Then one day, a famished and lonely Harvard freshman, having nothing in particular to do with his time (as is often the case with Harvard freshmen), wandered into the Fogg Art Museum, found himself mysteriously attracted to the painting with its delectable band, and picked off and ate the entire thing before a custodian managed to catch him in the act and turned him over to the Harvard judicial committee.

This committee, retaining the self-righteous rigor of its Puritan origins, but not the latter's sense of moral principle, and directing its ire not so much at acts of immorality as at acts of indiscretion, summarily dismissed our young man from the school.

He, in turn, didn't help his case by having declared a complete lack of any repentant attitude. He asserted boldly to his judges that he would do it again under any circumstances; it had been worth it.

Ballankirk matrons are fond of citing this final part of the story to reassure themselves that the pie is truly a gastronomic wonder, even though they have never, to their knowledge, actually tasted it. Also, the members of what is called the "egg" (or sometimes the "custard") party use this story to argue that the recipe does contain eggs because the band had stuck to the painting rather remarkably like tempura. Apparently, it had even deceived the scholars (not all that difficult a thing to accomplish in most circumstances).

Efforts to reach the poor evicted freshman with the intent to probe his memory have failed because he, like so many expellees of Ivy institutions in those days, had disappeared permanently into the impenetrable mazes of the Amazonian rainforests.

Meanwhile, the academic controversy about the painting dissolved into mutual recriminations, just as bitter as ever, between the two schools of academicians, each charging the other with having perpetrated a monstrous hoax on the scholarly world. The duke of Hallingforth's descendants launched international lawsuits against just about everybody for the defamation of their august ancestor — though the proceedings uncovered new information that proved that the duke may have been an even more cringing defector than anyone had previously suspected (though an alternate hypothesis also developed claiming that the duke actually abandoned the field in order to meet, munch, and mate with his newest mistress).

Despite such dishonorable revelations, the royal family, cravenly bowing to the Hallingforth family and to public opinion (as created and conveyed by the news media), insisted on an apology from the president of the United States.

The president of the United States, cravenly bowing to the royal family and to public opinion (as created and conveyed by the news media), gave it, though the president had never heard of Van Dyck, nor of the Roundheads and Cavaliers, nor, for that matter, of the royal family; and art museums around the world, cravenly bowing to curatorial hysteria and to public opinion (as created and conveyed by the news media), significantly tightened their security by denying all famished-looking visitors access to their collections.

The Ballankirk quest has continued nevertheless, for Aunt Jennie's Christmas pie is the bond that unites them. Of course, the clan gathers, either in part or as a whole, quite a few times a year at various familial domiciles around New England.

The Fourth of July is an important event, despite the original Ballankirk contribution to the "other side" and despite the opportunity afforded by the holiday to provide untoward "incidents" — often involving fireworks used to stun pets into more or less permanent states of zoological imbecility — that can be cited as grounds for conflict for years into the future.

Labor Day is spurned, and that's good — the very idea of Labor Day puts a typical Ballankirk into such a foul mood that it's just as well they don't convene. Instead, they mope around throughout the designated day in the isolation of their homes and sedulously cultivate their throbbing migraine headaches (migraine being the only impairment Ballankirks are subject to). In any event, how could one celebrate Labor Day if one doesn't believe that those who work for the companies one holds equities in shouldn't even get Sunday off? (And since the Ballankirks, collectively, own equities in virtually every American corporation, this conviction encompasses pretty much the entire industrial workforce of the United States.)

Thanksgiving, on the other hand, is permeated by an atmosphere of late-autumnal somnolence. The clan retires from a presumptively sumptuous repast in a calm and tranquilized mood. Indeed, despite all the burnt turkey and dried-out stuffing that makes sawdust taste wonderful by comparison, they resemble a roost of great roasted turkeys themselves, stuffed and bulging and basted in the juices of contentment. Moreover, the day subsides into the implacable boredom induced by the menfolk snoring and nodding before the television set, where a dazzling play or a sudden touchdown in a seemingly endless sequence of collegiate football games occasionally pops open their bleary eyes.

But Christmas, alas, is different. The New England winter has set in; one's spirit is alert and poised as it contemplates the onset of some great meteorological Battle of the Somme against an indomitable and wily foe. One's parsimonious propensities have been exacerbated into a paranoiac frenzy by the incessant barrage of Christmas catalogues, by armed sorties into glittering department stores and malls, and by children well advanced in the stages of holiday pandemonium; and one's greed has been assaulted at every street corner by a host of Santa Clauses ringing bells and collecting money for one cause or another — after all, what is wrong with all those dimwitted and indolent Santa Clauses? Why don't they go out like anyone else with a brain in their head and inherit fortunes? But above and beyond any such trivial considerations, Christmas means two things to a Ballankirk, each as deadly as the other: the ritual of gifts and the ritual of drinking.

I shall grant for the moment that whoever gave the first Christmas gift — one of the Magi, I presume — had only the very best intentions in mind. But history has changed, and Ballankirks have reversed much of that.

To begin with, Ballankirks, by nature, have little or no inclination to give gifts to anyone for any reason at all, but if social convention forces them into such an unwelcome procedure, as lamentably it often does, then they have a genius for turning the act into something more or less contrary to its accepted purpose.

Second, all Ballankirks have the congenital trait of being born with a full-scale cash register wedged in their cranial cavities somewhere between the two lobes of their brains, along with a permanently updated price list of all merchandise made and sold on the face of the earth.

Ballankirks, it must be known, are fond of memorizing sales catalogues (in fact, mountains of them) — they're the only sort of thing they do memorize, and once memorized, nothing is ever forgotten. This enables them to identify almost instantaneously the provenance of any gift — i.e., from what discount catalogue or bargain-basement sale it came and how much it cost.

In addition, Ballankirks are aware from birth that a complex set of rules applies to all acts of giving gifts in order to avoid giving offense: needless to say, it's important that these rules are *not* observed. We can itemize some of these rules as follows:

First, the value of a gift received must be equal to the value of a gift given. The only allowable method for determining in advance what the value of a future gift might be is psychic clairvoyance.

Second, no gift may duplicate anything the recipient of the gift has already in his or her possession, even if it has been hidden away in an attic for the last half a century and even if the recipient doesn't know he or she has it.

Third, the gift may not touch even remotely upon any disagreeable experience that the recipient has had in his or her past. For example, since Cousin

Beatrice was once stung by a bee on the end of her nose while sniffing a daffodil, it would be most unwise to give her a teapot with daffodils painted on it (it would be otiose to mention that she has received, nevertheless, innumerable gifts over the years with daffodil motifs engraved thereon).

Fourth, no drinkable or comestible gifts are allowed; an upset stomach or momentary indigestion caused by it is bound to elicit an immediate and irrefutable charge of poisoning.

Fifth, no gift can be too useless to its receiver ("What am I going to do with this thing?") or too useful ("I had to get one of these anyway").

Finally, the color of a gift must match the color of any possible thing in the recipient's household that the recipient could conceive of matching it with—a task made rather difficult by the Ballankirk inability to match a color with any other color anyway.

Well, none of these criteria could ever be met, but they're useful guides in knowing how best to fine-tune the offensiveness of the gift to its recipient. What a joy it is to see a full-blooded Ballankirk—and all Ballankirks are full-blooded Ballankirks, no matter how remote or exotic the origin of their non-Ballankirk ancestral lines may be—cautiously removing the wrapping paper from a gift (wrapping paper, I should add, that has been recycled at least a dozen times and that the recipient will use again).

And then there is that first shock of chagrin and derision, the mind whirring and clicking with the alacrity of a thousand IBM computers matching, pricing, remembering, comparing, plotting revenge. This is followed by a tilting of the head, a long, languorous turtle-like blink of the eyes, and a high-pitched, quavering wail: "Eeeooo, thay-yank yeeeuuu seeeuuu mooch!"—the final "mooch" being pronounced with a loud and ominous snap of the teeth.

Ah, yes, the ritual of giving lays out the battlefield.

Now for the ritual of drinking. Once again, I wouldn't want to disparage any venerable tradition of the Christmas season, least of all the fine old customs of wassail and good cheer. But I must admonish all who would attend a Ballankirk Christmas that a martini in the hands of a momentarily gracious Ballankirk matron is like a high explosive in the hands of a well-trained terrorist. How often have I watched those tilted glasses, the olive with its glowing pimento like a red-hot fuse, the chilled gin laced with vermouth like pure nitroglycerin about to be poured down into the entrails of a seething volcano! And those portly Ballankirk gents saturating themselves in heavy spirits so that their progressively addled faces appear like a hybrid of a brandied peach and a live hand grenade ready to burst! All it takes is just the right spark to get things going! And how they can get going!

There comes to mind one particular occasion that, to this day, is called The Battle of the Railroad Crossing. It all started over the high-speed collision of a freight train with the 20th Century Limited—a collision that resulted in the total derailment and partial destruction of both trains. No, this disaster didn't happen in the state of Kansas or someplace like that, where trains apparently go zooming about and crashing into one another; it happened on my brother's electric-train layout.

I was a child at the time. The clan decided to gather at my family's house for Christmas; all sixty-five extant members converged on our roomy domicile in southern Massachusetts for the festive occasion.

As usual in this season, we dragged the electric trains up from the basement and set them up in the library so that visitors could play with them. There was no difficulty about the children sharing them with adults, since children usually find electric trains insufferably boring after a short while, whereas male adults can play with them all day long.

As could be predicted, several of my uncles spent rather a considerable time at the trains, both before and after dinner—which was usually consumed in midafternoon, the dessert being put off until late in the evening. They drove the little trains around and around and around, and while they were doing this, they drank and drank and drank. Finally, only two uncles were left at the train set.

Uncle Henry, at that time in his life, was going through his riverboat phase. Though he lived on a bluff that overlooked the Connecticut River as it bends down from Hartford into the Long Island Sound, and occasionally ventured out on the river in his small cruiser, he came to fancy himself for a while as a Mississippi riverboat captain and as a dashing gambler enjoined by some unwritten law to wear a red silk vest with a small derringer tucked away in one of its pockets. He had dressed accordingly for the Christmas gathering and was now preoccupied at the train set in constructing an extraordinary network of tracks, switches, crossings, embankments, tunnels, and signal lights.

Across the table from him was Uncle Matt. He watched Uncle Henry's activities with no little irritation. He was also enormously "steeped," as they say.

Uncle Henry began to run a freight train carefully through his network to see if it would hold up; Uncle Matt determined that it would not. Just as the freight train was about to reach a crossing, he gave full power to his 20th Century Limited and brought it careening around a side track and broadside into the freight train as it arrived at the crossing, knocking down the entire network that Uncle Henry had spent so much time in building.

Immediately, Uncle Henry pulled his derringer on Uncle Matt. He did it to frighten him, of course. It was only a replica, anyway, without the power to shoot. But, simultaneously with Uncle Henry's little gesture, there was a short circuit on the track caused by the tangle of electric equipment and accompanied by a bang, a flash of light, and a puff of smoke.

Uncle Matt, who had just finished his eighth bourbon on the rocks, slipped underneath the table and lay silently on the floor.

Since it was now about seven in the evening, and everyone was sufficiently fatigued and "steeped," the scene was ripe for plenty of action. The whole company jumped from their armchairs, sofas, piano stools, and little circles around the fireplaces or in the pantry or by the liquor cabinet and dashed into the library. Uncle Henry stood by the train layout gaping in a rather bewildered way at his derringer and wondering if it had actually, for some utterly inconceivable reason, gone off.

Uncle Matt's legs protruded from underneath the table.

It is significant that Aunt Lizzy, Uncle Matt's wife, either jumped to the conclusion that her husband was dead or didn't care too much whether he was dead or not, or was engaging (as her enemies would, in later years, contend) in a bit of wishful thinking. Instead, her sole concern, at the moment, was to launch a full-scale verbal attack on Uncle Henry, reminding him vociferously of the devious and violent ways he had exhibited throughout his life, ever since the time he threw sand into her lemonade at the beach when she was three years old.

It became instantly clear that she really wanted to fight about the lemonade incident once again, and the apparent murder of her husband was merely a pretext for doing so.

Meanwhile, Uncle Matt was dragged from underneath the table, and everyone noted the rather silly smile on his face. His face was doused with a bucket of cold water (a therapeutic procedure learned from cowboy movies and, along with pouring whiskey over a wound and into a mouth, a standard Ballankirk way of dealing with any medical emergency). He opened his eyes and gazed upon the crowd gathered about him.

You can just imagine the disappointment when he was discovered to be alive. When Ballankirks get riled up over a tragedy and then find out there is no tragedy at all, they feel personally cheated. But this opportunity for a good row would not be allowed to slip by.

The clan immediately fractured into two warring groups. The fault lines of such fractures, as I've discovered over the years, are utterly unpredictable and utterly inexplicable. Each great quarrel has its own distinctive structure of hostilities. Even the size of the warring groups can differ dramatically. In this case, the groups were about equal; but sometimes minorities take on majorities of various dimensions and convictions.

I would like, at this point, to make special mention of my grandmother, of whom I, and everyone else, was especially proud. Like the great champions of ancient epic lore—Achilles and Roland and Aeneas and the Cid—she could advance into the fray and destroy anything or anyone who was in her way.

Even more, not unlike the redoubtable Cúchulainn of the Ulster Cycle, she could distort her body in the most terrible ways as she fought, sucking in one eye until it disappeared into her forehead while the other eye expanded into a bloodshot whirligig the size of a wagon wheel, and her hair meanwhile would change its color from fiery red to lethal yellow to deathly black and back again.

I mention her in this context because there was one occasion—it was her birthday party, and someone (we will never know who) put an extra candle on her birthday cake—when she took on the entire clan and fought them all to a standstill. She reminded me of one of those samurai swordsmen I've seen in Japanese films who single-handedly mow down small armies of a warlord's household retainers. The side fortunate enough to get her support in a family brawl was usually victorious.

She's deceased now, poor dear, but in her prime there was no warrior who could withstand her assault. I can't help but imagine that to this very day she assists old Charon himself by harrowing the hapless hordes of the dead into his flimsy craft and across the tumultuous waters of Styx.

The Battle of the Railroad Crossing followed the usual procedures, and it would be tiresome to go into all the details — for example, the tendency of the quarrel to move from room to room, to spread out at times into minor engagements, and subsequently to reconverge into major conflicts; the appointment of heroes and heroines from either side representing their group in individual combats conducted before the drawn-up hosts; the "fast draw" phenomenon when daring adversaries matched up for quick verbal exchanges of a particularly vicious nature; and the taking of hostages — i.e., shepherding your opponents' children together and pretending to whisper to them "dreadful secrets" about their parents (I've said "pretending" here because there are some depths to which even a Ballankirk will not descend). Indeed, the art of whispering is considered one of the most potent weapons, and a well-timed whisper can obliterate even the strongest man or woman.

Of course, in the midst of this there is the usual slamming of doors, stamping of feet, walking up and down staircases as if trying to make them collapse, running off for short periods into the wintry night without a coat (so as to punish an adversary by proposing — in theory, at least, though never in practice — to freeze oneself to death), threatening to leave and the angry bundling up of children in snowsuits, only to unbundle them again just as angrily (to demonstrate defiance), and the solemn promises, of immeasurable verbosity and length, never to speak to a certain person again.

It's also the custom at regular intervals for warring groups to break off and retreat into a place of privacy so that they can recoup their forces, plan strategy, and take nourishment to "settle the nerves" — primarily liquid and primarily very strong, of course.

These respites are particularly interesting because this is when the "spies" become active, circulating surreptitiously from one group to another, gathering information, and generally having the effect of heating up the situation to ever new pitches of excitement by telling people what others in the adversarial group are saying about them. There are also "double agents" who work for both sides. All of this ensures that the combatants will return to the attack more charged up and ferocious than ever.

In this particular battle I recall how Cousin Adele at one point ran screaming and wailing from the living room into the hallway and then stopped in front of the large mirror to admire herself because she thought she looked especially beautiful when her eyes were swollen and glistening with tears. Actually, Ballankirks in general take enormous pleasure in observing themselves in mirrors while in the throes of some passion.

They also use mirrors in the same way that a few especially deranged Roman emperors did—that is, to observe others indirectly—and that's why any Ballankirk house is filled with strategically placed mirrors. However, it's unclear to what extent the typical Ballankirk understands the optics of reflection by virtue of which to be able to observe another indirectly in a mirror is, in turn, to be able to be observed indirectly by that same person in that same mirror while in the act of indirectly observing, though such optics must be understood and even cherished, for such mutual indirect observation occurs frequently and is transformed instantaneously into mutual indirect glaring by way of the mirror—a particularly delightful variation on the normal mode of glaring at another.

The Battle of the Railroad Crossing ended as abruptly as it began—as is true of all Ballankirk conflicts. Cousin Karen of sweet and tender temperament (our most recent candidate for the Aunt Jennie of our generation) stepped into the no-man's-land between the entrenched foes and announced very demurely that coffee was ready and that fourteen of Aunt Jennie's Christmas pies, each prepared by a different family member, had been arrayed on the dining room table and were ready for the annual tasting.

All hostilities ceased instantaneously as if there had been no quarrel at all. Bitter enemies were transformed on the spot into old and intimate friends, as the clan filed slowly into the dining room to study the pies and commence the conversation that inevitably would ensue. Of course, there were differences of opinion, but the differences were amicable.

"Yes, this is superb," someone said as he or she delicately dipped his or her fork into the pie for another mouthful, "but it could use a touch more cinnamon." Another appreciated the candied fruits, but indicated that sherry, not rum, was the proper spirit for the fruits to be steeped in, and that more raisins and fewer currants were desirable. The "egg" party had its say; a recent Devonshire cream group had formed and advanced their cause with any number of compelling arguments.

The atmosphere was genuinely hearty and genteel. Though one could reasonably partake of only a few samples, given the richness of the pies, all the pies were genuinely good and rewarding to the palate.

Meanwhile, any outside guests or nonfamily members who had been invited for this particular occasion and who had been so unfortunate as to have witnessed the former altercation had to be coaxed, gasping and quivering, from closets and other hiding places and drawn, incredulously, into the merriment that now prevailed.

The tasting of the pies brought with it, as it always does, the funny stories that Ballankirks like to remember and recount for the millionth time as if no one has ever heard them before. Favorites are The Sinking of Aunt Ruth's Picnic Basket, The Revolt of Cousin Bill's Septic Tank, Who Put the Brick in Uncle Geo's Birthday Cake? (a still unsolved mystery, but evidence is still being gathered — or made up, as if that made any difference), and the time when Uncle Harnet had a nervous breakdown (so he claimed) when he discovered that someone had dumped scrambled eggs on top of his compost heap.

The story of Ossy of the Baleful Eye was rehearsed once more, and the loss of Great-Aunt Gwendolyn's research was appropriately lamented.

Again, speculations about the Harvard freshman abounded, one old fellow actually claiming to have seen his face in a background crowd in a newsreel filmed in Rangoon. No one believed this assertion for an instant and took it, rightfully so, as a sign of the old fellow's advancing senility (after all, no one had ever known what this mysterious person looked like in the first place).

But, for all this, the old house rang with laughter and goodwill.

Farewells are always lengthy affairs among the Ballankirks and may take hours to complete, as if dozens of important things to talk about are suddenly remembered only after the galoshes have been put on and heavy coats wrapped around the departing ones. Plans are made for summer visits on the Cape or in the Berkshires, or up in Maine somewhere, or by the New Hampshire lakes. Children suffer through these parting ceremonies with heroic patience and sometimes fall asleep in the back seats of cars as they wait for garrulous parents to start the engines, turn on the headlights, and drive off into the snowy December darkness. So it was this very night. Only two aged and rather inebriated bachelor uncles bedded down in the basement game room until they could safely leave on the following morning.

Now, I should remark that an outside observer, witnessing these terminal rituals of a Ballankirk Christmas, would be led to conclude that nowhere in the world could you find such a cheerful and happy group.

Certainly, as we know too well by now, such an observer would not be in possession of all the relevant facts. But then again, might not such an observer be right about this in some sense — that is, when all is said and done?

I mean, where would you find a group of people who have — let's face it — everything they want, and supremely so, and nothing, in the final analysis and according to their own lights, to regret?

We shall defer making a summary judgment about such a matter, as we must, I'm afraid to say, defer so many other similar judgments, to a time and a place somewhere well beyond our ken, somewhere well beyond what we can reasonably understand in this sad and sorry hither side of time.

And somewhere, too, I like to think that, under those frozen Vermont hills, under those wintry New England stars, Aunt Jennie hugs her infant sons closer to her breast, awaiting in her long hibernal sleep to be awakened to an infinitely more Hospitable Kingdom than the one she knew in her brief and gracious life so long ago, a Kingdom of Festivity, a Kingdom of Peace, like that once and future Christmas pie she bequeathed to us all — yes, to us all — so full of promise, so full of wonderment and joy.

Estampie

Stamp, stomp, leap, and hop,
Twine, twist, unloose the knot.
Bounce to right and bounce to left,
Give it lightness, give it heft.
Hoist your partner in the air,
Make her want to hover there.

> *Let's be blithesome, let's be free!*
> *Let's dance for all eternity.*

Tap with heel and tap with toe
Clogging, slogging, fast and slow.
Bluster, fluster, scold, and play.
Make all sorrows run away.
Sidle up and sidle down.
Make your kerchiefs swing around.

> *Let's be blithesome, let's be free!*
> *Let's dance for all eternity.*

Carp and caper, laugh and scream!
May joyfulness now reign supreme!
Hear the bagpipes skirl and tweet
As thumping tabors keep the beat.
Let our heart-chords twang awhile,
Our world encircled with a smile!

> *Let's be blithesome, let's be free!*
> *Let's dance for all eternity.*

Wobbly Jane

I called her Wobbly Jane because, when she walked along the street, she wobbled. She was tall, willowy, and — yes — remarkably sure-footed, and she walked with a short, brisk stride. Still, her head and shoulders had a funny little wobble in them as she walked. It made her look — I'll admit it — just a bit goofy, but it was an attractive kind of goofiness.

She always smiled, and her eyes were always smiling, too, as if the world was never anything less, nor anything more, than an amusing to place to look at. People, even the most complete strangers, smiled back when they saw her — smiled in a kindly way, but I don't think she was ever quite aware of that. I never knew what she was aware of.

I'm not sure she was ever really aware of me — except for one occasion, and I've always thought that that one occasion lasted for all of about two seconds.

She worked as a librarian in the New York Public Library on Forty-Second Street. She had a desk tucked away in a wood-paneled little alcove on the side of one of the big reading rooms. It was lit by a small, shaded lamp. I was never sure exactly what she did, but patrons of the library approached her desk, talked quietly with her, and were sent off in one direction or another. Whatever they came for, they got. An atmosphere of warmth and trust and cheerfulness seemed to emanate from that alcove. Even a kind of awe was there: I once saw some cocky but bright-looking college boys approach that alcove and be instantly tamed, if not quite subdued, by its curious aura.

I first saw Wobbly Jane one day when I was working in the library. I was at a reading station not far from her alcove, and she was returning from her lunch break. I saw her wobbling walk and pretty face and cheerful eyes. Then day after day, and week after week, I came to do my research and, more importantly, to look at her. I was continually trying to think of things that I could ask her about, but they always seemed so trivial that I never did approach her desk about them. I was conducting a research project in chemical engineering, and I felt awkward about asking for information on that subject. I wished I were a literary type, or something to that effect; then it would have been much easier.

I didn't actually make her acquaintance until I noticed her on the street one day. I recognized her from a block away by her wobble. No one else in the world wobbled like that. She was walking up Fifth Avenue to the Schrafft's on Forty-Eighth Street. I followed her. I would later learn that this was her regular place to go for lunch. She would sit at the soda fountain and almost always have the same lunch: a toasted cheese sandwich, a pickle, and a cup of tea. Sometimes she had a turkey sandwich with lettuce and mayonnaise, but the pickle and the cup of tea never varied. The regular soda jerks seemed to know her well, but I don't think she knew them. Anyway, I followed her into the restaurant and was lucky enough to get a place next to her at the soda fountain.

When we'd been served, and she was eating her sandwich by opening it up and pulling out one piece of turkey at a time, I started up a conversation. I asked her if she was going to see the St. Patrick's Day parade that would march up Fifth Avenue the following day. She didn't seem at all surprised or taken aback at being addressed by a stranger. Perhaps she was accustomed to it by working at her desk at the library. Anyway, she replied that she was planning to see the parade and that she never missed it.

I don't remember where things went from there, but I walked back with her to the library after lunch. I think we talked about everything. She told me, from memory, all the Major League Baseball scores from the previous day. I acted as if I was surprised at some scores, and disappointed by others, but really all I cared about was that she was telling them, because I have no interest in baseball, or in any other sport, for that matter. But I figured she did. Later I would come to know that she had no interest in baseball either, or in any other sport. But she always knew the scores, and she always told them to me. I wonder if that was one of the things people approached her for at her desk in the library. She never told me much about herself, her family, where she went to college, or how she came to work at the library, but I figured she was in her late twenties, though I never really knew.

Over the several years that I knew her, I accounted myself very fortunate if I could see her perhaps once or twice a week for lunch, or sometimes for dinner—but that was rare. On occasions we would walk together in Central Park. She knew all the statues in the park and made a special point of visiting each one of them regularly as if they were old friends. Especially she enjoyed the statue of Shakespeare, the busts of Schiller and of Balzac, and the statues of Sir Walter Scott and of Alexander von Humboldt over by the Museum of Natural History. And so many others. Balto, the husky who took the serum to Nome, was another favorite.

She loved New York in all its seasons, and I came to see New York through her eyes. She loved the Christmas decorations in the store windows—especially the big colorful Santa Clauses with wonderful sleds and dazzling reindeer pulling at the harness. They were particularly good if they were mechanized so that the figures tipped back and forth slowly, but with slightly—well, wobbly—motions. She seemed to have a peculiar attitude toward Santa Claus—as if she actually knew him as a real person and found it intensely amusing to see a familiar old friend portrayed in such comical guises. She also loved to gaze at the Christmas tree at Rockefeller Center and the skaters on the rink below. Often, we watched the children visit FAO Schwarz with their parents, but that was when FAO Schwarz was on the other side of the street and much smaller and a lot less showy than it is now.

In the spring and the fall, we watched the parades together. We went to the museums together. She was an endless source of information about everything we saw, and she was enchanted by it all. But somehow, in quite another way, none of this was really there for her. She saw things—but she didn't see them—as if she looked right through them at something else. That's the way she saw me too. She looked right through me, never at me.

I loved the way she dressed. Her clothes didn't look like anybody else's clothes. When she went out on the street, she wore narrow, creased garrison caps of the sort soldiers wear, except that her caps—she seemed to have quite a few of them—were very colorful and were worn jauntily tipped to the side of her head. She must have pinned them in some way to her fluffy brunette hair, or else I don't see how they could have stayed on her head, especially with that little wobble of hers. She also wore colorful scarves that matched her caps.

The effect was remarkable. No wonder everyone noticed her. The rest of her attire was simple and didn't change at all with the tide of fashion over those years, though it always looked fresh and crisp and impeccably clean. It occurred to me only after I'd known her for a while that she made all of her own clothing, and that's why it didn't look like anybody else's. Also, she wore no jewelry and very little makeup. She did have a thin golden chain around her neck with a tiny golden cross suspended from it. I never asked her about this, and she never brought it up.

I have to confess to something awful.

I have to confess to wishing, sometimes, that some little harm would come to Wobbly Jane—nothing big, you must understand, just a little thing like an unpleasant patron at the library, or spilled tea on her blouse, or, worst of all maybe, a sprained ankle at some curbside on her walk back to the library. I wanted anything that might make her seek out some sort of help—from somebody, from anybody, but especially from me.

How I longed to be of service to her, to aid her in a moment of crisis, to lift her up if she had slipped in a puddle, to fix something in her apartment, to stand heroically between her and a potential assailant, to wrest her rights from a penny-pinching landlord, to dry her tears with a fresh Kleenex extracted ever so expeditiously from a pocket where it was being faithfully stored for no other purpose than this.

It never happened.

For all her wobble, she never tripped. She never fell. She never needed me for anything. She never needed anyone for anything. If you'd poised her on a high, narrow pinnacle and tried to lure her off with all the promises the world can give, she would never have budged or even lost her balance for a moment. That's how she was.

There was one time when she actually invited me over to her apartment for lunch. This was on a day off. I was really quite surprised by the invitation. I'd never been in her apartment before, and this was for lunch! In fact, as I approached her building, practically dancing like Gene Kelly on the street, I flattered myself by thinking that I was at a critical turning point in our friendship.

Then, when I got there and she had let me into the apartment, I discovered that she'd completely forgotten about the invitation. I sat for a while in her sitting room as she busied herself with something in another room.

Like her alcove at the library, the apartment was warm and cheerful and filled with books. There were also flowers and little statues and some fine porcelain neatly displayed on shelves. Meanwhile, she suggested that I look into the refrigerator to see if there was something we could have for lunch. In the refrigerator I saw cartons of milk and orange juice, a package of Kraft American cheese slices, a few apples, a jar of pickles, an open can of Campbell's turkey noodle soup, and a loaf of Pepperidge Farm white bread. I noted especially the loaf of bread because I didn't keep bread in a refrigerator and because it was the same brand of bread that I buy.

Also in the refrigerator were several books and a purple scarf. If this had been anybody else's refrigerator, I would have been surprised by these latter items. But, as it was her refrigerator, I was not.

The kitchen seemed to have no other food in it. We ended up going to a Floxie's on Third Avenue, the place that has the "Hamburgers with a College Education." I was still in an exuberant mood, so I ordered their specialty, the Hamburger with the Ph.D. (it's also called "Professor Burger" and has onions, bacon, and cheese on it), and she had her usual toasted cheese sandwich with a pickle and a cup of tea.

I never quite knew what Wobbly Jane did on Sundays. She had a way of disappearing. Or, at least, she didn't answer her phone and was never available for anything. I could never figure it out. She didn't seem to have any relatives, or at least anyone she ever spoke of. She didn't have friends either.

Where did she go? What did she do?

Perhaps she just vanished like some fairy princess into that world of books that surrounded her. Was there a magic king somewhere that she sought out? I could see her, like the characters we see sometimes in a movie, stepping into a page of a book and appearing on the other side in a land of enchantment. With what a funny wobble would she take that step! How I would have followed her — followed her anywhere!

One time when we were talking about something, we got on the subject of St. Louis. There was a curious confusion that ensued, when she said some things that didn't make any sense to me. She talked about going to visit St. Louis. I thought we were talking about the city of St. Louis, so I got going about the great arch and the Mississippi and whatever. Then something about a St. Michael got in there too! St. Michael? Where's that? Is there someplace called St. Michael? We never did get around to clearing up the confusion.

Only a long time afterward did I realize what the misunderstanding was all about. I'd stepped into St. Patrick's Cathedral one day to get out of the rain and found myself exploring the interior of the church. In the aisle that runs around the back of the choir and the main altar, I discovered a little side altar dedicated to St. Louis, the king of France. On one side of the altar is a statue of St. Louis; on the other side is a statue of St. Michael the Archangel.

Why did that side altar remind me of the alcove in the library? Of her apartment? Of her?

Did she come here? What did she do when she was here? Was St. Louis another one of her friends? Was this the magic king sought out by the fairy princess? But I knew in truth that she wasn't a fairy princess and that the king she sought wasn't magic. St. Louis was a friend — just a friend and that was all.

Once, and only once, in a conversation, I — how should I put it? — "declared" myself to her. Is that the expression? I told you I'm not a literary type, but if that expression seems a little awkward, it's nowhere close to being as awkward as what I actually said to her. The occasion was in a restaurant somewhere. We were sitting together at a table, so that we were facing one another. That was unusual because Wobbly Jane always preferred to sit at soda fountains. I don't remember what we were talking about, but suddenly, out of nowhere, I said the stupidest thing that, in the history of the world, any would-be courting gentleman ever said to his fair lady.

I said, "You know, I think you're a *humdinger*."

How could I have said that?

I swear to you, I'd never used that word before in my life. I've never used it since—except, of course, to tell you what happened. I don't even know where I could have gotten it or how it could have entered my vocabulary. But there it was, popping out of my verbal reservoir like the plucky head of an otter out of a silent, woodland lake. In retrospect, I figure it was just the sort of whimsical remark that Wobbly Jane could be most expected to appreciate. But I was embarrassed, instantaneously.

Wobbly Jane cocked her head just slightly like a little puppy and looked at me for about two seconds. I think it was two seconds. I think that during those two seconds she was really looking at me—that is, really seeing me for the first time and not looking through me at something else.

Despite my embarrassment, those two seconds were the best two seconds in my entire life. In fact, those two seconds were better than my entire life has been, or ever will be. Then she said something that changed the subject, and she didn't see me anymore.

When I received a job offer in Seattle, I thought that, at last, Wobbly Jane might take some serious notice of me. Certainly, she would regret that I was leaving New York, perhaps never to return. Certainly, she would protest and try to get me to change my mind. But I don't think she regretted it one bit. Instead, she congratulated me and wished me well. She never protested, and she never even hinted I should change my mind.

When I said goodbye to her on the steps of the public library, she stood on a step higher than mine, framed in my line of vision by the great sculpted lions at the portals, and good-naturedly leaned over and kissed me on the bridge of my nose.

It's the only time she ever kissed me, and it's the only time I've ever been kissed on the bridge of my nose. I've seen people kiss dogs on the bridges of their noses, and she might as well have been kissing a dog goodbye.

That was the end of it. I watched her wobble up the stairs and into the library.

She never looked back.

From Seattle I sent her Christmas cards every year. I went through a special effort to find what she might like—big colorful cards with jolly

Santa Clauses on them. I even found one on which Santa's beard was made of real cotton and stuck out from the card in a little fluff.

But I never received a card in return. I figure she probably loved the cards but just forgot to answer them. One year the card came back still in its envelope. It was stamped by the post office. It couldn't be delivered, and there was no forwarding address.

A few years later, I came to New York on a business trip. I tried to look her up, but she was gone. The alcove in the public library was occupied by someone else. The Schrafft's where she had had her lunch had been turned into a boutique for fur coats.

I even went to her apartment building and spoke to the landlord — the landlord I'd once hoped to defend her from. But he was a very nice guy. He said that one day she just left.

What about her stuff? I asked. She sold everything she had, he said, didn't take it with her, gave the proceeds of the sale to a poor family several blocks away. He had no idea where she went.

I wonder where she is now. I can't imagine her being away from her alcove in the public library, or away from Fifth Avenue, or away from New York.

Did she finally wobble off forever into one of those books of hers whose pages she turned with such delicacy and affection?

Did she find in an ivory palace somewhere a Royal Spouse, adorned with gold and anointed with frankincense and myrrh, whose mysterious and beautiful realm she was always gazing at through the appearances of this world?

I hope I'll see her again someday.

Maybe I will. I think I will. But all of this happened so long ago.

I don't think I've ever loved anybody as much as I loved Wobbly Jane.

Pup

What gratitude would I not give
To have you, Pup, back home to live,
To see you coursing o'er the field
Or through the brushwood half-concealed.

The hall and hearth are not the same
As when you dozed before the flame,
Heeding in dream the sounding horn
Or chasing woodcocks from the thorn.

Your hazel eyes and golden fur
Would autumn pastures yet bestir.
Your life was filled with vim and grace;
Your love could all my love outpace.

> *Beyond these hills I know you run,*
> *Beyond the thickets of the sun,*
> *Where ages hence we'll reunite*
> *In boundless forests ever bright.*

Galileo: A Letter to His Daughter

(Arcetri, March 1634)

Maria Celeste, your citron jam and candied quinces
  Regale my learned guests; the phial of rosemary-waters
Commends your convent's fine distillery.
  No, my "imprisonment" at home is not as arduous as you think —
After all, the view is superb: Florence, the Duomo,
  The leafy hills beyond the Arno; and I am close to you at last.
I thank you for your offer to recite each week
  Those seven penitential psalms prescribed for me;
What soul could protest an innocence without them?
  Yet I stand, in this case, innocent in my witness to the truth.
For who could disparage such a notion as they hold —
  A whirring glazier's disc, bathed in gulfs of immortal fire:
Earth no more, really, than a mote
  Dead-center, stationary, held in vague sublunary derision
While God's regal wand spins out the planispheres
  Into orbs of searing light and epicycles like webs of glass,
So crystalline and delicate? It's gorgeous to imagine
  (Though not as gorgeous as what I have actually seen!).
Then am I so audacious as to claim,
  As our Tuscan poet said, mounting the terraces of repentance,
"Si come mostra esperienza ed arte,"
  That God would hurl us like a brazen spearhead
Through immeasurable space,
  Whorl upon whorl redounding all about us,
Ourselves a whorl amid such shaggy planets
  And flaming stars, each arc inscribed so perfectly, so just —

A Universe not hyaline and brittle
        But made of fiery brass and tooled precision;
And all dancing, not to different tunes
        But in one cosmic galliard that measures and ordains
Both the starry lodgements
        And the fall of acorns on hazy autumn afternoons?
We, too, take our part,
        And do not merely gawk like idlers at a country fair.
But be not scandalized at my scruffy waywardness;
        Scholars, not saints, have thus sequestered me.
They, too — call them what you will:
        Philosophers, men of science, members of esteemed academies —
Coddle their own assemblies of fondly nodding heads
        And skittish tongues. Protest a detail here or there,
Probe a technicality, suggest a "new" interpretation,
        And they'll frown, tilt sagacious eyes, murmur a word or two —
Maybe even land you in a prestigious job!
        But call the entire *modus operandi* into doubt,
And you'll end up a-bubbling in a sordid stew.
        They, no less than anyone, will use, if they can,
Engines of relentless power to resolve a squabble
        Or to refurbish a broken pride before the world.
        Yet I hesitate to think what I myself have done
To prejudice or forestall an argument
        Or bludgeon a compeer's intellect before he spoke,
Incurring, thereby, the lash of scorpions' tails.
        Could I not proclaim that the Glorious Lamp of the Universe,
The Parded Sun, aslant upon its golden hinges,
        And all its variant gestures of discovery and prognosis
Have brought upon my head this acrimonious charade?
        As for my adversaries, did not Aristotle muster his precedents
Only to exemplify or confute, never to demonstrate?
        And did Aquinas spar with magisterial hearts and minds

Not to sift, and test, and understand,
     But to expatiate over pompous and mellifluous inconsistencies?
Had the two of them seen the "givens" through my vitreous tube,
   They should have soundly boxed the ears of their unctuous children!
And no mere talk of "saving appearances" for them;
     With loving eyes they would have courteously embraced
The one, unalterable structure of the Universe Itself.
   Yet they knew, as all wisdom must, the limits of presumption.
Protect me, in time, from my own protectors.
          There is no school of thought
But, without fresh insight and vigorous refinement,
     Distends with age to sophistry and pretension.
And why do those who love the ancients scarcely read them?
   Archimedes, Pythagoras, and Augustine would most gladly share
A cup of wine at my humble board
   And wonder who stood without and was battering down my door.
Ah! Maffeo Barberini, how he and I could douse
        A torrid Roman night with goblets of cool Marsala,
Meandering through the gardens of Trinità dei Monti
     And babbling all the while about nodes and parallaxes,
Like two old sots
   Rocking back and forth on the lucid horns of a crescent moon!
Now he shuffles along the corridors of the Vatican labyrinth
   Feeling "personally" betrayed, while the Jesuitical gang at court
Meticulously gnaws the innards of his papal ear.
     (The Jesuits know I'm right and read my books in secret;
Benedictines and Carmelites line up on my side.)
   Meanwhile, the archbishop of Siena does what he can for me;
And Niccolini shunts from Rome to Florence,
     Braving the cold winds of the *tramontana* and hoping to dispel
The mists of malefaction. Barberini mumbles and demurs,
   Then declares for all to hear, "We believe it. We believe it." —
Yet sends no reprieve of that seditious edict he never signed.
   (His own nephew, the Chief-Inquisitor, would not sign it either!)

Maria Celeste, I pray you pray for me;
     And do not worry—in the end, truth will speak in my favor.
The orange trees you asked about are blooming at my window;
     Last week's hailstorm did not hurt them in the least.
And "my lady mule" has recovered from her ailment.
     Beneficent old Geppo will load her up with spice-cakes
And bring them to the convent tomorrow afternoon.
     Tell Mother Achilea I have some new sonatas for her organ—
She will like them; and yes, my lute has been repaired.
     And I beg you, in your sick-room duties, be not so overzealous—
Leave something for the novices to do.
          (As if I could tell you that, knowing whose heart you bear!)
And do not yield to dark presentiments—
     You know I could not thrive without your kindly ministrations.
Inscribe your own fine arc, Maria Celeste,
          Through all your days and nights
     In perfect rest and ceaseless energy,
Maria Celeste, Heavenly Star,
          Brightest star in all the firmament for me.

Three "Friends"

"Friends"? And "three" of them? Hardly. At least not with one another. (I was supposed to be one of them but scarcely knew the other two.)

I'm not given, in most circumstances, to casting myself in what some might call "dramatic" roles, momentarily and rather self-consciously assumed, but it does happen occasionally, and it could hardly have been avoided when I visited Dorothea Lindstrom a month or so after the death—reported as the result of an accident while fishing—of her husband Sven.

Part of it was the setting: for Dorothea had somehow managed to fashion a diminutive sitting room in a glassy, closed-in porch whose special function it was to engage presumably select and privileged visitors in precisely the kind of formal conversation we were to have.

The room, so refined and delicate in all its deportment, so filled with light and glowing surfaces, contrasted severely with the rest of the house, which had something dark, massive, and ungainly about it and which deployed its oversized furniture into such a set of obstacles that to get across a room was to engage in a dance of physical distortions not unlike that of a football halfback maneuvering through a tightly congested line of scrimmage.

I was always a bit mystified by that house, frankly, for it was so unlike Sven—the Sven I knew or thought I knew—and the appended sitting room was so like Dorothea: reclusive, translucent, "off to the side," impeccably tidy, fragile but poised as if "bearing up" as ever under some kind of strain I could scarcely be expected to comprehend.

Entering that room (it was the first time for me, as often as I had been in that house) was like making an entrance into one of those small stage sets sometimes positioned to the front and side of the main stage — often a garden bower or some such thing where more intimate relations among characters are entertained, and perhaps resolved.

I had never felt before, in visiting anybody, that I was a "caller" in the old-fashioned sense, that the object of my visit was both ceremonial as well as personal, and that, even as an old friend, I had been somehow prompted to this interview not only by Dorothea's invitation but also by a summons of curiosity and conscience on my part, however obscure that summons may have been at the time.

Was there something important I was meant to know?

Dorothea's role in the interview was as distinctly ceremonial as I had expected it to be. She sat resolutely upright in a small, rigid chair, a tall and chiseled Swedish beauty with blond hair braided in a crown around her head. She had a number of pronouncements to make in that mellow voice of hers, declarations of a sort that would round off and conclude the events not only of the past few months but of the past years of her life with Sven as this had affected both his (and, through him, her) interactions with me — as few, really, as these latter had been.

I no longer remember many of the details enumerated in her carefully rehearsed litany, to which I listened attentively, nodding politely at every affirmation, frowning sympathetically at every negation, and even wondering why she was telling me all of this. Naturally I expressed some concern for her financial situation, but she assured me that all was well in that respect (indeed, almost overwhelming in the unexpected size and scope of the legacy she had been bequeathed).

But there was one point I could never forget, the climactic point at which everything else was aimed and which she quite obviously regarded as urgent to communicate to me. She told me that Sven had said to her, several weeks before his fatal fishing accident, that he had treasured three friends especially in his life — that these three friends were Jaleb Brooks, Martin Casey, and myself, Nat Thompson. Moreover, she imparted this information to me in a most peculiar way: on one hand—let's call it, in the ceremonial guise—she seemed to be conferring some sort of honor upon me, a medal or certificate, as it were, of esteem and recognition; on the other hand—let's call it, in the personal guise—she made her bestowal with an odd tone in her voice while peering at me intently, her head tilted a bit to the side, like a bluejay studying an especially tempting berry of some sort. Was there a question in her mind, both perhaps about herself and about my reaction, that held something in abeyance, that called into doubt just how honorific this honor might actually be?

Furthermore, I was not sure at the time why she told me this. Was there something I should do with the information? Was there a commission involved? Did I now have the obligation to perpetuate something about Sven—for example, by being friends with his former friends? I didn't know the others very well—actually, almost not at all. At the time, I tried to accept her declaration simply as a compliment—as I still do, in a way—remembering uneasily the jostling and pushing that took place when the three of us were among the six pallbearers at Sven's obsequies. The other three pallbearers were Sven's son—called "Winkee," for some reason; Art Bailey, Sven's former partner in his law firm; and Brian O'Grady, Sven's old fishing buddy.

I don't know why all that jostling took place. Too much difference in body types, I suppose, made coordinating movements difficult. But I remember Jaleb Brooks, a huge, broad-shouldered, bearded man, swearing under his breath at Martin Casey, a limp, spiny insect of a man who seemed unable to hold up his corner of the casket.

I also remember when, before the funeral began and I was introduced to the other pallbearers (I already knew Winkee, for better or worse), Jaleb leered at me and muttered insolently "So *you're* that teacher guy!" He stared at me for a moment, laughed, and turned his attention to the hired and nowadays indispensable bagpiper, kilt and all, with the same scorn he had directed at me. I was glad that at least he had delivered himself of whatever pronouncement he thought I merited and that I didn't have to deal with his disdain while the casket wrenched and jolted around in our hands, his powerful grasp constantly pulling the others off balance.

Only Winkee, dressed in uniform—he was on leave from military service—seemed to take pleasure in the proceedings and glanced knowingly at Jaleb from time to time.

My interview with Dorothea concluded, I felt "discharged." Our personal postmortem was over, a psychological inquest brought to a proper finish—or so I thought at the time. Years would pass without much further contact with Dorothea. Eventually she took up a new life, vanished for a while, as much as Sven had vanished, perhaps even more so, for I had been, however indirectly, initiated into a company whose only cohesive point had been Sven himself, or so it seemed—three friends who didn't know one another, who were certainly not friends with one another, but whose presence together was occasionally marked by a fortuitous brush at the hardware store or by the gasoline pumps or at the town dump.

I wondered if the others had been recipients of the same officious declaration from Dorothea, though my guess is that, if they had been, they dismissed it rather quickly and gave it no further thought. I can't say that they came to know me—at least they never seemed to recognize me—but I recognized them, and I think I eventually came to know something about them.

I should say, at this point, that both Sven and Dorothea had not been "natives," as the expression goes, having come from somewhere in the midwest to the township of East Gilead in northern New Hampshire about fifteen years ago. Sven, in addition to being an astute lawyer, was an ardent fly fisherman, and I always imagined that his attraction to the locale was based on the many well-stocked trout streams that flow down into the adjacent valleys from the White Mountains.

He met, it was said, his sudden demise by slipping on a mossy rock close to one of those streams and hitting his head against a jagged shard of New Hampshire granite. Jaleb Brooks was with him at the time and was the only witness.

I should mention that I, too, am an outsider and teach history and languages at the East Gilead regional high school.

About Sven: well, what can I say?

Would that I had a stock of heroic epithets I could apply, something Homeric, something vast and breathless and evocative of boundless space and airy heights, for Sven was an eagle of a man for me, with eyes that could see tiny things at great distances and a mind that could stretch its wings over mountain ranges. Okay, I grant it must appear inordinately strange to engage in such sublime hyperbole; but genuine intelligence is rare enough among humankind, and Sven had it, the real thing, I mean. There was a sort of Odysseus in him — a tall, energetic man, a wave of blond hair setting off a broad, luminous face, steely blue eyes, a man "many-minded," adventurous, destined — if anyone was ever so destined — for roaming over the "wide-bosomed earth" and the "wine-dark sea."

I first discovered all this by chance at an open house at my high school, when, among the milling, ingratiating, apologetic parents (who nevertheless regard teachers as a version of latter-day household slaves), Sven emerged, not with his son (whom, for some odd, reason I never did have in class and who avoided me as much as his father later sought me out) but to ask me some abstruse question about a point in grammar. You must know something about the inimitable "tribe of grammarians" to know what discussion of an abstruse point in grammar can lead to.

In this case it led to a great deal.

It turned out that Sven knew an enormous amount about language, about classical and modern languages even, and much more than that. He was a polymath, reading voluminously everything that came to hand. Inquiries, subsequent to our first meeting, would reveal not only that, superior to the teachers who taught them, he had a command of almost all the subjects taught at the school but that he was considered an exceptionally qualified attorney whose persuasive skills made him the man most to be avoided in local legal altercations.

I was able to hold my own ground with him, even surpass him in those things that I knew well; and I could follow him into arenas where we were equals. But whereas I had leisure to pursue matters of mutual interest, he didn't; and hence his penetration to the core of issues — with some of which he had the barest acquaintance — never failed to be astonishing.

Our friendship was based on this.

It's odd that Winkee, his son, had a reputation in the school of being a ne'er-do-well, a bounder, a tramp, a "punk."

It's even odder than Sven didn't seem to care about this.

Sure, Sven and I had so many lunches together I couldn't number them—sometimes at a café near the school, sometimes at his home. Or, standing on the sidelines of a high school soccer game, we would unravel the latest version of the "Big Bang" theory, critique what Chomsky had (or had not) accomplished in linguistics, or consider whether Wittgenstein was all that he was stacked up to be. Sven seemed to know some of the Platonic dialogues by memory, though he was equally conversant with the Devonian rock formations that appeared by the streams when he went fishing up in the mountains. And, of course, we talked history, endlessly, scrupulously, taking apart the strategy (or lack of it) at Antietam or Shiloh, or discussing recent excavations of Viking settlements along the rivers of Southern Russia.

Our infrequent discussion of those redoubtable Norse marauders, whom Sven identified vaguely as his remote ancestors, brought out a brief but curiously rough edge in him, a boisterous guffaw that always surprised me but which I took to be his momentary impersonation of such venerable ancient spirits.

And all of this was mixed in with no little fascination with matters such as the permutation of subjunctive verb forms among the various Romance languages out of their original Latin roots.

Most remarkably, there was never a hint of the trivial, an absorption in a mass of irrelevance, involved here. Sven spoke lucidly, learnedly, elegantly, ever with the slightest touch of humor, with an intellectual detachment as refined as it was gentle. He was a bright light in a world in which almost everybody regards knowing anything as a dangerous extravagance and as a serious flaw in character.

Of course, I knew that I occupied a small niche in Sven's life—I rarely saw him in the evening, or at his work, or on the weekends. In any event, that light went out for me—too suddenly, too prematurely. Whatever else I might come to think about Sven in future years, this much has remained for me an unsullied and irrefragable source of admiration.

But why had I never known these other friends of his, fellow compatriots of the select group, the privileged threesome in which belatedly I found myself included?

Sven had never spoken of them. I had never seen him in their company. When I was introduced to them at the funeral, I recognized them as people I had seen around town. It was difficult not to notice Jaleb Brooks now and then, with his great overbearing stride, his unkempt beard flecked with axle grease and wood chips, his pickup truck unspeakably filthy and belching clouds of exhaust from a broken muffler. I was surprised to see this hitherto macabre but obtrusive figure show up at the funeral of someone like Sven Lindstrom.

Martin Casey was also not totally unfamiliar: a tall, angular man, as thin as a stalk of hollyhock, lethargically sprouting great rangy, insect-like limbs, with a drooping head, a long red nose, and spectacles an inch thick. He ran an antique shop in the center of town, and I often saw him—I hate to use the expression—"slithering" furtively in and out of that curiously malevolent den, jammed as it was with the detritus of a moribund rural culture that he sold to tourists at exorbitant prices.

Beyond that, I had no further impressions. Yet we were the three friends of Sven: honored presumably, revered for that fact, sharing something in common, for Sven, if he was nothing else, was an exceptional man; his friends must be exceptional in some sense too.

Were they ever!

About a year after Sven's demise, I was discussing some points of American colonial history with my senior class. What comes up in such classes is sometimes remarkable, for some of the students are descendants of the earliest families that came to these hills around East Gilead in the mid-eighteenth century, and their familial lore has retained fragments of regional history, though what may be factual and what most certainly belongs to the genre "tall tale" needs to be carefully distinguished. If such students happen to be minimally articulate, they have interesting things to say, and the occasional explosive laughter of the other students helps to differentiate the particular family account from the universally understood fabrication.

Local real estate agents, of course, in their marketing efforts, have so embellished some of these stories that it's now more difficult than ever to know what is true anymore: history is a good selling point for them. For example, the traditional "root cellars" in all the old houses put up for sale in the area nowadays have been retroactively transfigured into pre–Civil War "underground railroad" hiding places for runaway slaves on their way to the Canadian border.

The well-heeled urban purchasers of these houses as summer homes accept this fiction without hesitation, not knowing about a farming family's need to store turnips and potatoes through a cold winter and all too glad to be able to palliate their affluently guilty consciences with this effervescent link to one of the more tragic episodes in American history.

In any case, a year or so after Sven's death I happened to mention to my students something about the famous workshops around Boston in the eighteenth century that produced what is now considered invaluable colonial furniture. I discovered, to my surprise, that some of the students recognized a name here and there, but they were surprised when I told them that such furniture was very difficult to find and expensive to buy. One student even brought up the name of Chippendale: his grandmother had owned a genuine Chippendale chair. I asked him what had happened to the chair.

The student told me: Martin Casey, the antique man, had bought it — bought it for fifty dollars, which his grandmother was happy to get because she was a bit short of cash that year. Other students told similar stories. Martin Casey would come to their houses and purchase furniture of all kinds — cabinets, desks, dry sinks, harvest tables, grandfather clocks, old canopied beds, everything. The families were glad to get the money. I recognized that they obviously had no idea what these items were really worth.

And, oh yes, that lawyer, "Winkee's dad, don't yuh know," always came with him.

Sven?

Yes. Sven and Martin Casey.

I guess I should have left things alone at this point, but I didn't. I decided to visit Martin's dreadful little shop, located in the center of town and hideously named "Knick-Knacks, Gee-Gaws, 'n' What-Not." I wanted to see his furniture.

"Furniture?" he croaked at me from behind a desk festooned overhead with a row of battered tin lanterns. "I carry no furniture."

I stood there before him, surrounded by the most amazing collection of dreary junk the world has ever seen, junk in cabinets, junk hanging from the walls and suspended from the ceiling, junk spilling out of barrels and large wicker baskets and old brass-studded leather trunks, junk originally spewed out in vast quantities by nineteenth-century mills and sold over the past 150 years in five-and-dime stores to a parsimonious rural population. His great red nose pointed at me like the beak of a vulture ready to peck at my entrails, and his almost blind eyes were monstrously magnified by his thick spectacles.

"But I understand you buy furniture from the local farmsteads …"

He lifted and fanned out a long-fingered hand at me. "Well, well … I do, we did, that, ahyuh, but no longah. An' I shipped it off, yuh know … ta New Yark, Bahston … no market for it heyah, but in New Yark, Bahston …"

"Where to?" I asked. "To Sotheby's, Christie's, I suppose?"

"It could fetch a handsome price at places like that. They was glad to have it. Sven and I … yuh know … it worked very nicely for us, very nicely indeed." His lanky body convulsed in a weird, clucking laughter.

"Sven and you …?" I repeated.

He rose from his desk, his head bent forward so as not to collide with all the objects suspended from hooks in the ceiling. He slid out from behind the crowded desk and made his way through a narrow corridor of shelves filled with old pottery, canning jars, and glass medicinal bottles. He stooped down and began to sort through a wooden barrel filled with broken metallic toys.

"Sven seemed ta know everythin'. Knew his furniture, he did—could identify the really priceless stuff in a second," Martin mumbled. "Course, I couldn't—couldn't see it anyhows, even if I knew. But even plain old pine furniture became valuable for collectors.

"We got it all. We combed the areah from Centah Alliston right through ta Perry's Junction. Made a small fortune, if yuh wanta know. Sven knew how ta get inta othah people's houses, could spot the good stuff right off, outa the cornah a' his eye without lookin' like he was noticin' it.

"What a line he had! He understood old Yankee psychology ta a tee— 'Ain't nothin' heyah for sale, but go ahead an' make an offah anyhow.' Afta bikerin' 'bout some junk—actin' like it were great stuff an' he were real disappointed not ta get it, he'd turn his attention ta what he really wanted, but puttin' on like he just didn't wanta return home empty-handed. They were nevah ready for this. He sure was good at it. He could talk anybody outa any heirloom they had.

"Great friends we were—Sven an' I. I guess Jaleb Brooks was anothah friend. That makes sense, knowin' the both a' them. There was anothah fellah he hung around with sometimes—some teachah fellah at the school. Don't remembah his name. I guess he was anothah one a' them pallbearers at Sven's funeral. Couldn't see him anyhow. That was a heck of a time, I tell yuh, at that funeral with Jaleb bein' his usual piss-ass self an' pushin' ever'body else around an' that damned bagpihpah-man gnawin' out my middle ears with all that high-pitched squealin' like some damned pig in a poke."

Martin fished out a black Lionel steam locomotive from the toys. He looked like a deformed blue heron plucking a lobster out of a tangled morass of seaweed. Its paint was scratched, and its wheels and wires dangled loosely from its base. He glanced at me: "A fellah who collects Lionel trains called me yestaday. Just tryin' ta help him out. I wonda if I be havin' a caboose somewheyah in heyah. He's lookin' especially for a caboose.

"Anyways—what was I sayin'? Yep, we'd buy the stuff, an' then Sven an' Jaleb Brooks would go out an' fetch it in his pickup truck an' bring it inta my shed. From there I'd ship it off. Didn't want ta be sellin' it around heyah—that's for shuwah. Didn't want the folks 'round heyah ta get wind of what this stuff was worth.

"That Jaleb is something else, let me tell yuh—a good match for Sven. It's funny though; eventually they began ta bring furniture in that I had nevah seen befowah. Great stuff, I tell yuh. I don't know wheyah they got that stuff, but I shipped it on too. Didn't ask no questions 'bout that, an' the people who got it didn't either."

He slid his long fingers back into the mound of toys. "By the way," he added, "yuh interested in old baseball cards? I got a whole shipment a' them this mornin'."

"No," I replied. "Tell me about Jaleb. What do you know about him?"

"Nothin' much. He's rough, all right, an' maybe even dangerous. Yuh wouldn't wanta cross him, yuh wouldn't. But for all his blustah, he's a smaht man, maybe the smahtest man 'roun', 'cept for Sven when he were alive. Much smahtah than that othah fellah Sven hung 'roun' with whom I can't remembah. Sven used to say about that othah fellah that he was like the fool in some Russian folk tale who went ta the county fair an' spent so much time lookin' at the exhibits a' little things, he nevah saw a great big ol' chained bear standin' right in front a' him."

"Oh, really . . . how like Sven to know a Russian folk tale!"

"Yuh wanta know what else Sven thought a' that teachah fellah?"

"No, I don't think so."

I said goodbye and left the shop.

Weeks later, promptings of no especially beneficent nature, I'm sure, drove me to enter the law offices of what was still called "Lindstrom and Bailey" upon some pretext I no longer remember. Art Bailey was not busy at the moment and had time to chat. He recognized me and invited me into his office. He sat in a large aluminum and leather chair that tipped back rather alarmingly. He was a short man, a bit chubby and bald, with a thin moustache and a curious propensity to tap his head rather loudly with his right index finger whenever engaged in what was meant to be taken as an act of thinking. His head sounded curiously hollow. Sometimes he would grasp his head in both hands and lift that same finger upright so that it looked like a small stubby antenna attached to the top of his skull; he would then waggle that finger around as if the antenna were trying to pick up a signal. As we talked, he did a great deal of that tapping and grasping as well as rocking back and forth in the chair, which at times would suddenly catapult him from an almost reclining position to an upright position so violently that it looked as if it would hurl him right across the desk—in my direction, unfortunately—antenna and all pointed directly at me.

We spoke of what we had in common: our memories of Sven. He was visibly nervous about that but was able to acknowledge how brilliant Sven was. Indeed, the law practice had certainly declined since the time of Sven's accident. But there was a curious lack of remorse in his whole manner of speaking. Late in our rambling discourse, he mentioned something about a "ghastly incident."

"And what was that?" I inquired.

"Well, well," he said. "It was that pal of Sven's, that bearded barbarian, Jaleb Brooks. A few days after Sven's accident, he barged in here and demanded several items of furniture that were in Sven's office. I had assumed they were antiques of some sort. He said they were his, that *he had made them.* Of course, I protested, threatened to call the police, all the rest you know. I was met with language so coarse, so abusive, so intimidating that I decided to let the things go. I thought he was going to kill me. He would have killed anyone over those antiques. What did it matter to me? I just let them go. Sven had seemed rather fond of them, however. They were very nice pieces—completely unlike the grotesque hunks he filled his house with."

"That must have been pretty shocking—after all those years with a gentleman like Sven, to be treated so crudely like that."

Art allowed his chair to come slowly to an upright position. He took his hands away from his head and folded them on the desk in front of him. He looked down at his hands.

"Not really," he allowed. "That was not the shocking part. Sven, you know, always treated me like that too. Sven was a coarse and violent man, given to the most uncouth oaths and violent tempers I've ever witnessed. Surely you knew about that, Mr. Thompson. Surely you knew that about Sven. And he had met in Jaleb a man as violent and coarse as he was, except perhaps a bit more so. If the two of them, for some reason, had gone at each other, the consequences wouldn't have been pleasant."

I was astonished. "No. I didn't know."

"But the shocking part—that was the admission by Jaleb that he had made those antiques—those 'antiques,' if you understand the contradiction in terms."

"He must be very skilled."

"Skilled indeed! I've made some inquiries since then. Only Sven could have figured out all the details of how to do that—the right glues, the right wood and pegs and nails, all extracted from genuine old pieces of no real value, then recrafted to a perfect set of specifications. It took Jaleb to do the actual carpentry, and, yes, he must be very good at that, judging from those pieces we had here in the office. I guess they had quite a business going from what I can reckon, all funneled through Martin Casey, who never had an idea of what was going on. Even the experts were fooled."

"And have you tried to bring this out, expose this …?"

"There's no point in doing that. I learned a lot about law from Sven. What little success I've had is due to him. Anyway, he's dead. And anyway …"

"Yes?"

"I wouldn't want to get on the wrong side of Jaleb Brooks. He's too dangerous a man. He wouldn't stop at anything."

I turned to go. As I opened the office door I heard Art Bailey murmur, "And I never believed, never for a moment, that Sven died from hitting his head on a rock. Never believed that, never did."

That evening, hours after my brief interview with Art Bailey, I could swear I saw Jaleb Brooks roar down the main street of East Gilead in his old pickup truck, his beard aflame in the evening sun, his eyes intent with demonic fury, and his truck rattling like an infernal chariot loosed upon the unhappy denizens of this world.

Years later, I happened to go to a teachers' conference in Minneapolis. Such affairs, as anyone knows who has ever been to one, are so dreadful that any excuse to get away for a while is quite welcome. I decided to rent a car and drive out to a pleasant suburb where I had learned that Dorothea now lived. I found a somewhat more robust and happier woman than I had remembered, less tense, living with a new husband amid decorous surroundings. We talked about life back in East Gilead, what had happened to whom, who was doing what, and about her life and what she was doing.

We talked about Winkee, too, but he rarely kept in touch with his mother. He had been in trouble a number of times—a dishonorable discharge from the army, drugs, alcoholism, a short prison term, a short-lived marriage. Dorothea was clearly sad about him.

Toward the end of our conversation, I felt impelled, really in spite of myself, to allude to her pronouncement, made so many years before, about the three friends.

"I knew," she said, "how much you admired Sven, and I thought you might be honored to know what he told me he thought of you. And I am so glad you remembered that."

"I did remember," I answered. "And I was honored."

"I considered telling the others the same thing, you know — Jaleb Brooks and Martin Casey. But I never did. I would have felt just a little awkward mentioning it to Jaleb because in the last week or so before the accident there had been hard feelings between Jaleb and Sven. It was something about furniture in Sven's law office.

"Sven had a few pieces of furniture in his office that I guess Jaleb thought belonged to him and Sven was unwilling to give up. I never saw this furniture. I wonder if it was as awful as what our house was furnished with.

"Anyway, I found out because Jaleb called at the house once — something he never normally did. Jaleb was in a terrible state at the time.

"I couldn't imagine the two of them as having any interest in furniture. Furniture! That's so unlike them. Anyway, they must have resolved the disagreement, whatever it was."

Dorothea tilted her head in a slightly odd way, in that same curious bluejay way I had seen years before, and watched for my reaction.

"Why do you say that?" I replied.

"Because of the fishing trip — when the accident occurred."

"What about the fishing trip?"

"Usually, Sven went fishing with Brian O'Grady. He often spent evenings and sometimes weekends with Jaleb doing I don't know what. But that weekend he went fishing with Jaleb. They wouldn't have gone fishing together if there still were hard feelings between them, would they?"

I was silent. I knew she was testing me. "I mean, they must have resolved that issue about the furniture."

I was still silent. I knew that they hadn't resolved that issue. I knew that she realized that as well.

"And Jaleb was so nice about it." Dorothea dropped her eyes. "He supplied all the fishing gear. Sven didn't take his; I guess his ties were getting old and were not so effective anymore at luring the fish. I didn't even know that Sven had gone off on a fishing trip that day."

Dorothea looked at me again. "I'm so glad you came by. You were such a good friend with Sven. That's why I told you back then about yourself, and Jaleb Brooks, and Martin Casey. I just wanted you to ... to know; I just wanted someone other than myself to know. And I knew that you would finally work it out … that you would put all the pieces together. I gave you the foundation for what you needed to find out."

"Find out what?"

"You know very well what I mean."

"Who …" I hesitated.

"Yes," she smiled. "Who Sven really was, and …"

"And …?" I repeated.

"What he was up to, and …"

"And …?" I repeated yet again.

"… what actually happened to him."

Two Sisters

This is the story of two sisters whose names were Marcia and Constance. They were tall, slender girls with fine features, and though Marcia was born three years earlier than Constance, they almost looked like twins. I can tell you that more intelligent, more accomplished, and more lovely girls you couldn't find anywhere in the world.

But things didn't turn out too well for them, as you will see. All of this happened quite some time ago. I must warn you that this is an unhappy story—a very unhappy story. If you don't like unhappy stories, you shouldn't read it.

Marcia and Constance grew up in Newton, just outside Boston, back when the town still had a vaguely rural quality about it. Their father was a distinguished lawyer who died while the girls were still children. Their mother was a beautiful woman, remote and elegant, who managed her household in an old-fashioned way. She rarely left her house. Over the years she maintained a small staff of domestic servants—butlers, maids, chauffeurs, gardeners—who performed the various errands that kept the household well supplied or took her daughters to church, or to school, or to the various lessons that girls of that time needed in order to acquire the appropriate social graces. Though she never accepted engagements outside her own home, she did bring many guests into the house and entertained them in regal fashion. She insisted, all of her life, on dressing in the long, beaded, corseted gowns stylish several decades earlier, at the time of her courtship with her late husband. It made her something of an oddity in the social circles of Newton in the 1920s — but, I should add — a pleasant oddity, a living memorial to what so often the young assume to have been a more settled, more ceremonious, and less demanding age.

Marcia and Constance had many friends who enjoyed coming over to their house. To catch a glimpse of their mother moving like an apparition through a distant hallway was considered something of a privilege. It would be talked about for days afterward.

Newton was a wonderful place to grow up in. Tree-lined, shady streets; fine houses adorned by well-groomed gardens and lawns; the succession of seasons, each with its own inimitable charms and delights; the various little village centers here and there throughout the larger township whose pharmacy soda fountains made ideal destinations for leisurely bicycle rides: all of these surrounded the girls with what can only be described as a kind of domestic paradise. The years revolved slowly and dreamily, marked by events that, however commonplace they might be for the experienced eye, were a source of boundless excitement for the girls. Their mother was always there, somewhere in the background, ordering and cherishing their lives with an aloof but patient tenderness. And they got along splendidly together, Marcia and Constance: in their childish games when they were younger, and in whisperings and flutterings when they were older and began attending country-club dances, involving themselves, as they inevitably would, in the whimsical stratagems that so enthrall adolescent hearts.

Their college years were just as good: Marcia went to nearby Wellesley, and Constance, three years later, packed off for what was regarded as somewhat distant Skidmore College. Those years were filled with interesting courses about things such as Gothic cathedrals, French poetry, and Russian novels, and with sporting events and dances on weekends and occasional trips to New York or to other college campuses throughout New England. Warm, golden summers were spent on Cape Cod, when their mother sent them off with half of the domestic help to occupy their old but sunny house perched on a grassy dune overlooking the beach. Things couldn't have been better for them. Never could the future have held out more fecund promises, more assurances that the blissful, dreamy years could go on forever.

It's too bad it didn't.

When Asherton Bricklawn first appeared on the scene, it seemed like the confirmation of everything the girls had ever anticipated. He was handsome, rich, well educated, robust, and full of derring-do—well, with too much of this latter quality, as it would turn out. He went to Harvard, where he was a catcher on the varsity baseball team. A goodly crowd would turn out on sunny afternoons in the spring to see the team play, and especially to see Asherton, because of his dramatic leaps after bunted balls, his playing perilously close to the swings of the batter, and his daredevil pursuits of pop flies. One time, in pursuit of just such a pop fly, he ran full speed into a post of his team's dugout and knocked himself unconscious. He was borne off the field like a slain warrior or like a knight felled in a joust, and the crowd applauded loudly.

Marcia was in that crowd. She could, verily, have swooned. Six months later she was engaged to be married to Asherton Bricklawn. He was certainly the most dashing, the most wonderful man she had ever met. He was so much like the adventurous men you used to read about in the weekly magazines back in those times—who flew open-cockpit aircraft over desert wastelands, who traveled to the heart of Africa, or who climbed the Himalayas and visited the Dalai Lama.

Constance couldn't have been more excited about it, too, or happier for Marcia. The two of them began laying the most detailed plans for an elegant wedding—knowing full well, of course, that their mother would finally plan it all in her own way, in her own house, and do a much better job of it than they could dream of doing.

The engagement turned out to be a long one. Asherton, having graduated from Harvard, was trying to get established in a brokerage firm in downtown Boston. His intelligence and vitality naturally recommended him highly to his superiors, and the way looked clear for a meteoric rise in his profession. But delays occurred. In his first year of work, he was in an automobile accident and was hospitalized for two months during his recovery. He broke both legs the following winter by trying to ski Tuckerman's Ravine in New Hampshire at a time when few attempted to do it on those old-fashioned wooden skis. In the spring, he took up airplane flying and flipped a small biplane upside down on the runway while trying to take off, though he emerged miraculously unscathed by that adventure.

Marcia spent a lot of time that year in hospital rooms and guiding Asherton around in wheelchairs as he urged her continually to run with the wheelchair and send him careening off down a hallway or a lawn or a steep sidewalk. He once even tried to persuade her to let him loose at the top of a staircase in the wheelchair. He would lift his arms and wave his hands and fingers around as if trying to clutch the air above him and cry out, "Marcia, push me, push!"

His lively spirits were irrepressible — irrepressible indeed! Often Marcia, keeping faithful watch at his hospital bedside, had to hear him talking for hours about how unfortunate it was that there was no war for him to go to. He dreamed of charges into hails of machine-gun fire. At his job he did get into serious trouble when he lost a small fortune for an important client of the firm by investing funds in an extremely risky venture, one that his superiors had vigorously warned him against. It's fortunate that he didn't lose his job at the time, for his supervisors decided to give him another chance. New clients were drawn by his verve and good looks. Of course, Asherton didn't really need a job — he had a trust fund that made him independently wealthy.

The wedding finally did occur. It was just as glorious as one could expect, except for when Asherton, grasping a bottle of champagne in one hand and a tall-stemmed glass in the other, climbed up to the roof of the porch and jumped, with a great shout, into the garden fishpond from there. The guests were horrified — most human beings could not have survived such a jump, but Asherton stepped, dripping and laughing, out of the pond still grasping his bottle of champagne, though the tall-stemmed glass had vanished somewhere in the murky waters. A tangle of lily fronds was wrapped about his neck. Marcia tried to laugh but could not. She decided it was time for them to be on their way, and after the bride and groom had changed their clothing, they departed with much fanfare in the open Pierce-Arrow coupe that Asherton liked to drive at breakneck speeds. They were driving north to Maine for their honeymoon at Boothbay Harbor.

Several hours later, they pulled up at a scenic outlook where some rocky cliffs dropped rather abruptly into the sea below. It was early evening, and Asherton said he needed a short rest from the driving. The couple stood at the side of the cliff, arms around each other's waists, and watched the easy rolling of the sea and the breaking of the surf on the rocks far beneath them. Marcia couldn't have been happier; she knew that Asherton, now a married man, wouldn't take so many risks and would settle down to a more reasonably tranquil way of life. Suddenly, Asherton lurched out in front of Marcia, stood teetering at the very brink of the cliff, and raised his arms into the sky, wildly waving his hands and fingers. He cried out, "Marcia, Marcia! Push me! Push me! Push me!" Marcia was terrified; these were words from the wheelchair games he had liked to play, but now the circumstances were too real, too dangerous. She lifted her hands to grab hold of his shoulders so that he wouldn't fall, but, as she made contact with his shoulders, it was like touching off a powerful spring or trap. He was not there anymore—just the sea and sky in front of her. Instantly she heard a thud from the depths below.

It was good that Marcia had Constance to look after her in the first few years after Asherton's death. Marcia was convinced that she had killed her husband on her wedding day. In another way, of course, she knew that this was not true. She had not pushed him; he had jumped. But it didn't matter. She sat for hours on the porch, looking into the distance. Often she imagined Asherton rising up out of that fishpond with a shimmering skein of wet water lilies wreathed gruesomely around him; the image would make her tremble violently. Her life was crushed under a load of remorse and suffering. The girls' mother was as gracious and as remote as ever; she was able to do little to alleviate her daughter's grief.

Then came Bob.

Who could forget Bob? His full name was Bob Shreveman—a graduate of Colgate University and an aspiring estates lawyer. Constance met him at a "mixer" while in her junior year at Skidmore. I don't think anyone ever liked Bob, except for Constance. If there ever was a man who preened himself, it was Bob. He combed his hair; he straightened his tie; he made sure his cuffs came out of his coat sleeves just exactly the proper length; he looked into the mirror at himself from several angles and worried and fussed about himself constantly.

Whenever he was about to sit down, he examined the chair to make sure there was nothing there to stain his suit. He had a clean handkerchief that was perpetually in use, patting this or dusting that or insulting any number of mortified hostesses by wiping their silverware and the rims of their glasses and cups before he would deign to use them. He also went in for extravagant clothing and was fond of long silk scarves that he would sweep dramatically around his neck and let drop almost to his knees on both sides. But Constance had an absolute passion for him because he was so good-looking, so well spoken, so courteous almost to a fault.

Bob gloried in her worship of him; she was his fan club, his adoring audience. He could parade himself up and down in front of her and know that her attentive eyes would appreciate every detail, every finely attuned color and line in his invariably matchless attire.

An occasional doubt about Bob, however, sometimes flickered through Constance's mind. He almost never touched her. He held her hand once after a date, but when her hand became a bit sweaty, he released it abruptly and wiped his own hand with his handkerchief. There were a few kisses now and then, to be sure, but Constance quickly realized that if there were the slightest hint of moisture on her lips, the kiss would be met with repugnance. He also didn't like contact with lipstick—he regarded it as "slimy," which was an important word for him and which he used to describe anything he didn't like. Practically everything was "slimy" for him—and especially anything bodily, wet, warm, earthy, protoplasmic. His obsession with clothes was to keep things covered up, disguised, and out of sight. She also felt hurt sometimes when he wouldn't drink from the same cup she had drunk from or take a bite of a sandwich or cake that she had previously tasted. He was constantly afraid of "germs."

Just about any woman in the world would have dismissed Bob without further ado, but Constance loved him. Perhaps he reminded her of her mother somehow—so reserved, so elegant, so detached. There must be passion, somewhere, under all that reserve, she thought.

They got married. It wasn't a big wedding such as Marcia had. Bob had no friends to speak of, Marcia was just coming back to something like an active life again, and their mother had retreated deeper into the recesses of her aging household. Constance, for her part, was more than ready to depart the household and make a life of her own.

On the wedding night Bob emerged from the bathroom in the hotel suite dressed in a pair of red silk pajamas with a black silk bathrobe. He exuded the most powerful fragrance of *eau de cologne*. After studying himself for some time in a full-length mirror, he walked proudly about the room, turning and posing like a model and basking in his own admiration. Constance knelt on the bed and clapped her hands and giggled. She was practically jumping up and down with excitement. She was dressed in a short nightgown. Her slender arms and legs were bare. She felt so supremely glamorous, as if she were a girl in an advertisement. She just knew that Bob's reserve would turn into the passion she had been longing for so long.

But there was no passion. He wasn't even looking at her. He removed his bathrobe, got into bed, and fell fast asleep.

It was not until two years later, after the marriage had ended, that Constance was able to confide in Marcia about what had happened. She had a difficult time putting it directly. She said that Bob just didn't like any-thing—well, messy; anything "slimy"; anything that involved getting too close; anything that was not … not … sufficiently dressed. She said all of this in tears, in a stumbling and humiliated voice. But Marcia got the mes-sage; there had never been a marriage in a physical sense; it had just never happened. Constance, whatever she thought of Bob, could no longer live with his ever-present disgust at her physical existence.

The saddest thing about Constance was that she didn't get over her ado-ration of Bob for quite a while. For the next three years, Constance lived by herself in an apartment in Boston that overlooked Kenmore Square. She did this solely to be able to see Bob every morning punctually at 8:35 driv-ing his car down Commonwealth Avenue to work. She loved it especially when he would stop at the red light at the intersection of Commonwealth and Beacon Street so that she could have a minute or so to gaze at him. The same viewing was repeated every evening at 5:35 when he returned home from work.

Some seasons of the year were more difficult than others in this regard, for the early winter nights and headlights often made it difficult to see him. But he was always so impeccably dressed, and Constance found it a matter of great curiosity to see what he would wear each day. She came to know all of his various outfits and was delighted to see a new one show up from time to time. In the summer he would drive to work in his convertible, often with one of his long silk scarves trailing in the breeze as he drove. He was so gallant! She organized her entire life around this effort to see him drive by twice a day.

One morning on his way to work, one of those long silk scarves was blown to the side by a gust of wind and got caught in the left rear tire. It reeled in like a fishing line and grabbed hold. It snapped his neck as it yanked him out of the driver's seat and down onto the road. The convertible bolted around to the right and drove into the large front window of a beauty parlor, dragging poor Bob behind it. Luckily, the beauty parlor had not opened up for business yet and no one was hurt.

Constance noted that he didn't appear that day at the intersection, but she was accustomed to his occasional failure to show up. When she read about his accident in the newspapers the following day, she was very sad about it—but not too sad.

In later years she would come to interpret her momentary relief at the news of his death as an expression of satisfaction that some force of destiny had finally exacted a just revenge on the person whose vanity had cast such a malevolent spell over her life. As she grew older, this "spite," as she came to understand her relief, would become a source of endless self-reproach.

In the meantime, the girls' mother had passed away, and Marcia was living alone in the house in Newton, attended by a now substantially diminished staff of domestic servants. Things were getting a bit shabby at this point; the gardens were overgrown with weeds and shrubs; and the fishpond, no doubt deliberately, was allowed to vanish under a heap of dead vegetation that had accumulated on top of it through the years. Despite all this, Constance decided to give up her apartment in Kenmore Square and to move back to live with Marcia. Both were still young women, and it was unfortunate that they resolved to withdraw so prematurely into an isolated life. Financially, they were well off. Inheritances came to them from their mother, as well as from their deceased husbands. Marcia and Constance let themselves be known to the outside world, respectively, as Mrs. Bricklawn and Mrs. Shreveman. Like their mother, they retired into what seemed to be a dignified widowhood, though neither of them — and rightly so — had any sense of having ever actually been married.

As they saw it, they had wounds to heal, though the measures they took to heal them ensured that these wounds would remain open for the rest of their lives. Shortly thereafter, they decided to sell the house in Newton and to live year-round in the old beach house at Cape Cod.

How can I describe the mode of life that they lived now in that tall, lonely beach house in all seasons of the year? Mostly, of course, it was very good — at least good for a decade or so. They inhabited a kind of tense but unreal postscript to a life that had never happened — or more accurately, since most of their conversation dwelled on those beautiful childhood and adolescent years whose memories were made most poignant by recalling the dreams of the future that they once had, it might be proper to say, as paradoxical as it sounds, that they inhabited a prelude to a future that was irrevocably past.

For all of this, they managed to live well together, to enjoy long walks on the beach, the flowers and vegetables they cultivated, their care of the house (for they no longer had servants), their literary excursions, the occasional guest from Boston or New York, the unusual and imaginative cooking they did, their boundless fascination for the seabirds that flew overhead and for the schools of whales that sometimes passed along the coast. Winter, of course, was bleak, but it had its consolations in the cheery fire that burned in the hearth, in the hot cocoa they loved so much, and in the endless stacks of novels they read with passion and discussed from week to week. Curiously, the only season that posed any real difficulty for them was summer, when tourist traffic clogged the local villages, and the beach in front of their house was overrun with bathers carrying noisy radios and leaving behind rubbish strewn over the dunes. In fact, in a moment of what we might call lavish eccentricity, and partly as a reaction to the summer crowds, they decided to have a spacious sundeck built on the roof of their house. Since the house was three stories tall, the venture would involve a rather costly and skillful feat of carpentry. They could use it during the summer, watching the sea from there when it was not so pleasant to go down to the beach. The sundeck finally was built. They called it their "widows' walk" and were amused, initially, by this ironic appropriation of a relatively harmless architectural term to fit the circumstances of their lives. The "widows' walk" was reached by a long wooden staircase and gave a superb view over the dunes to the sea beyond.

In quite another sense, things were not so good between the sisters. The tragedies of their marriages, the remorseless ambiguity of having been, and similarly of not having been, married, occupied their home and their life together like great blocks of silent granite around which they had to move and squeeze and scrape themselves day after day—a vast, unfathomable vacancy as immovable, as impenetrable, as stone.

Because they lived so much in the past, they kept that unspoken vacancy, that unfulfilled promise, continually in mind. At times it would produce tension that would explode in a hail of bitter words between them. But they quickly brought things back under control and were easily reconciled.

Perhaps the most injurious development, however, was their beginning to make jokes about each other's predicament. At first, such a practice might have looked salutary; they were being lighthearted, jocular about matters that preoccupied them too seriously. Certainly a few jokes now and then, some kindly teasing, would help to deflate the burden of those somber feelings that still dominated their lives.

Marcia would express either discontent about things in general, or disapproval about Constance in particular, by invoking the language of Bob and using one of his favorite terms, such as "slimy." She would dress with inordinate attention to detail and press Constance, in a jovial way, to admire and flatter her for her achievement.

Or Constance would dare Marcia to do various things, more ostensibly than actually risky, or act as if she herself was about to engage in some monstrously daredevil act. Then both would laugh and think it was terribly amusing and call each other Mrs. Bricklawn and Mrs. Shreveman in ways that mimicked the voices of the former husbands.

As the years passed, however, such exchanges became less amusing. Marcia began to act and think like Bob and to relate to Constance in the way that Bob had. She began to hate anything bodily, putatively unclean, "slimy." She began to detest her younger sister's physical presence. She would do everything to avoid any contact with her. Personal items belonging to or associated with Constance, such as a toothbrush or a comb or a stray hair, became objects of loathing for her. Marcia also grew inordinately protective of her eating utensils, segregating them meticulously from anything that Constance ever used. Finally, she became almost unbearably timid—afraid to swim, to climb a stepladder, or even to drive a car.

Constance, in turn, became intolerably reckless, taking on the personality of Asherton and acting toward Marcia as he had done. Marcia's abandonment of car driving gave Constance the opportunity she wanted to drive irresponsibly, sometimes spinning the car out onto the beach, getting it stuck in the sand so that the local tow truck would have to recover the car while the rising tide came ever closer and closer to it. Sometimes, when driving with Marcia along the causeway that passed over the salt marshes to the local village, she would bring the car to a screeching halt, leap out of the door and onto the railing of the causeway, and dive from there into the shallow murky waters below with a shriek of delight. On these occasions, Marcia not only would be painfully reminded of similar episodes with Asherton but also would be terrified for Constance's safety.

Even more, Constance took to frightening Marcia with slimy crabs and spiders and garden snakes. She did everything, too, to make herself unpleasant: walking around the house in torn clothes or leaving wet underwear to dry over the kitchen sink. But, worst of all, she would suddenly dare Marcia to push her anywhere, anyhow—from chairs (which she had climbed on specifically and solely for this purpose), from door stoops, from sand dunes, from boating docks—as she grappled the air with wildly twitching fingers.

One summer, an unbearably hot, humid, overcast day settled over a sea as flat and colorless as a tile of gray slate. Not a single breeze stirred the grass on the dunes, and the seabirds were nowhere to be seen. A few knots of tourists dotted the beach here and there, but they seemed as listless and as torpid as the sea. A single radio blared its thumping cacophonous music across the length of the beach. In the midst of this heat, Marcia and Constance decided to mount the wooden stairway to their "widows' walk" in the hope of catching any cooling breeze that might come their way.

Marcia climbed the long flight of stairs with some trepidation, as she now usually did; she held tightly to the railing and wouldn't look down. At the top she lay down on a lounge chair with her eyes closed and rested for a while. She wore a kind of red terry-cloth robe which made her even hotter than she was, but she insisted on wearing it. Body exposure had become repellent to her.

Constance, on the other hand, virtually danced up the stairs and flung her robe aside, sitting down somewhat precariously on the broad railing of the sundeck in her bathing suit. She was sweating profusely. She took a plastic bottle of suntan lotion out of her beach bag and, squeezing some of the lotion into her hand, began rubbing herself all over with the white, oily substance. Marcia opened her eyes for a moment and watched. "Ugh," she said, "how revolting! Do you have to use that stuff?"

Constance shot back, "Begging your pardon, Mrs. Bricklawn, but it's well-known that hazy days like this can give one serious sunburns."

Marcia groaned. "How intolerably hot and slimy you look today, Mrs. Shreveman! Do you have to offend my eyes this way? It's making me feel sick." She closed her eyes again.

"Go ahead and feel sick!" Constance retorted.

"And your body—you're too old for swimsuits like that, Mrs. Shreveman! I would rather look at a decaying fish whose eyes have been plucked out by the gulls!"

Constance glared at Marcia. Tears flooded her eyes.

Suddenly, she tossed the suntan lotion back into her beach bag, jumped up from the railing, and skipped over to the head of the long wooden stairway, and, looking out to the sea, she shrieked, "Push me!" She lifted up her arms and waved her hands and fingers around in the gray sky. "Push me! Push me, Marcia! Marcia, push me!" To make it even worse, she began to teeter back and forth on her heels and toes at the brink of the stairway.

Marcia opened her eyes again. She stared at Constance's glistening back with its streaks of white suntan lotion mixed with sweat. She thought how slippery and gruesome it would be to touch. But an inexplicable rage overwhelmed her. The image of her husband at the edge of the cliff that had so haunted and obsessed her all these years took furious possession of her mind. Even more, though, she was gripped, as so often happened, by a terror for her sister's safety, of seeing her sister tumble off that dangerous perch. Unaccountably, and to her own shock and surprise, she bounded from the lounge chair and tried to grab hold of her sister's shoulders and pull her back, but the momentum of the bound and the slippage of her hands downward on Constance's oily back resulted in a push. It was an unintentional but an actual push this time.

After the thumping and screaming and banging were over, everything was silent. A few bathers on the beach in the distance stood up and looked with astonishment toward the beach house. They were not sure what they had observed and didn't know, at that moment, what to do. Marcia sat at the top of the stairs. She had shrunk into a little ball, her legs pressed up beneath her, her face buried in her knees, her arms wrapped over her head, and her hands tearing at her hair. At the bottom of the stairs, Constance lay sprawled and motionless. Her head was tilted in the coyest, sweetest way. Her neck was grotesquely broken.

Marcia spent the rest of her life in a mental institution. She would spend the day—day after day—weeping and moaning and butting her head against the walls and floor of her room. But it was a very nice place just outside Boston, with courteous and mindful attendants, with flourishing trees and well-tended lawns, with rose gardens and fountains, and with twittering birds fluttering through the trellised arbors, and … and … well, enough of this.

I told you that you shouldn't read this story.

Le Danse du Diable

Byron Langley was not the first in his affluent suburban community to discover between the pages of a glossy mail-order catalogue some strange and initially inchoate resuscitation of a long-forgotten dream. Indeed, the very merchandising principle of many such catalogues depends upon producing precisely this effect in their unwary customers. You may never have actually engaged in homesteading in Alaska, or in climbing a Himalayan peak, or in managing a tropical plantation, or in breasting the ice-cold waves of an arctic sea in your private windjammer; but you can purchase the appropriate outfit for doing so, even if it's to be worn only on a Saturday excursion to the liquor store and even if the setting is no more exotic than a comfortable and exquisitely landscaped suburb of New York City, such as that of Upper Paragon, New Jersey.

Many of Byron's neighbors had succumbed, at one time or another, to the temptation. In fact, Milton Barnaby, an eminent Wall Street lawyer who lived only three houses away from the Langleys, purchased an entire lumberjack's outfit, along with a huge double-headed axe of Paul Bunyan vintage, in order to fell a dead rhododendron bush in his backyard. Across the street from Milton Barnaby, Jonathan Birdsell purchased an Australian field jacket to go with his new Land Rover, a vehicle he needed for the presumably arduous journey over the rugged outback that separated his commodious "shack" from the local supermarket. Yet another neighbor, whose name discretion forbids us to mention, had the custom, during autumnal windstorms, of standing for long periods of time on his back "deck" dressed in a Norwegian fisherman's outfit as he scanned, with a brass telescope, little more than the brook that babbled down from his neighbors' yards and past his house, all the while sipping hot tea laced with potent naval rum from, of course, an appropriately weather-beaten tin cup.

An advantage of the so-called anonymity of suburban life, as well as of the copious leafage of trees and hedges with which we conceal our dwellings, is that we can indulge such private fantasies without too much public attention to the fact, though such attention, implicitly and finally, is the point of it all. Our neighbors may have to make quite an effort to see what we're up to, but it's important that such an effort be made and that it be, in any case, well rewarded.

In Byron's case, the long-forgotten dream was stirred by what might be described as a particularly undistinguished and, in one sense of the word at least, "modest" article of clothing to be found in the pages of L.L. Bean — a pair of red-flannel long underwear.

Byron probably had little idea of why he was so attracted to this underwear; but, after all, long-forgotten dreams are like that. The clear, imaginative, improbably detailed pictures of youth are replaced only by the longings connected originally to them. We struggle with these longings, often — though in vain — trying to define them, and even more assiduously trying to repress and restrain them, especially when they arise at some inconvenient time, such as in the middle of a business conference or while we're trying to negotiate some particularly tenuous agreement. But then again, everything in our environment perpetually urges us to give in to such impulses, to "throw off our fetters," to be outrageous, to indulge, to buy.

It all comes down to the same thing in the end.

Byron, however, did struggle with the temptation for several years. We must give him credit for that, but the insistent arrival of catalogue after catalogue, in season after season, broke down his resistance at last. He felt, finally, a devilish streak coming out in him (and how ominous is this talk of "temptation" and "devilish," considering the outcome of all of this). In any event, he said, as we all finally say when submitting to a whim, "Why not?"

Byron's wife, Midge, was consulted. She was a little surprised by his desire for this odd item of clothing but had no objections. The item was ordered.

Several weeks later, Byron came home on the evening commuter train from New York, where he pursued a mildly successful career in international investment banking. There he found, leaning against his front door, a large brown shipping envelope from L.L. Bean. He picked it up and carried it into the living room, where he laid it on the long maple coffee table. Midge arrived home a few minutes later. Byron didn't hurry to open the parcel. Instead, he waited until he'd changed into his casual wear and until both Midge and he could settle down for their cocktail hour with tall, cool highballs propped before them on the coffee table. When all was ready and calm, he ceremoniously pried open the end of the envelope. A small plastic bag with the bright red garment tightly folded up inside it slid out onto his lap.

His initial reaction was, as one suspects it often is in these situations, one of acute disappointment. For part of a reverie has abruptly materialized with agonizing literalness, all neatly folded in an antiseptic and paltry-looking plastic bag.

Where is the rest of it? Where are the glaciers, the wind-blown sea, the banana trees sweltering in the tropical sun? Why are they not in the package too? After all, the catalogues show these things, if not always to the eyes, then at least to the spirit. Aren't they part of the bargain? Did they forget to send them along?

"Well," Byron asserted, as he was accustomed to do in such matters, "you take what you can get." That was one of his favorite expressions.

After the initial letdown, Byron removed the garment from the plastic bag and, lifting it up, allowed it to unfold before him. A long vertical row of small white buttons, contrasting sharply with the brilliant red of the flannel, secured the two sides of the garment all the way from the neckline down to the crotch. Suddenly, Midge giggled.

"What's the matter?" Byron asked, a tone of alarm in his voice.

"Look at the back! Turn it around!" she cried.

He swung the garment around and discovered a long slit in the back end, held together—demurely, you might almost be inclined to say—with a single white button. He was awestruck! This startling aperture seemed at once to galvanize for him some part of the long-forgotten dream. Obviously, this was the perfect garment to wear in the middle of the night to some remote outhouse perched precariously on the edge of a jagged cliff.

It all came to him now—or so he thought—a smoky cabin high in the Ozarks, the hound dogs, the moonshine, the hogs submerged in their own swill. How he would stun and horrify the neighbors! How jealous they would be to see him lolling about in front of his house on hot summer evenings, dirty, chewing tobacco, barefoot, with nothing on but a pair of old overalls, held up by suspenders over his red-flannel long underwear, which would soon be splotched with sweat, dust, and streaks of tobacco juice that, not successfully expectorated across the yard, had been drooled down over a crudely unshaven chin and onto his chest. Even Milton Barnaby would be thoroughly abashed, his lumberjack duds ignominiously reduced to the status of slick professional wear.

Byron let out a whoop—what he presumed to be, no doubt, some version of a rebel yell—downed his highball in one great gulp and lunged from the couch into the bedroom to try on his new underwear. Meanwhile, Midge sat nervously in her chair and listened to Byron's voice expostulating on his newfound role in life.

Suddenly there was a long, studied silence. Not a motion, not a sound from the bedroom! Then, just as suddenly, Byron appeared in the doorway.

Midge shrieked. His tall, angular body, frozen into a contorted posture that resembled a Picasso *saltimbanque*, straddled the doorway in its blazing red, skin-tight outfit. His eyes had the look of wild astonishment in them, and his mouth was held tautly open as if he were in the throes of some monumental decision. The decision, whatever it was, was made. With a single grandiose movement of arms and legs, he bounded into the center of the room, almost hitting his head on the ceiling, and came to a perfect rest in a *demi-plié*.

"Byron!" Midge screamed. "You look like ..."

"I know! I know!" he declaimed. All thoughts of outhouses, hound dogs, and little brown jugs had been instantly banished from his mind.

"I'm the Devil!" he shouted. "I'm the red Devil, come to accuse the world of its sins!"

At this juncture, you might be impelled to inquire about the long-forgotten dream. Did it all have its origins in the frustration of a little boy who didn't get the costume he wanted on some teary-eyed Halloween of yore? Such a conjecture might well be reasonable, except that the sporting of this marvelous devil apparel quickly assumed dimensions inexplicable by such a simple hypothesis.

For Byron, after his dramatic leap into the center of the living room, proceeded to engage in a very bizarre sort of dance. It resembled initially an odd combination of ballet, kickboxing, and mime. He glided across the living room into the dining room and back, his arms and legs flailing in every direction. Now and then he would shake his fists, parrying and jabbing like a boxer.

At last, he broke into a whirling Russian folk dance, kicking his legs out and shouting, "I accuse. I accuse. I am *diabolus*. I am the adversary. I am the Devil who accuses the world. *J'accuse. J'accuse.*"

With that, his leg hooked by mistake around the leg of the coffee table, throwing it over, breaking the highball glasses, and pitching him over the couch where he landed in the narrow space between the picture window and the couch. Midge jumped from her chair and ran to the couch. She saw him reclining there, flat on his back, with a huge, if fatuous, smile on his face.

"How do you like it?" he asked.

"Like what?" she asked in return.

"My dance. My Dance of the Devil."

"Well ..."

"I'll call it, *Le Danse du Diable*. Sounds classier in French."

"Why not *El Danza del Diablo*?" she suggested with a laugh. "Sounds more ferocious, more intense ..."

"And like some kind of tequila drink with hot peppers in it," he replied quite seriously.

"Or how about *Der Tanz des Teufels*? You know — Faustian, Walpurgisnacht, and all that."

"Too Teutonic. Too Wagnerian. Not for me."

"Then *Le Danse du Diable* it is. Now let's have dinner and forget about it as soon as possible. I'll have to clean up these broken glasses, since I assume you're in too distracted a state to do it yourself."

Midge went to get a broom to sweep up the broken glass while Byron still lay behind the couch, wrapped in deep thought. When she finished, he was still there. She urged him to get dressed for dinner, but he didn't seem to hear.

As she went into the kitchen, she kept thinking about the chaotic dance she'd just witnessed. Of course, you could regard it as a kind of a travesty, a grotesque mimicry, a satire on dance; she'd seen Byron do this kind of thing before, but never with the energy and persistence he'd just exhibited.

Midge had trained as a dancer in her girlhood and had kept up a lively interest in it ever since, though she prided herself on her ability to keep a critical distance from the fads and obsessions that, in her view, so dominated and diminished the seriousness of the dance world.

Byron, on the other hand, never professed anything but a deep contempt for dance as an art, never lost an opportunity to ridicule it, or to assume, at the oddest moments and in the oddest places, some hideous and contorted variation of a conventional dance move. Midge always felt that he did this at times to amuse her and at other times to tease her about her abiding interest in various dance styles. But now, for the first time, he'd executed an entire dance routine before her eyes.

As improvised and absurd as it was, Midge was nevertheless deeply troubled by it. For in the process of the dance and between bouts of the most frantic whirling of arms and legs, Byron again and again, for only split seconds at a time, executed moves that only a professional dancer would know how to do. Further, even in the wildest of gestures, he always seemed to have an almost perfect control over his movement and an innate sense of how to blend one movement into the following one, no matter how incongruent the subsequent movement happened to be.

Well, there was an explanation after all. At the Upper Paragon Racket Club, Byron was rather well known for his ability to do imitations. He did imitations of how fellow club members walked, how they lifted a glass of beer, how they got in and out of cars, and how they played tennis. Nor did he need to devote much study to their movements prior to the convincing imitations he could render of them; some brief observation was sufficient to enable him to do it naturally and spontaneously.

He also did the most astonishing imitations of animals — of elephants eating foliage with their trunks, of moths beating around light bulbs, of dogs throwing up, of cats licking their paws, of daddy longlegs slowly picking their way over a garden fence, of cobras coiling upward out of some basket to the tune of a reedy pipe. His hilarious and most popular imitation was that of a matador locked in mortal combat with a raging bull wherein he mimicked both the movements of the matador and the movements of the bull *simultaneously*.

Anything that moved he could imitate; it made sense, then, didn't it, that he could imitate, with startling grace and demeanor, the positions of classical ballet, as well as the gestures and modes of other dance styles?

The crowd that had watched him in the bar of the Racket Club found his antics to be the most wonderful entertainment. His mimicry of flamenco and the tango had his audience practically hurting with laughter. He could imitate the tap dancing of Fred Astaire, the leaps of Gene Kelly, and the gyrations of Elvis Presley.

Midge, naturally, found most of this to be rather embarrassing for her; nevertheless, she was frequently just as surprised and amused as the rest of the audience by what Byron could do, and there never seemed to be an end to what he could do.

She only regretted that his contempt for dancing prevented him from engaging in any ballroom dancing with her. She loved ballroom dancing, and the only time she'd ever danced with him was at their wedding, where social propriety and an insistent, even if brand new, mother-in-law had forced him into it. But, to her surprise, he knew the dances and executed them with a perfection she'd never experienced in a partner before.

She also regretted that she had to seek out her old friends in the dance world to accompany her to the performances in New York that she so treasured and delighted in. Her teacher, Madame Schernovsky, had retired recently from her studio in New York to an adjoining township, and Midge enjoyed staying in touch with her and renewing her enthusiasm for the dance through sharing her occasional companionship.

She'd succeeded only once in compelling Byron to attend a dance performance—and that with the promise of a good restaurant that she'd discovered near the theater. He'd been restless throughout the performance, shifting in his seat and shielding his eyes in the most brazen way so that he could not see the stage. He even was the source of some mortification when, at one point during the performance, he burst out loudly, "They don't know what they're doing!" The people in the surrounding seats turned to glare angrily at him, while Midge hid her face in her hands.

The problem was: she'd already, at that point, realized that the dance company was a sham, and the performance was incompetent. Byron, for reasons that utterly defied any explanation, had been right in his judgment.

So much for *Le Danse du Diable*, she thought. It's come and gone, like all the rest.

Perhaps it had something to do with her. Perhaps some malevolent spirit really had entered into Byron under the guise of that long red underwear to accuse not the world but her of insufficiently dedicating herself to an object of artistic devotion, of having prematurely abandoned a demanding and uncompromising vocation.

Dance, in its demonic mode, had arisen to reproach her through the antics of her husband. She decided to put aside these questions and ponder them no further.

But *Le Danse du Diable* didn't go away.

On the following day, at the time of the cocktail hour, a reinvigorated Byron donned his red-flannel underwear once again and flailed across the living room floor, kicking and jabbing, stabbing and bolting, swirling and flaring. This time he had pushed aside any potential obstacles to the dance, such as the coffee table. Once again, the dance was accompanied by sporadic outbursts of accusations leveled against just about everything in the world.

Midge watched this spectacle from the safe distance of the door leading into the kitchen. She held a highball in her hands and sipped from it. She noted a new set of variations introduced into the dance that seemed to have some relationship with oriental martial arts, including karate, tai chi, and samurai swordplay.

She decided to play the role of critic and declared that the chops and swings didn't match well with the Russian folk-dance motifs that were occasionally resumed. Without ceasing to dance, Byron shouted back that her remark was "insensitive" and "philistine" and that he was trying to create a "disturbing, disjointed" image that would cause people to "rethink their lives and values."

Midge laughed; yet she was slightly shaken by this mention of "people." Was someone actually supposed to look, someday, at this?

After a few more whirls around the room, Byron shouted again, "I'm synthesizing Eastern and Western Man in my dance! I'm creating a universal language!"

Midge shouted back, "Don't forget about Ancient Man and Renaissance Man, and Neanderthal Man and New Jersey Man and Peking Man! Or was it Peking duck?"

Byron was undaunted by this challenge. "Don't worry! I'll get to all of those in time."

On the third day, Midge was startled by yet another set of innovations. Byron took up a number of very odd positions, puffed out his cheeks, rolled his eyes, and rocked his head back and forth on his neck. He pounced backward and forward, flapping his arms and slapping his bare feet against the floor. His fingers moved rapidly through dozens of complex formations as he danced.

"Hindu temple dancing!" Midge thought. "Or at least some preposterous version of it! How would he know how to do that?"

She called out through the kitchen door, "Indra fights the great dragon, Vrtra! The monsoon rains are coming!"

Byron stopped short. "Not at all!" he shouted back, after a hesitation. "I am Shiva, god of destruction. I stamp down the demons of the underworld. In my cosmic dance, I contend with the powers of darkness."

"I thought you were a demon, the Demon King himself, the Erlkönig, the power of darkness personified."

"So I am. So I am. I dwell in paradox and ambiguity!"

"The ironic Mephistopheles!"

"Whatever!"

He resumed his dance, waving his arms so quickly through so many gestures and positions, his fingers and palms twisting into a rapid succession of precise "mudras," that it looked as if he had, indeed, six arms like the god Shiva himself.

Then he began to point wildly in one direction after another while shouting, "I accuse you, and you, and you, and you, and you!"

He stopped again.

"Midge," he cried, "what can I do in this dance that would really offend an audience, really bring home its complicity in socio-, politico-, cosmological evil?"

The mention of an audience was a bit disconcerting; but she answered, "I do have a suggestion, but you may not like it."

"I'm open to all suggestions."

"You know that opening in the posterior of your costume?"

"Yeah."

"Well, at the climactic point of the dance, you just turn your back to the audience and . . ."

"Midge! You're not being serious about this at all!"

"Is anyone being serious about anything?"

"I'm no longer open to suggestions."

The dance now shifted to something like an Australian aboriginal shuffle, filled with abrupt stops, a frozen position held for a few seconds, and, just as abruptly, a resumption of jagged, up-and-down movements, as if Byron had an imaginary spear in his hand and was shaking it at some recalcitrant kangaroo in the bush somewhere.

Midge retreated to the kitchen. She'd come to detest *Le Dance du Diable* and to regard it as something distinctly—well, diabolical.

Two months after the arrival of the accursed parcel, the dance had, as the expression goes, "taken over their lives." It was always the first thing that Byron did when he arrived home from work. He danced his silent, savage dance until he was exhausted. Eventually, he took up the dance on weekends as well, spending much of Saturday morning engaged in his—as he claimed—"perfecting" of it. Only on Sunday did he consider it appropriate to desist, perhaps out of some deeply residual, if subconscious, respect for the Sabbath.

Midge could no longer stand to watch or even be close to it. She found somewhere in the house, or out of the house, to be away during its daily performance. She no longer noticed the almost infinite permutations it passed through, though she did become aware that it transformed gradually into a quieter dance with less thumping and banging in its process. Meanwhile, Byron was neglecting his lawn and garden work and had given up playing tennis at the Racket Club.

Midge finally decided to take action. One evening at dinner, while Byron was ravenously slurping up his cream of artichoke soup, Midge calmly inquired, "Byron, don't you think it's time to give a performance of your work?"

"H'mm," he answered without looking up from his soup. "I perform it almost every day."

"Yes, but I mean a public performance—before a real audience. You don't want to go around accusing imaginary people. You need to accuse real people."

"I'm not ready for that yet. The dance must be perfected."

Midge stirred her soup for a moment. She said, "Well, Byron, I understand why you think that. Every true *artiste* strives for perfection. But I wonder if an *artiste* can truly perfect something without some exposure to a public. That's a way of finding out, sometimes, if an *oeuvre* is working or not."

"Sometimes!" Byron replied, looking up from his soup. "That's the catch. You can't trust an audience. Audiences mostly have the standards that someone else tells them to have."

"Perhaps. But an art needs a public resonance of some sort." Midge responded. Then she added, somewhat dramatically, "If it's pursued purely in private, it will ultimately turn in on itself and wither and die. *You wouldn't want that to happen, would you?*"

Byron eyed Midge suspiciously. He looked down at his soup and scooped out an artichoke leaf with his spoon. "There's a spike on the end of this leaf," he said. "It could catch in my throat, couldn't it? A person could very well choke and die on it, couldn't he?"

Midge continued. "Actually, Byron, I've made an arrangement—nothing too ambitious, you understand ..."

"An arrangement! What arrangement?" He pushed aside his soup with the potentially deadly leaf left floating on its surface.

"For a performance—you know, at the annual Racket Club Talent Night next month."

"What?" Bryon rose out of his seat, his mouth open, his eyes bulging. Midge was glad he wasn't wearing his devil outfit at the moment. The eyes of the Accuser were supremely accusatory.

"The Racket Club Talent Night? *Le Danse du Diable* at the Racket Club Talent Night? Are you crazy?"

"Byron, it's already on the program. It will be wonderful!"

"Midge, this is serious work I'm doing. Am I going to be sandwiched in between Bee Bee Hagen's rendition of the Nocturne in E-Flat and Kim Dougherty's slides of India?"

"Bee Bee does a very nice Nocturne in E-Flat. After all, it's the only piece of music she knows."

"She always messes up the trill at the end. And as for Kim Dougherty—why does she think that hideous photographs of Bombay prostitutes are somehow artistic, just because . . ."

"They're 'socially relevant,' my dear. She trying to accuse us of something with them, thinks they make us feel somehow responsible—the same thing that you're trying to do."

"Not quite, actually."

"Anyway, she's back in India right now."

"Photographing more prostitutes, in Calcutta maybe . . . ?"

"She won't be on the program. In fact, yours will be the last performance, the highlight of the evening, so to speak. It's all very exciting, don't you think?"

"This is absurd, Midge, out of the question! I won't do it."

Byron sat down again and glared at Midge from across the table. "Besides, what sort of audience would that be? It's the very heart and soul of consumer society. New Jersey Man is Consumer Man."

"Just the audience you're trying to reach!" Midge retorted. "You take what you can get, as you would say. If your message isn't effective here, it won't be effective anywhere."

"But they'll hate it!"

"Isn't that what you want—for them to hate it?"

Byron's eyes brightened at the suggestion. "I could really give them hell, couldn't I?"

"You certainly could. Your choice of words is most apposite, in more ways than one."

"It will be *Le Sacre du Printemps* all over again. A riot. A storm of protest. I could make them feel really guilty."

"Yes, and they'll love how guilty you make them feel."

"But then they won't hate me."

"They'll hate you because they'll hate themselves for loving to feel guilty, and that will make them feel even more guilty, and then they'll blame you for making them do something they love to do."

"That doesn't make any sense. I won't do it." Byron fell into a resentful silence.

Midge had one final ploy left. "Byron, do you know what I think you need?"

"What?"

"A grant."

"A grant?" he repeated. The word had a certain ring to it.

"That's what I said — a grant. What *artiste* these days is without a grant? And conversely, without a grant, how can you be an *artiste*? You see my point, don't you?"

"I suppose so, though the purpose of these grants seems to be to ensure that any art form is as bad as it can possibly be."

"That may be true. But in any case, to get a grant, you need some kind of performance record. And you know that everybody has to start somewhere. The Racket Club is as good a place as any. After all, these people, despite whatever shortcomings they may have, are the support of the arts in our time, the patrons of the modern age. Look at all the paintings they lavish all that money on in New York galleries! Their toleration for the ugly is limitless."

She winked as she said this, but Byron missed the innuendo.

"Okay," he said. "I'll do it. But there's a problem with the costume. I can't simply go out on the stage with a pair of long underwear on, especially with that opening in the back."

"Don't worry. By the time we're finished working on the costume, no one will recognize it as a pair of ornery long johns fresh in from Dogpatch. We'll sew up the back, add some lace cuffs to the collar and to the sleeves, and . . ."

"Yes, and I can cover my face with some kind of red paint with a black stripe coming down over my forehead, nose, and chin, giving me a kind a 'divided' look." Byron leapt from his chair and assumed a series of his official "marionette" poses, his arms and legs lifting and falling in weirdly contorted gestures, as if pulled by strings, and his head bobbing mechanically up and down.

"And your hair can be spiked up into horns …"

"Well, we'll have to think about that."

"And music? How about Tartini — you know, 'The Devil's Sonata?' "

"I don't think I recall that."

"Or Stravinsky — 'The Triumph of the Devil' from *L'Histoire du Soldat?*"

"Too fast. Too noisy. Too much drumming."

"As if you know the piece! Nobody knows it!"

"I do! Only too well. 'The Devil's Dance' in it is more subdued."

"I guess you do know it!"

"But I don't care for that either. No music anyway. I require silence." Byron waggled his head raffishly while twirling about, stooping, and twirling about again.

"You would have made a great Petrushka," Midge exclaimed.

"I did, apparently."

"You did? You did what?"

"There are those who said I did make a great Petrushka," Byron shouted back as he whirled once more. "Just not great enough for … for me."

"What are you talking about? You're really crazy! How do you come up with such complete nonsense? I can't believe a word you say," she laughed.

Byron sat down at the table again, and they finished their meal. Midge was satisfied with the plans. But she knew the risk she was taking. An unusually large audience would probably flock to the Talent Show to see Byron. They would expect his performance to be — and understand it as — an immensely funny satire on avant-garde dancing. They would laugh throughout the dance and perhaps even shout and make jokes.

She was still not certain what was going on in Byron's mind about the dance; she continued to suspect that the dance was some kind of enormous ruse calculated to result in precisely the hilarious outcome it would have on the evening of the Talent Show. It wasn't inconceivable for Byron to think up and carry out just such a practical joke on her and on everybody else in the community.

She could just see him, at the end of the dance, assuming some Dying Pierrot gesture with a silly smile on his face and his arms twisted grotesquely around his neck as the audience roared with laughter and the curtain dropped ridiculously, calamitously, on top of his head.

And yet there was something else involved that she couldn't understand. Much of Byron's life was a mystery to her. He never spoke about his college years. She'd no idea what he had studied or what had done. It was as if he were hiding something from himself, as well as from her.

After college he spent three or four years abroad, in France mainly. She always assumed that he'd studied international finance there or had worked for some multinational organization in Paris or Strasbourg or Brussels, though a recent vacation in Paris had revealed his rather deep intimacy with that city.

But he never discussed those years either, though his fluency in several foreign languages had helped him to land a reasonably good job with the international division of an investment bank on Wall Street. Curiously, however, he never expressed any interest in his job; he just did it.

The only thing he ever seemed to enjoy was … to put it simply, to move. Just to move—like a cat walking along a picket fence, like a swallow darting through the evening air, like a cheetah, lithe and lean and swift, gliding and swerving across the African veldt. To watch Byron play tennis was a source of wonderment for anyone who happened to be a witness of it. Unfortunately, though, he couldn't hit the ball.

And now there was this dreadful, chaotic dance. Midge didn't know what to make of it.

Byron intensified his efforts at developing the dance, especially in the final weeks before the performance, when he took his annual vacation solely for this purpose, destroying Midge's plans for a tour of Austria. But she was willing to make this sacrifice. She was convinced somehow that one performance would be sufficient to bring *Le Danse du Diable* to its predestined and certainly cataclysmic finale. She thought of Berlioz's *Damnation of Faust* and the hectic ride of its doomed protagonist through the belching, sulfurous, cacophonous grottos of Hell.

The performance was scheduled for an evening in late June. The stage at one end of the ballroom at the Racket Club was ideal for performances of various kinds and was often rented out for children's piano and dance recitals, as well as for occasional professional and amateur groups, such as jazz bands, string quartets, choral societies, and the local Gilbert and Sullivan Association, which used the facility for its annual operatic fête.

As Midge had anticipated, the Talent Show drew an unusually large audience. Word had gotten around. Who would want to miss seeing Byron Langley in a full-scale travesty of modern dance? It was a fine, warm evening, and the audience was in a buoyant mood; its only challenge would be to survive most of the performances that would precede the notorious *Le Danse du Diable*, which, even though yet unseen, had a reputation that had burgeoned beyond all bounds in the imaginations of its prospective audience.

Even Madame Schernovsky showed up, much to Midge's mortification. She motioned to Midge as she entered the ballroom. "I hear your husband is just too amusing," she said. "I look forward so much to seeing him." She went off to her seat with a little backward wave and a chuckle.

The sequence of acts proceeded with the usual results. A slightly bored, restless, inattentive audience managed, more or less, to suffer through the various performances, though there were bright spots, such as the country music trio of the Emory sisters, all corporation lawyers, who sang and hooted through a number of Nashville pieces while swirling their fluffy orange skirts; the magic show of Ruddy Lindstrom—invariably delightful for all its mistakes, including Ruddy's having to chase his rabbit up the center aisle of the ballroom while the audience both jeered and cheered him on; and Dick Oleander, who did a seriously fine Cajun banjo routine. Bee Bee Hagen played her usual Nocturne in E-Flat, sighing, rolling her eyes, and swaying her body as if wafted away in some ethereal ecstasy. She messed up the long trill at the end, as everyone could predict she would. The audience now braced itself for the event of the evening—*Le Danse du Diable*!

Midge had worked assiduously on the costume and, on the evening of the performance, helped Byron with his red and black makeup. His hair was left natural. When everything was in place—Byron standing ready behind the curtain and the lights ready to flash on as the curtain opened—Midge exited the stage area from the back door and fled across the lawn to the clubhouse tavern. It was closed. She remembered then that it was always closed during the Talent Show to keep people from sneaking out during the performances for surreptitious drinks.

She sat on the steps and decided to wait out the horror that was about to ensue. She could imagine Byron there on the stage, the bright lights aimed on him, the red underwear with the lacy cuffs, the wild pointing and gesticulating he would do.

Sure, he might be funny, and yet it was all so awful anyway. She suffered for him, and she suffered for herself. She wished, for once in her life, that she smoked cigarettes, for that seemed the appropriate thing to do in situations like this. She also wished she could disappear for a while, vanish into a fairy forest, be out in the middle of some vast sandy steppe dining voraciously on locusts and honey, be secluded away in a shed built atop a giant baobab tree in Tanzania with baboons clustered on neighboring boughs and screeching their hearts out ...

A roar of laughter ripped through the ballroom. The curtain must have opened! Midge wanted to run away. "Run," she thought. "Run, Midge, run." There was more laughter a few seconds later, though now not quite so loud.

Midge got up to run. She would run out to the tennis courts. There she would be safe from all the humiliation. A bit more laughter — though now hesitant and nervous. Several seconds later a single loud guffaw echoed from the ballroom and was cut short by its own guffawer.

Silence.

Absolute silence.

Deathly, still, stony silence.

Midge was still, too, listening to the silence, although images of running still flooded her head. She saw herself running down a wet Parisian street in the depths of the night, fog curling through the dark alleyways and around the lamp posts, running, running, to a bridge over the Seine, where underneath its arches the black foamy waters eddied and swirled, the dark Parisian night, Paris, the silence ...!

The silence.

Suddenly something in her screamed: "He was a dancer once! He was a professional dancer! That's what he was doing when he lived in Paris! How did I fail to see that all these years?"

Just as suddenly, she wanted to see what everybody was so silent about. Instead of running away, she ran to the entrance of the ballroom and slipped into the rear of the audience.

The audience was spellbound. It was locked in a breathless panoply of crooked necks, torsos bent forward, tilted heads with mouths open, and eyes hypnotized by the spectacle in front of it. The angular figure on stage, glaring red in the stage lights, looked twice as big as life. Midge could hardly believe it was Byron.

He moved slowly, rhythmically, through a set of modulated gestures, every limb and sinew blending together in a perfect synthesis of bodily form, a kind of sculpture in kinesis, fascinating in every detail of slant, dimension, and control, confinement and freedom, rhythm gathering into architecture and resolving back into rhythm again.

Midge was astonished. She'd never seen anything like this before. He was doing things, combining movements in a way and with a complexity that she'd never envisaged was possible. Every movement flowed with perfect necessity and yet with utter unpredictability from its preceding movement, drawing out and perpetuating the quintessence of its form while transmuting it into something fresh and startling.

And there was no sign, no hint, that he even thought of an audience in front of him, no crazy posturing, no accusations, no message to be delivered. It was just pure design exquisitely internalized, exquisitely folded in on itself like the play of refractions in a lucid gemstone as it's turned around in the light of the sun.

Too soon it was over. She'd missed most of it. The curtain dropped as he assumed a final pose.

After a short period of dead stillness, the audience seemed to awaken from a trance, and a genteel, subdued applause passed through it. The curtain didn't come up for a bow, and the audience slowly began to rise, look around at one another, faces bewildered and mystified, and file out in silence, not talking or laughing or having much to say to one another. There was no rush to the tavern, which was just opening its doors; the people went to their cars and drove home.

Midge was at the back of the ballroom and, as friends and neighbors passed her, pushing through the exit, they looked strangely at her.

Bee Bee Hagen went up to her and took hold of her hands. There were tears in her eyes. "I'm so embarrassed," she whispered. "I'll never play my Nocturne again. After that, how could anyone do anything again?"

The once and future Norwegian sea captain, whose name we dare not mention, stopped by her, looked her in the eye, and said, "I've never seen anything so beautiful, not even a narwhale arcing through the icy floes of an arctic sea." This was high praise from a man who had never been anywhere close to an arctic sea.

Dick Oleander, carrying his banjo case, commented, "You should have told us. It was remarkable. It was more than that—it was great."

Midge cringed when she was approached by Madame Schernovsky, who looked hard and puzzled at Midge. "How long have you known about this?" she asked.

"Known about what? I don't know what you mean," Midge responded.

Madame Schernovsky shook her head. "I've never seen anything like it. Give me a call in the morning. We must—*we must*—talk." She walked off to her car.

The usual socializing and banter that followed Talent Show was neglected. The tavern opened and then closed shortly afterward because no customers came.

Midge found herself alone. She turned and worked her way back through the remaining crowd in the ballroom and up to the stage, where the curtain was still closed. She groped for the center of the curtain and pushed her way through.

Byron was sitting cross-legged on the floor, his head bent, his hands in his lap, the stage lights still illuminating with sharp intensity his bright-red costume, which was now darkened by large, round stains of sweat. Long streams of sweat from his hair and brow had run little crevasses through the red and black greasepaint on his face. He seemed to be so exhausted that he could not move.

Midge came up to him and knelt down beside him. "Byron, do you realize what you have done?"

He didn't reply. He sat as if in a trance, looking straight before him. Finally, he said, "Yes, I know. It was awful."

"Awful? Byron, it was great! The audience was stunned by it, reduced to gaping idiots by it. You took them out of themselves. But it's more than that. Byron, you've made a revolution. It's like the invention of polyphony, like the discovery of the triadic chord; nothing will be the same again."

"It was awful, that's all."

"Byron, I tell you this was a moment in dance history, a ..."

"Midge, did we throw out that catalogue from the place in Seattle?"

"What? What are you talking about?"

"You know, the catalogue from the Yukon outfitters. I thought I could pan for gold in the brook that runs past our backyard. They have all the stuff you need ..."

"But *Le Danse du Diable*!"

"I won't need these anymore," Byron proclaimed as he stirred into action and ripped the white cuffs off his sleeves. "My red-flannel underwear will be perfect for a 'forty-niner' *redivivus*!"

"Byron," Midge shouted. She jumped to her feet, pursed her lips, and raised her fists in a militant gesture, suggestive of old Soviet posters. "Down with global evil! Don't give up the ship! Damn the torpedoes! Don't tread on me and all that! *Le Danse du Diable* will change the world! With a few refinements, it will create riots in every capital city in the world! There's no end to whom we can accuse! The new order is coming!"

"I'll need a floppy, wide-brimmed hat and some high boots."

"Down with consumer society!"

"Quit it, Midge. You know as well as I do that dancing has nothing to do with all that nonsense. I've no one to accuse—except myself."

Byron, now refreshed and his spirits lifted, sprang nimbly to his feet. His face twisted into the sharp-eyed leer of a Hollywood actor impersonating the archetypical ruthless business tycoon about ready to close an unscrupulous deal. "Midge, you and I are going to make a million. Panning for gold is just the beginning."

"But *Le Danse du Diable*!"

"Just wait and see all the stuff we're going to consume." Byron glided off the stage and into a back room to change.

"*Le Danse du Diable*," Midge wailed.

The following morning, Midge waited to make her call to Madame Schernovsky until after breakfast, when Byron had gone out to the yard. As she dialed the number, she noticed Byron pacing back and forth on the lawn and occasionally going over to the brook at the far end of the yard, as if studying it for some obscure purpose. Madame Schernovsky answered her phone but didn't have a chance to say much until after Midge had impetuously summarized the events of the past few months, including the post-dance denouement. When Midge finished, Madame Schernovsky was silent. Midge could hear her carefully measured breathing over the phone.

Finally, she spoke. "About the professional training, of course — that we can find out easily enough, if he hasn't, for some reason, changed his name. I doubt that he has. It's quite inconceivable that there would not be people who would remember him — remember him perhaps as the most extraordinary dancer they had ever encountered — and who would not, even to this day, feel about him as I feel now — an unspeakable sadness. I could almost die with the sadness I feel. And yes, I do remember some curious gossip that once wafted through the downtown studios and lofts where we worked — it was so long ago. Just a mention … just a hint. A great Petrushka, it was said … discovered in Europe … Someone whose name no one seemed to know … Forgotten about soon enough."

"Madame Schernovsky, I just don't understand what you're saying, I don't …"

"Ah, my dear, I've seen this kind of thing perhaps only once or twice before in dancing. I've heard of it in the other arts as well, and I imagine it happens in everything that humans do. So often we're under the illusion that when there's a person endowed with a great intelligence for some activity, an innate sensibility beyond anything most of us can imagine, it will express itself naturally and irresistibly. But nothing could be further from the truth.

"I suppose there may be a hundred reasons why such an intelligence fails to flourish as it should, but the saddest of all is this: in some people, its penetration of an activity is so prodigious and so complex that it paralyzes the person's ability to pursue the activity. Where we ordinary mortals see moderate success at least, even sometimes great success, such people see only devastating failure, in themselves and others. Where we're willing to abide, to be patient with, to a greater or lesser extent, all the mediocrity, the sham, the pretentiousness that goes on in any art, they are not; they're simply too embarrassed, too disgraced, too ashamed by it.

"I think this is the case with your husband. Such people become exiles; exiles from the art, exiles from themselves. It's a deeply tragic thing. And the loss to the art itself is beyond all calculation. I wonder if I've ever seen, except among a few of the greatest *artistes*, a genius for bodily movement such as your husband has, as trained or untrained as it may be. He's a 'natural' — and you know well enough, Midge, how guardedly I use an expression like that, as committed as I am to the discipline of training. But that's not all; what we saw last night was simply extraordinary. There was a whole new definition of dance there."

"The audience was mesmerized by his performance," Midge protested.

"As it should have been," Madame Schernovsky replied. "It will probably not see its like again. Audiences often have an intuitive sense for what is good, and sometimes they recognize it when they see it. The problem is that they have also been conditioned to distrust their own perceptions, to submit to the opinions of cultural mandarins and to accept bad things as good. That's the problem. In the last analysis, however they may respond to a work in the immediacy of the situation, they can't put that response together with a larger, a more total picture.

"People like your husband know how arbitrary it all is, because for such people, none of it is arbitrary at all. They understand what is involved. They grasp the foundations of it, the essence that pulls it all together. You said that, originally, he wanted the audience to hate him; but, in reality, it's the audience that he hates — hating it for its fickleness, its lack of steady discrimination. Even more, he hates the dance world for having made it that way. He also hates himself because he cannot do what he thinks he should be able to do and gives it up in frustration. He cannot live up to his own standards."

"And this stuff about accusing the world, consumer culture, all the rest?"

"It's not at all unusual for someone like your husband to express himself in the most ridiculous and irrelevant fashion about something at one level that he really only understands at another level, that is, in terms of the practice of it. If there was any 'statement' in that dance at all initially, it was directed at the world of dance itself. That was the object of accusation. And all that clowning, that irony, that preposterous rhetoric — are these not signs of his own alienation from what he loves best?

"But statement or no statement, he created an artistically beautiful dance of unbelievable richness, and that's all that matters; and under all that silly chatter he knows that that's all that matters—which is the core and heart of his tragedy. In the final analysis, he sees through the rhetoric of art with remorseless accuracy, even as he can mimic it with remorseless invective. I know that I'm saying very direct things to you, Midge, and perhaps you don't want to hear them, but it's my own sorrow that urges me. I love my art and grieve for anything that fails to make it as good a thing as it can be. I know it's difficult, ultimately, to conjecture a thing like this, but the world may have lost, in him, one of the greatest dancers in its history."

"Then you think there's nothing we can do, nothing that can salvage the situation."

"Nothing. Nothing at all that I know of. Genius, Midge—even the most extraordinary sort of genius, such as I'm convinced your husband has—is one thing; quite another thing is the motivation and confidence and will-power and circumstances efficacious to make that genius flower as it should."

After Midge had hung up the telephone, she watched Byron out in the yard as he continued to study the course of the brook. He seemed to be making plans for the gold-panning operation. Then he backed up from the brook, braced himself, and began to run toward it. "He's going to jump across the brook!" Midge gasped.

As he approached the edge of the brook, he rose from the ground in a perfect *saut de chat*, his arms outstretched, his head tilted back, one leg curved beneath him as he sailed in a tall arc above the glistening waters, and landed, gracefully, flawlessly, on the bank beyond, where he stood for a moment, his arms curved down by his waist and face bent backward, radiant and serene in the glow of the morning sun.

He turned to study the brook momentarily and then as quickly lost interest. Once again, he backed up several yards and ran toward the brook. Halfway across the brook, suspended almost, as it were, in midair, he executed a triple pirouette and descended lithely on the other side on a single leg, his other leg and one arm extended together in a perfect symmetrical curve.

It was a perfect finale, a perfect finishing touch, Midge thought to herself. She laughed. Could it really be any better than this?

"You take what you can get," she said to herself, and she was content.

A Lament: for Gilgamesh of Uruk

(In two voices)

"Have you seen him?
    He has bound the whirlwinds of the sun
And yoked the wide-pronged rivers in his hands.
    He has pitched his tent beyond the mountains
And girt the hills with splendor,
    For the wilderness has flourished in his name.
And the Golden Horns of Uruk
    He has raised above all cities;
He has sheathed its walls with brightness
    And perched its verdant terraces in the sky.
Have you seen him?"

                "I have seen him.
        He has walked among the Gardens of the Sea.
        He has tasted their pure waters.
        He shall not come again."

"Have you seen him?
    He was the wild bull of the forest,

The wild bull of the plains,
    For he strode the fallow parklands clad in thunder.
Before him danced the lion and the ibex;
    The gazelle and spotted leopard rejoiced to hear his call.
For his arrival was the dawn on river marches,
    Where the sacred ibis rose to glory in his sight;
And his departure was the twilight in the desert,
    Shedding stars like fiery spoors through the night.
Have you seen him?"

                    "I have seen him.
            He has gone to the Cedar Mountain.
            He has rested in its shade.
            He shall not come again."

"Have you seen him?
    He trod the dusty byways of this world.
He only looked before him as he roamed—
    And his heart knelt down inside him.
He mourned upon the ramparts of the city.
    He mourned at the azure gates and by the broad canals.
He mourned in the towered enclaves of the gods,
    For the cup of all his love lay shattered on the stones.
Who, besides him, shall sift the grain aright?
    Who, besides him, shall hew the arrow of his people?
        Who, besides him, shall loose its shaft unto the ages?
Have you seen him?"

                    "I have seen him.
            He sleeps among the Rainbows.
            His lids are closed forever.
            He shall not come again."

The Bulls of Bashan

> *O that I were*
> *Upon the hill of Basan to outroar*
> *The hornèd herd.*
>
> Shakespeare

> *Many bulls have compassed me;*
> *Strong bulls of Bashan have beset me round.*
>
> Psalm 22:12

Wild Bulls of Bashan, stout and free!
Who dares approach them, dares to see?
In chaff, in whorls, in storms of dust,
Forward pitching, leap and thrust,
Thrashing down the mountainsides,
Landslides of brawny, glossy hides,
Haunches taut and streaked with sweat,
Brindled shoulders, humped and wet;
Their nostrils panting, eyes aglow,
Blue-tongued, slavering maws below
Snorting, lowing, bellowing loud;
Horns uplifted, rapacious, proud,
They heave and shudder, bound and lunge,
Buckle, hurtle, downward plunge
Through thorn-brake, thistle, briars thick,
Through stony gulches, staunch and quick;
Hooves as sharp as hardened wedges
Punching turf like iron sledges.
Flee the valleys! Flee the glens!
Flee the vineyards, roadside dens!
Flee the groves, the village square!
For nothing will they slight or spare:

Ploughlands, pastures, seats of pleasure,
Contrivances of trade and treasure,
Flowering gardens, parkland pools,
Theaters, palaces, and schools
Perish beneath their brute stampede.
These are not herds of human breed —
Their roars are roars of nature's right,
Their strength is strength of nature's might.

Lord of Whirlwinds, Lord of Thunder,
Breach and break these herds asunder!
From Bulls of Bashan, wild and free,
Make haste, great Lord, to salvage me.

Bordeaux, A.D. 408

(In two voices)

"At anchor in the harbor now,
    Galleys of the western fleet prepare to sail.
The sun rides low beyond the ocean;
    On our table, a cruet of Burdigalan wine
Glows fiery-red in evening light,
    And we watch the somber nightfall
        Lean its brow upon the sea."

"Should we not prepare to leave as well?"

    "Where would we go?
The Augustan legions are withdrawn;
    The Rhine frontier has fallen.
Like bats in a gutted tower,
    The *foederati* flutter through the empire
Seeking a blackened perch amid the ruins.
    And Alaric turns his raven's eye
Down the Flaminian viaducts,
    Down to the Alban Hills, and — dare I say it? —
'The walls of lofty Rome.'
    The stays of the imperium cannot hold."

"But the matter of perpetuity!"

    "Ah, we can but cherish what has been bestowed;
We can but praise what lived before us,
    And will yield its gracious foison to the ages.
Perpetuity renders us
    But is not ours to render; all human excellence
Alone is quarried in the hands of God.

But look, upon the darkening waves,
The galleys trim their starboard lamps."

"When will they depart?"

"They sail with the tide, those ships;
    They will not come again.
Lucinius has joined them.
    He stuffed his earthen jars with scraps:
Souvenirs of the old campaigns—
    A battered eagle or two, medallions from Trier.
What does it matter? He sails for Spain.
    The *barbaroi* will be there to meet him.
Shall he embark for Africa?
    Numidian grainfields shall be red with blood
Before he unpacks his wares."

"And us?"

"... compose the hymns
Which they at morning will intone
    To laud the newborn sun, the ancient land,
The same ripened apples
    Loaded into carts at harvest-time.
Someday they, too, shall walk these hills
    And take the poplars for their song
And sing a lady's beauty.
    Someday they, too, shall aptly raise
Basilicas of thought into the heavens."

"Until then ...?"

"Until then ...?
    The wine, my friend, a final cup;

209

The night is growing heavy,
    And I must homeward bend my way
To stave my lids, my weary soul,
    Against that long-encroaching,
        That dark and ageless sea.
May Roman peace betide us
    Among the solemn groves,
The sepulchres of our fathers in their sleep."

Brünnhilde

I think she merited the soubriquet Brünnhilde, among various other reasons, because wherever she went, she never seemed to walk. Like Brünnhilde, *prima donna* of the tempestuous Valkyries, she flew. She flew into rooms, even as she flew out of them when it was time to leave. She flew around them while she was in them, except for those moments, now and then, when she alighted upon a chair or sofa or piano stool like a short, stocky eaglet upon a branch or rocky outcrop, arching her neck slightly forward, flexing her muscular wings, fixing her gaze upon a target, and waiting to swoop once again. She flew up and down staircases. She flew along the streets and in and out of buildings. She didn't, of course, fly upon a six-legged horse and bear the shades of slain warriors into Valhalla, but she could fly, with unparalleled energy, over the keys of a pianoforte and bear thereupon, with enthusiasm and devotion, the sublime spirits of the grand opera into the high empyrean of hearts and souls. She flew, in a sense, into my life, even as later she flew out of it.

She resided in an old five-story edifice on Central Park South close to Columbus Circle with a magisterially sculpted façade and a gorgeous view of Central Park—a proper nest for the Muses (and for Valkyries) if there ever was one. Therein she waged, for decades, a cosmic war against a band of real estate developers who, if they could finally succeed in dislodging her from her studio loft on the fourth floor, would be able to vacate the building of its final tenant and tear it down, replacing it, as Fáfnir and Fasolt would certainly have done, with yet another shimmering titanic spear puncturing the firmament over Manhattan. But she had an unbreakable rental contract from decades earlier — one of those sacrosanct bonds that quasi-divine figures so often seem to have — and a character as tenacious and well-accoutered in psychic panoply as any other Valkyrie in this world could ever boast. That lovely building is gone now, and she has gone, too, in the only way she would have ever consented to go, chanting until the end of time, as I would imagine, her joyous death song as she flew to whatever ring of flames, upon whatever mountain peak, shall in our memories be pleased to blaze around her.

I should say up front that my relationship to her was scarcely as dramatic as all that. After all, I was only twelve years old at the time. Each year she took — condescended, perhaps, to take — a limited number of students for music lessons. These were, in some sense, "special" students, though I could never figure out what was special about me, and I could never get over the feeling that, whoever and whatever it was that made the recommendation necessary for my entry into her minuscule but ever so elite *conservatoire*, had sorely miscalculated the level of my abilities, and even more the level of my motivation. That selection may have hinged more upon Brünnhilde's friendship with one of my aunts than upon any putative talent that I might have displayed in some momentary and largely gratuitous skid into virtuosity.

My aunt's meteoric rise and fall so many years before as an international opera singer had peaked in the small opera houses of Cremona and Mantua and bottomed out before a half-empty house at Covent Garden. Although Brünnhilde had been her coach and guardian, efficacious and sheltering, in this finally hapless trajectory of events, she wasn't able to protect my aunt from all those serendipitous consequences that affect the lives and careers of even the greatest artists.

For all of this, as I said, she flew into my first lesson and flew out of my last: the former with boundless hope and the latter with boundless grief. But there was no point, for her, in regretting what regrets could not repair. When it was appropriate (as well as expedient), she could be tragic, but she had no regrets. Quite candidly, I, too, have few regrets about all of this, though I do have some regrets about having few regrets. I don't doubt that the proper judgment was made in the end; it was she who was disappointed, and I didn't enjoy disappointing such a formidable spirit. If my destiny had lain in that direction, it would have been a beneficent destiny, and her guidance would have been the best thing about it. If she knew — knew better than anyone else I've ever known — the heights to which great artistry can rise, she also knew — knew better than anyone else I've ever known — the stupendous labor without which all great artistry cannot flourish. She knew, and made a point of emphasizing again and again, that the fineness of the fine arts resides in the maximum of precision and control.

She stood, as firmly and strongly as the Valkyrie she was, against the "expressionist" understanding of the arts that prevails in so much of modernity, though many of those who knew her would regard her as the most expressive person they had ever encountered. And she was; but she could distinguish clearly between what it means to express a real passion (a passion about something and for something) and what it means to express an artistically controlled imitation of a passion (i.e., to be passionate about the skill of pretending to be passionate). And if anyone knew what it meant to be passionate, about anything, it was Brünnhilde.

Most people didn't see the laborious and painstaking tasks she submitted herself to — they saw only the Valkyrie result, the exuberant, stormy side of her, not appreciating that Valkyries are what they are because of the enormously pedestrian preparation they put into what they do. I suppose it was that part of it that I couldn't, in the end, abide, at least in regard to this particular pursuit, and that made my efforts futile and worthless. There's no point in hankering after supernal beauty when you can't discipline yourself to spend hours a day doing finger exercises and counting out beats in measure until you're ready to keel over with exhaustion.

I'll never know, of course, since I was too young at the time, how big the world of opera was that surrounded Brünnhilde in those days. She seemed to know everyone in that world, all the singers and musicians, the performances, the ins and outs of the opera stage, what was going on all over Europe and the United States. She'd been born in the American South, in Alabama, I think, and spoke with a heavy Southern drawl. But her early years in Europe taught her Italian, French, and German. She could imitate the accents of each of these languages in English (which she often did in a most comical way); she could speak the languages fluently as well as speak (again, for comic effect) in elaborate, nonsense mimicries of these languages. It would appear that she'd been in every great opera house in the world, at La Scala and Bayreuth and Vienna and Glyndebourne and everywhere else (I imagined her flying from one locale to the next on her winged, mythic six-legged horse).

It was to the Metropolitan Opera House in New York that the steed of her professional life was most closely tethered, and much of her work was calibrated to its repertoire and ambiance. She'd been a piano accompanist to a myriad of singers, a few great and most otherwise, and she'd performed with them on their tours and recitals. She had an encyclopedic knowledge of operatic scores and librettos and could, on the spur of the moment and if offered a piano worthy of her robust renditions, regale the guests at a social occasion with the most dazzling stories drawn from the entire range of operatic literature, so much of which she seemed to know by memory, and which she could embellish with endless anecdotes about what this diva had done with such and such a passage and how that *Heldentenor* had faltered at just the wrong moment in *Tristan und Isolde*. All of this was reinforced, naturally, by her virtuoso playing on the piano as accompaniment to herself and her vivid storytelling.

She wasn't a singer herself but developed an ability to speak the words of an aria dramatically as she played its stirring music on the piano; the effect was beyond description. She could assume all the roles in a libretto, acting them out in sequence as she proceeded through the text (usually abridged, of course, to high points only). Her lively narrative filled in the scenic details and the stagecraft. What's more, she could present all of this with enthusiasm and humor, making people laugh at what is inveterately funny about opera (and especially about opera librettos) even as they sighed over what is great. She could turn high seriousness into high comedy with a single note—a single note played flat and out of key. She could mock what she loved, making it just that much more lovable. She was, almost, as it were, in such a situation, an entire operatic performance encompassed in a single person.

She even did this sort of thing professionally, I should add, occasionally renting out one of the ballrooms in a downtown hotel for the purpose. But

I never attended one of those professional afternoon entertainments. I was too young for that and would have been too out of place among the well-heeled, matronly entourage for whom they were intended. My viewings were private—yes, private, if you can envisage that. On several big family occasions, she was there and would sometimes demonstrate some small portion of what she could do. My aunt, retaining after many years some measure of her former abilities, might help out here and there. But at my lessons, after what always was a grueling session, my tears were brushed away by a modest offering of chocolates and little maple-sugar soldiers and by her playing a selection from an opera.

In my time with her I must have been presented with, albeit in pieces and fragments, just about all of *Aida* and *Don Giovanni* and *Lohengrin*. I cannot attend to these operas to this day without thinking of her, without thinking of the ceremonial Egyptian beard she made out of something or other and attached at times to her chin when she was being the pharaoh, or of the sheaf of papers she brandished in her hand between snatches of Leporello's catalogue aria. And her recitation of "In fernem Land," the piano swelling with Wagnerian cadences, shall resonate with me for all my days. It was almost too good to be true.

There were many other sides to Brünnhilde's life that I knew practically nothing about—as is true about everybody we know, even those we know most intimately. She'd spent several years in Milan when she was young—my aunt told me about that—and there had been a young, gallant military officer in her life. Mussolini's contribution to the war had cut that marriage tragically short. Her husband responded to his mobilization orders, as he felt his military oath and regimental fealty required him to do, even as she departed for home until things should get "back to normal" again. Things never got—generally never do get—"back to normal." He was killed in Africa. Nevertheless, she proudly bore his Italianate surname as her own surname for the rest of her life.

Her Italian years had endowed her with a knowledge of Italian cuisine, especially Northern Italian cuisine, long before it became widely known in the United States, and among her many operatic friends her loft on Central Park South was noted for its fine Italian fare. Her specialty was a beef brisket simmered in a fragrant sauce, served *con patate*, and what *patate* they were! I had it once at a family occasion.

But the configurations of our lives change, like the changing forms of a kaleidoscope as it's slowly turned — the pieces staying the same, in a way, the relationships altering moment by moment, sorting into new patterns with every turn. So, as time passed, her piece for me slid into some obscure spot at the edge, I suppose — still there, but no longer as prominent as it once was.

To this day, I can't help but think of Brünnhilde soaring off somewhere in the exuberance of her flight. I can't help but think of her asleep upon that fire-moated mountain until, as in one of the greatest moments in opera, encased in her glittering armor, her Valkyrie eyes widen again, as luminous as the luminosity they gaze upon, her very words in that magical awakening being everything that she was in life for me and for so many others:

> *Hail to thee, O Sun!*
> *Hail to thee, O Light!*
> *Hail to thee, O brightening Day!*

Leviathan

Leviathan was a horse: a large white horse with a long white mane that drooped down below his neck and a long white tail that swayed back and forth in the prairie winds. He wasn't an especially beautiful horse. He was old and had a sagging belly and knobby knees; his mane and tail were unkempt and dirty and snarled with burrs and shreds of grass; his fetlocks and hooves were encrusted with dried mud; there was dust and grit all over his body. His right ear was oddly torn and always seemed to tilt backward on his head like an ear of corn partially broken off at its base and hanging, just barely, from its stalk.

But his neck was as strong and as firm as an arch of antique marble and he had enormous blue eyes, as bright as sapphires. He loved to gaze at things with those glowing eyes, gaze at all kinds of things for a long time, as if he understood them, as if he'd known them all his life. His eyes were like orbs plucked from the deep-blue Wyoming sky and dropped from their heights into his sculpted and noble head.

Nobody knew where Leviathan came from. He just showed up one day, trailing along after a herd of cattle in one of the southeast pastures of the Pronghorn spread. One of us saw him there, Riley it was, when he was laying down some salt licks for the herds in that area. Riley told us about him, and as soon as we could make the arrangements, some of us borrowed his car to look for him. I don't know why. There were plenty of other horses around: in the ranch corrals and stables; in the pastures; in the upland woods where we went to hew down trees and haul them back for wooden fence posts. Sometimes we even saw wild horses grazing along the edge of the high escarpment that ran for miles along one side of the valley.

These were all fine and beautiful horses, filled with energy and life, but not like old Leviathan. Not like him at all. We went to see Leviathan because, as Riley had said, there was nothing quite like him. He looked like a creature from another age, another place, another world altogether. We could never fully explain this impression, but that's what he looked like. One of us, Jon, who was a literary type, called him Leviathan because he reminded Jon of the white whale named Moby Dick, and "leviathan" is taken to mean "whale" in the Bible. Just like Moby Dick, this creature seemed to come from that other world that was more this world than this world seems to be. How can I explain that?

At our insistence, Mr. Garret, the ranch owner, made some inquiries. None of the other ranchers up and down the valley could identify the horse. Some had seen him wander by in recent weeks, stop by their pastures, sniff at a few items, move on. No one came looking for him; there were no notices for lost horses and no signs that anyone owned him or wanted him back. He was apparently not shy of human beings; indeed, he was friendly and docile and appreciated a human approaching him, petting him, looking him over, and wondering who he was.

He appeared to have the ability to get in and out of fenced-in pastures, to join up for a while with a herd of cattle and then leave, even gathering together with some fellow horses for a bit now and then before showing up somewhere else a few miles farther up the valley. Did he have the ability to open gates—and then to close them, most considerately, behind himself when he left?

As you would expect, Mr. Garret was pretty puzzled. He figured that Leviathan might have been a packhorse—the sort that some outlanders use for hauling supplies when heading off into the mountains for a hunting safari. Perhaps Leviathan had been lost; perhaps he'd just drifted off from some encampment during the night and nobody especially noticed or cared. It was curious that he had no bridle or halter on him, nothing to indicate a human claim. Maybe he was just set loose and shooed off so that an original owner wouldn't have to cart him from the high country of Wyoming back to Cheyenne or Omaha or Denver or wherever he came from. Lots of people did that sort of thing with their dogs and cats and other animals: just left them someplace rural, thinking that they were being given their "freedom" and could survive perfectly fine in the wild, though what, in fact, these people were doing was leaving their pets to die difficult and lonely deaths.

Whatever Mr. Garret thought about Leviathan's origins, he was initially resistant when we proposed that we venture into the valley lowlands, find Leviathan, "capture" him, in a sense, and lead him back to the ranch. His argument in opposition was very simple and could be summarized in two words: "Then what?" But we were young, and the chain of reasoning that began with "Then what?" hadn't been too perfectly branded on our brains yet. The future could take care of itself. I think, in retrospect, that it probably did; but we were lucky that it did. Anyway, Mr. Garret consented, much to our surprise, issuing in the meantime a number of curtly framed caveats. The horse, under any circumstances, was not to be a nuisance, either to the ranch personnel or to property or to other livestock. We agreed to assume all responsibility.

Including Riley, there were nine of us at the ranch that year. We were "the summer help," recruited with ads put in a number of newspapers, to assist the regular staff of ranch hands from June through the end of August. We came from everywhere—from the East, from California, from several Midwestern states. The ranch was located in one of those high valleys in Wyoming that cut through treeless grasslands, ascending upward through foothills and plateaus, and terminating in dense conifer forests and in the towering, snowcapped peaks of the Absaroka Range. The valleys have rivers of various sizes flowing through them, bordered sometimes by marshes and groves of aspen and cottonwood. The valleys also have, here and there, wide, lush hayfields.

During the summer, the cattle are driven up to the higher pastures in the foothills and even to the narrower valleys in the mountains while the fields below are harvested for their hay. The herds return to the lower valleys for the winter. Our job was to mow, rake, buck, and stack the hay, which would provide winter fodder for the herds. It was a demanding physical job requiring long days and many-sided operations. We were glad to get whatever leisure we could. Leviathan was a diversion that several of us — Jon, Walt, and I — would welcome. For a week or two before we sought him out, we talked endlessly about him and what we would do once we had him in our keeping.

The "hunting" and "capture" of Leviathan, if I may dignify our expedition with such expressions, turned out to be more daunting than we had expected. It had rained heavily during the night, so the fields were soaked, and we couldn't engage in the haying operation until things had dried out somewhat. So we had the day off. We would devote it to the pursuit of Leviathan. I should say that Leviathan himself was the easy part. When we finally found him, he welcomed us as if we'd been long-lost friends. Tracking him down was the hard part. Having seen him as an incongruous member of a cattle herd several days prior to our search led us to believe that we should have no trouble at all in spotting him in open country. Obviously, Leviathan, in the meantime, had ambled off, in his slow, measured way, into the marshlands of the river bottom.

After several hours of driving around in Riley's car and finally concluding that that's where he may have gone, we decided that our search required abandoning the car and sloshing around in knee-deep mud for hours, pushing brambles and razor-sharp thistles out of our way, being attacked by billows of aggressive mosquitoes more copious we ever imagined could exist, tripping over submerged roots and landing face down in the mud, and being deceived again and again by a species of white flowering bush whose mirage of attaining our goal produced an endless series of disappointments.

When we did find Leviathan, it was something of a shock. First, we encountered a white apparition hovering in the underbrush close to us. We decided not to be fooled once more by one of those flowering bushes. Then suddenly the white apparition reared its massive head upward through the branches, and he was there, right in front of us, looking at us through the foliage with those great blue eyes and seeming to say: "Where were you? I've been here all this time waiting for you to show up. Goodness, what a mess you've made of yourselves." Well, he wasn't all that pristine himself. A small armada of dragonflies circled around him and finished off any mosquitoes so impudent as to invade his territory. It was also shocking to be so close to what we'd seen previously only at a great distance. Leviathan was much larger than we had expected. There was also something bizarre about him, as if we'd stumbled upon a unicorn standing in the middle of a primeval Druids' grove.

We had a halter and a rope with us, and he took to those without the slightest protest. But it wasn't so easy to lead him out of the swamp: he had to struggle as much as we did with the difficult footing and the deep mud. It might have looked rather comical to an observer: Leviathan and the three of us, like four clowns together, fumbling through the muck, falling and rising, pushing our way through the dense brush, and bumping into one another and pulling each other down, though Leviathan was the most stable and provided our support on many an awkward occasion.

Gradually we learned that he should be leading us, rather than vice versa. And he did. We followed him toward the river, and there we cleaned ourselves off, splashing water on each other and washing off Leviathan, even though the water was bitterly cold, as these snowfield run-off rivers usually are. We walked along the shallow edge of the river until we found a place where we could get back up to high ground again without having to traverse the marsh. Then two of us returned with him to the ranch. It was a long walk but well worth it. Jon found the car and drove it back. We had, at last, our Leviathan.

Did we ever clean him up! What an act of grooming, currying, clipping, washing, rubbing, and polishing went on! By the time we finished, he looked like a great chalk horse carved out of the side of some ancient Britannic hillside. He looked like a horse fit to be ridden by Marcus Aurelius on the summit of the Capitoline Hill. He looked like one of those Lipizzaner stallions ready to perform in front of the Viennese court accompanied by the music of Johann Strauss. He looked as grand and as mysterious as the great white whale after whom he was, indirectly, named. We were proud of our job, and he was proud of it too.

I admit that Mr. Garret, to say nothing of the sundry ranch hands, was puzzled by this treatment but not unappreciative. I mean, after all was said and done, Leviathan was still an old "nag" who had wandered in from the prairies.

Initially we bedded Leviathan down in a small, dilapidated stable not far from the main compound of buildings that comprised the Pronghorn Ranch. We brought him plenty of fresh water, hay, some oats now and then, gave him the exercise he needed, swept out his stall, and kept him immaculately groomed. An elderly, mostly retired cowboy — the only fellow at the ranch, from what we could make out, who actually would use that term to refer to himself and who would dress accordingly — was our consultant about how to take care of Leviathan: to look after health problems, teeth, hooves, and the like. He took a lot of pleasure in advising us "greenhorns" about what to do. For our part, we had never imagined that so much work was involved in taking care of a horse.

It's difficult to know what Leviathan thought about all this fussing that went on about him. I think he liked it, but he made it clear, before too long, that he didn't really need it. He started, quite regularly, to get out of his enclosure. We didn't know how he did it. He would do it in the middle of the night when no one could see. During the day, he would mosey around the ranch and the adjoining pastures, on his "own recognizance" as it were, minding his own business in a way, even as he was, in fact, rather busily minding everybody else's. He watched old Frank, the mechanic, fix broken tractors; he watched Mrs. Carter, the cook, select vegetables from the kitchen garden for the evening chow (and always offering him a carrot or two); and he watched Olaf Swenson, who spent his life sharpening things and liked to sing as he whirled his millstone while the sparks flew in every direction.

Funny thing, too, but everybody talked to Leviathan just as a matter of course. We wanted to talk to him because he was the only thing around that seemed to care and would actually listen. How often I talked to him, telling him everything I was planning to do in my life. He was so understanding and so patient. Did the amused and skeptical glint in his eyes show that he knew already that I would never actually do any of it?

Anyway, he followed us around, doing his own thing, coming and going when he felt like it, often ambling after our great wobbling processions of machinery as we moved from field to field over rough ground, harvesting and stacking the hay. Finally, we gave up trying to keep him in his little stable.

We never knew where he spent the night. He didn't bother anyone, and we just let him do what he wanted to do. Even Mr. Garret didn't seem to mind, though Leviathan and we were violating some of his rules.

Eventually we borrowed a saddle and put it on Leviathan and took turns riding him. These were not particularly adventurous rides, for it was difficult to prod him to move much faster than a slow canter, and even that would last for only a short time. Walt preferred to ride him bareback; Walt was a kind of gymnast and could do all kinds of dexterous things. Leviathan was amenable to anything we wanted to do. He enjoyed our company, and I have to admit that often, when I went out for a ride, I did it more for his entertainment than for mine. We did enjoy following deer paths through the many ravines that provided access from the lower valley up through riffs in the escarpment. Then we would ride along the edge of the escarpment. I don't know if horses take pleasure in things like "views"; I've always rather doubted that they do. When they stand someplace for a while, they avert and shake their heads in that bored, impatient way that indicates they would rather be doing something else.

But Leviathan certainly seemed to like the scenery, if that doesn't sound too absurd, and he could watch over the distant canyons and cloud formations for long periods of time with what looked like rapt attention. In fact, he paid more attention to things than do most human beings I know. As for averting the head in a bored, impatient way, well, that describes just as many of my friends as any horses I know.

We did have fun, on a few occasions, finding suitable shelter from sudden cloudbursts that swept over the mountains and descended into the valleys like golden eagles swooping down on their prey. The claps of thunder and the streaks of lightning fragmenting the sky were more frightening to me than they were to Leviathan. I always let him lead the way and find the best refuge, which he did, often seconds before the first wave of colossal hailstones ripped through the air like what I imagine a discharge of musket shot would have been in a Civil War battle, followed by huge, isolated raindrops smacking into your face like the big wet kisses that many a child doesn't particularly want to have. As we watched the storm pass over us, I'd whisper "the thunderbird" into Leviathan's sagging ear, and he would shake his head in understanding, as if he were one mythical critter acknowledging the domain and authority of another.

One time, when we were making our way up a ravine and passing through a clump of brush and pine trees, we startled some mule deer. A stag and three does jumped out of the grove, bounced up the ravine in a zigzag pattern for about fifty yards through some sagebrush, then turned to stare at us. We stared back, just as surprised as they were, and continued on our way up the ravine. They continued to watch us. Soon the does were grazing on some patches of grass, even as we passed close by, and had no further concern. The stag continued to eye us but without anxiety. He seemed to say: "So it's you, after all. Did you have to give us a start like that? And who's that goofball sitting on your back?"

I think that Leviathan was pleased by these encounters with his feral brethren. He also seemed to know some of the mustangs that lived on the plateau beyond the escarpment. Once we were rambling along a stretch of prairie when a pronghorn antelope showed up in the distance. The antelope moved up to about fifty yards behind us and followed us for several miles, or for about half an hour, before it finally cavorted off across the prairie and disappeared. During this little pageant, Leviathan would sometimes stop, swish his head around, and look at the antelope before proceeding further. I began to wonder if they were friends too and I was the "third party" making old ties between them difficult to renew.

As I said, Walt liked to ride Leviathan bareback. One evening, after a difficult day in the fields, we went out to join Leviathan for a little after-dinner company. Walt got the idea of riding Leviathan around in a circle inside a training corral. He managed to get Leviathan up to his customary slow canter. Then, just as a silly stunt, I suppose, and with no little bravado, Walt crouched on Leviathan's back and then stood up there. I couldn't believe what I was seeing. Leviathan was prancing around in a circle with Walt standing on his back. What was even more unbelievable—and sometimes I think it must have been more my imagination than real—Leviathan's gait became wonderfully elegant and measured. He looked as if he was dancing, lifting his legs in an odd sort of way. He looked as if he was doing what he was meant to do. It occurred to me then, and I still think about it now, that Leviathan, in some part of his past, may have been a circus horse.

All of this didn't last very long. Walt attempted to flip upside down and do a handstand on Leviathan's back and almost immediately fell off. Leviathan ceased his trot and looked around at Walt with a kindly but somewhat reproachful glance. After all, Leviathan had done what he was supposed to do; why had Walt not lived up to his part of the bargain?

It never happened again. Sometimes I wonder if inadvertently we had penetrated some treasured but inviolate secret that Leviathan harbored in the depths of his heart, one of those memories that are finally too precious to reveal except in the momentary but capricious display of them. I'll never know the answer to this, but I'll also never lose my memory of what went on in my mind at the time: the sense of a circus band, the big tent, the ringmaster, beautiful young women in glittering array under the lights, a thousand laughing, cheering children, and Leviathan at the center of it, looking out at it all, enjoying every minute of it.

Leviathan — hadn't I known it all along? — was, in the end, not just a performer but also a spectator, a spectator of spectators, in love with the razzle-dazzle of the world, inside and outside of a gorgeous circus tent.

There's one special event regarding Leviathan that merits attention. Each day, Mr. Garret would have to decide which field the crew would go to for the day's work. Then something like a mechanized military column would assemble in the ranch compound and advance out to the designated hayfield. All told, a column might consist of seven or eight tractors of different sizes bearing different kinds of attachments. There were also several trucks as well as Mr. Garret's somewhat antiquated Land Rover and a huge, movable catapult-like rig for building haystacks as tall as a three-story building.

Some of these fields were difficult to get to. The procession might have to ford the river several times, pass through circuitous and hazardous cutbacks, and negotiate an occasional treacherous bog (I once saw three tractors get embedded in the same bog — the ranch bulldozer had to be sent for to get them out), long stretches through wooded lanes where boughs and fallen trees might have to be cleared out of the way, and gates whose rusty locks and joints required nothing less than crowbars to get us through.

The only one who had an easier time getting to a worksite was Leviathan, who simply walked straight to it, crossing over whatever needed crossing over, and not paying attention to what our heavy machines demanded of us. Sometimes he arrived at a worksite before we did, and we could not figure out how he could have known where we were going.

On this occasion, the usual process was set up. It took four men to build a stack, and we "temporary" ranch hands often got stuck with this dirty, physically exhausting, and often dangerous job. The four men would stand at each corner of where the stack was projected to be, tear apart with their pitchforks an immense swath of hay that was dumped in the middle of them by the hay rig, and drag hay over to the sides to build up the corners. Gradually the stack would rise beneath them. It was dirty work because each swath of hay would land on the stack with a huge puff of dust and chaff, and the abrasiveness of tromping around in the hay could wear out a new pair of dungarees in two weeks, to say nothing of what it did to a pair of boots. It was dangerous work because the stack buckled and swayed as it was constructed and, as I mentioned, was close to three stories tall by the time in was finished. Falling off the stack was always a threat.

Well, one day, one of us fell off. It was Josh — I haven't mentioned him yet. He was a star football player from some Southern school who thought that ranch work would toughen him up for the coming football season. He was tough enough, I would reckon. But when he fell off the stack and then discovered that two tines of his pitchfork had penetrated the palm of his right hand and had exited out the back, he fainted dead away. I don't blame him. I probably would have done the same.

The problem now was how to get him to an emergency room. The closest hospital was sixty miles away at least. But that could happen only after we got him out to the nearest road. That was the real problem. The journey into the field that morning had been excruciating. The journey out, to someone in his condition, would be even worse. There was a road only a mile away as the crow flies, but it was a three-mile trip through unbelievable obstacles if done by machine.

Leviathan to the rescue! I'm not kidding. Who would ever have thought it?

Leviathan just moved into position on his own. Josh did regain consciousness but wasn't able to do much. It was quite an effort for a few of us to lift Josh's big defensive-tackle hulk onto Leviathan's back while one person braced that pitchfork still dangling from his hand (we didn't dare to pull it out ourselves). Then, holding on to Josh from both sides, we walked alongside Leviathan and allowed him to find the shortest, most convenient route to the road. He carried his burden with the utmost care, stepping gently over obstacles and avoiding sudden movements of any kind.

By the time we reached the road, Mr. Garret had brought the Land Rover from the field by hurtling wildly over the uneven terrain of the "bucking bronco" trail (as he later described it) and was able to load Josh into the passenger seat and rush him to the hospital. But first, figuring that leaving the pitchfork in the hand until it could be removed by a professional health provider probably entailed greater risks than removing it himself, he yanked it out of Josh's hand and wrapped a first-aid bandage around the wound. Oddly, there was little blood. Josh let out a yelp none of us were likely ever to forget and once again fainted away.

Immediately afterward, before getting into the Land Rover, Mr. Garret strolled quickly over to Leviathan, slapped him firmly on his neck, and proclaimed: "Good job, old boy!" Even those of us who were "summer help" knew by now that Mr. Garret never said "good job" to anyone who had done a good job. He said it only to someone who had done a spectacular job.

Of course, summer came to an end. That's when Mr. Garrett's initial admonition "Then what?" came back to us with a great deal more than its original force. We had to depart. We had to go home. What would happen to Leviathan?

During those final weeks, we discussed, consulted, pleaded, lamented, and agonized over what we were going to do. It was the old, retired cowboy who finally settled it for us. He told us to let Leviathan decide for himself. We asked him if a horse could actually decide for itself. He said he didn't know; but, if it could, Leviathan was the one who could do it, and he would certainly know what to do.

Two days before we left, I rode Leviathan, bareback this time, out to a high, rocky hill about five miles from the ranch. Jon and Walt followed along in the Land Rover. About five hundred yards from the summit of the hill, they stopped the vehicle, disembarked, and accompanied us on foot to the summit. There we all stood for a while, looking out over the panorama before us: the prairies, the hills, the forests, the mountains. Then we removed the halter from Leviathan, said our goodbyes, and walked back down to the Land Rover.

We were very sad about this and could hardly talk to one another. We couldn't help but wonder if, like an original owner, we were not leaving Leviathan to a sad and lonely death. We had heard a great deal about how long and bitter were the Wyoming winters. But Leviathan continued to gaze out over the landscape. Soon it would be autumn and the herds would return to the lower valleys. Would Leviathan be with them? We got into the Land Rover. Before we started up the engine, we saw Leviathan sweep his neck in our direction and look at us for a moment with his brilliant blue eyes. He seemed to be saying, "Thank you." Then he turned back again to face the wilderness, walked slowly away, and disappeared over the crest of the hill.

We knew, of course, that we were the ones who really had to be thankful. And we were. We started the engine and drove back to the ranch. Leviathan didn't show up the next morning, as we thought he might possibly do. On the following day, the three of us, plus Riley, were heading in Riley's car eastward out of the valley. We were on our way home—home to the Mississippi valley, to the Atlantic coast. We couldn't help but keep a lookout for a solitary white horse somewhere up in the rangeland around us. But we didn't see anything.

The following spring, I wrote a letter to Mr. Garret asking him if he, or anyone else, had seen Leviathan or heard anything about him. He wrote back telling me that Leviathan had vanished—indeed, had vanished that very day we had taken him out to the hill where we had left him, had vanished back into the prairies whence he, on some curious day in the past, had mysteriously come and now had just as mysteriously gone. I should have felt worried, I guess; but I didn't.

I'm confident that Leviathan is out there somewhere, doing what he always does, taking care of himself, his long white tail swooshing in the prairie winds, his great blue eyes affixed patiently, lovingly, on the far horizon.

The Stonemason: A Journal

Day One

His name is Anpu. That's what he told me. At least, that's what I think he
told me. I don't know what kind of name that is, or even whether it's a first
or last name. Rural New England abounds in exotic names, though I never
heard that one before. If his name is odd, it's even more odd that he ap-
proached us exactly when he did.

How did he find us?

I don't know how he knew we were thinking about having a stone wall
built in front of our house. I suppose we may have spoken about it casually
with some of our neighbors—they often walk along this lane and have seen
me dallying about, studying the front yard, musing, measuring, consider-
ing. Naturally, they've asked me about the object of my studiousness, and
I've told them. I've also mentioned the prospect with some of the people
who had been working on our house recently. And maybe we'd begun to
make some initial inquiries, though I don't recall whom I spoke to about
that. But obviously the word had gotten around. He came to the door this
morning and asked me if the job was available. I was a little taken aback
by this query. I hadn't really decided anything yet, and his inquiry was, in
a way, forcing me into a decision. So I decided right there and then, and I
said, "Yes, there's a job available."

He asked me what I had in mind—where the wall would be located, how
long it would be, other such matters. I wasn't quite prepared for this either,
despite all my preliminary but vague fantasies. I knew that the wall would
serve as a border between our front yard and the country lane that runs by
our house, that it would be made in the "dry" fieldstone style traditional
in our locale, and that it would be fifty to sixty feet long. It would have a

gate or entrance. Other than that, I'd settled on few details of the project; indeed, I knew so little about what was involved that I didn't even know what there was to settle.

As is common in such a situation, I sought his advice, and he was more than happy to explain some of the technical problems that would have to be solved and what some of my options were. He spoke learnedly and confidently about his subject. I said I would give it some thought and discuss it later with my wife.

He asked me where the stones would be coming from. I said I had a plentiful supply of stones. I don't own a lot of acreage, but I own enough to have, as so many landowners in the area do, sizable stone walls of some antiquity running obscurely through dense second-growth woodlands. Such walls once formed the boundaries of pastures that have long since been reclaimed by the forest; now, though often difficult to get to, they're a good source of nicely weathered fieldstones that can be dragged off and used for the construction of ornamental walls in more conspicuous places. Even better than that — since I'd rather not tamper with old walls, even if they're hidden — I have a number of large fieldstone piles located close to my fields. I asked if he wanted to examine the resources I had, and he said it was unnecessary.

I asked about an estimate. How much might it cost?

He looked rather vacantly into the sky for a moment, as if he were doing some calculations. Yet somehow, I don't think he was doing any calculations. I think he was studying a cloud formation that was drifting overhead. Then he gave me a price, not an estimate.

The price was very low. I didn't believe it when he said it. I still don't believe it.

After saying he would come by again in a few days, he departed. I don't know where he lives or what his telephone number is. I don't know anything about him — except for his name: Anpu.

Day Two

So I've made inquiries. Of course, it's difficult to make them because I can't even identify who he is. Anyway, nobody knows him: nobody even knows of him. Nobody has heard of Anpu. I've spoken to a few construction people.

They're acquainted with all the stonemasons around, and since this fellow isn't in one of their familiar groups, he must be a newcomer, which already makes him suspect.

Naturally, they warn me against him. I need to take their admonitions with a grain of salt, for local people warn against everybody and anybody—that's just what they do.

They're all, however, incredulous about the price. A wall of the sort we're planning should cost about four or five times as much. So that makes them really suspicious. Such a low price must mean that he does very low-quality work.

I don't know what to make of all of this. Could he be giving me a low price and then intend to jack it up monumentally as he runs into the supposedly unexpected but inevitable problems? That's a game that all the local construction people know how to play, and he would be no exception in that regard.

How do I get in touch with him?

Day Three

He showed up again this morning. Came in out of nowhere. Has a dirty, crumpled-up-looking van, curiously box-shaped, with indecipherable markings on it. I wonder if he lives in that van.

Was I interested in having him work? Yes, I was interested—that is, interested enough to pursue the issue.

I asked him if there was a stone wall somewhere in the neighborhood that he had built that I could look at. Well, no; he's new to the area. (I guess we all had that right.)

Does he have references? No, he doesn't have any references. He informs me of that in a way that implies that the question is unnecessary and impertinent. Apparently, according to him, he doesn't need references.

When could he start on the job? Anytime I wanted him to start.

Could he start tomorrow? Yes, he could start tomorrow.

I'm a bit confounded. Now, my normal procedure in situations like this would be to get several bids from different masons. But for reasons I can't unravel, I'm willing, in this case, to bypass that procedure.

Why do I have confidence in him? On that first day he discoursed so eloquently about his métier that I was convinced he knew what he was talking about (a dangerous inference to make, under any circumstances). Also, I know I won't get a price like that from anybody else.

So am I just being stingy? After all, I don't know what I'm going to get for that price. Indeed, I tend, by and large, to be susceptible to the dynamics of what people call "value perception"—that paying a higher price entails getting a better product. So I know I'm not stingy, not in principle anyway. I like things of quality and am willing to pay for them what they're worth, though I know that "value perception" psychology can often be deceptive.

In any case, I'm not the obsessive bargain hunter who fills his life with junk, nor the shrewd financier who, more often than not, is the long-term victim, if also maybe the short-term beneficiary, of his own connivance.

I ask Anpu how I should contact him. He doesn't seem to have an address or telephone number yet. He says he'll contact me. As I said, he just came into the area.

In addition to the price, I'm also attracted to the immediacy of when he can begin work. At least I don't have to wait some indeterminate length of time before things get underway. That's a relief.

Sometimes I think I'm crazy. I must be crazy. I offer him the job. I offer him the job on the spot. I've never done that before.

Does he want an advance? No, he doesn't want an advance.

Anpu doesn't want an advance.

Day Four

He arrives early in the morning, and I must interrupt my leisurely breakfast hour to accompany him to the woods and show him the mounds that will serve as the source for the new wall. I also show him the walls that belong to me, and I'm careful to distinguish them from other walls that run close by and that are boundaries between my land and the adjoining woodlots of my neighbors. I don't know who's considered to own walls like these, but I assume we shouldn't touch them, and I don't.

Anpu has no difficulty grasping the logistics of the situation.

When I ask him if the supply will be sufficient, he laughs. There's enough stone there to build a wall ten times the length of the one being planned.

He notes that I have a tractor parked behind my barn and asks if he can use it to haul stones from the forest to the front of the house. I agree to that. We go to the tractor, and I explain a few things about the hydraulics and the clutching system and a few other gadgets, just in case he's not familiar with this kind of tractor. But he doesn't seem to need this information. He's soon at work, and I return to my coffee cup and newspaper. All day long I hear that tractor going in and out of the woods.

Day Five

The fieldstone heap he's created already is amazing. Gigantic. I can't figure out how he's moving some of these stones. The front-end loader of the tractor can carry them, of course, but how does he get them into it in the first place? And stones of so many shapes and colors and sizes? On those mounds up in the woods they all looked more or less the same: grey, rounded, covered with lichens, sedate, ordinary. Maybe I just never looked carefully at them.

Here they have sharp edges, sculpted projections and bulges, flat sides and rounded sides, rectangular lines and pyramidal shapes and brilliant hues, all aglitter with embedded mica or shot through with jagged veins of dazzling white quartz or encrusted with coppery sheaths.

No two are alike.

I don't know how to identify stone, despite that one course in geology I took at college (one of several random "science" requirements), but there must be dozens and dozens of different kinds of stones here. Those glaciers of old must have scooped and gouged deeply into the strata of the earth to yield such a variegated harvest. I can't imagine how he's going to put them all together.

Many of my neighbors, who regularly walk along the street for their daily exercise, are now aware that something fairly dramatic is going on and stop to gape at the huge mound of stones. All day long Anpu keeps adding stones to the pile, slowly and methodically. Sometimes he stands for a while, with that curious vacant look, studying the clouds in the sky, but he gets a lot done, though it's impossible to figure out how he does it.

It's difficult not to watch him at times.

I keep thinking he looks familiar to me, but I don't know why. He doesn't look at all like you would imagine a stonemason should look. He's not hefty, round-shouldered, thick, or rugged like the stones he moves about. He's medium height and slender as a reed and has a sallow, pleasant face; his nose and chin project somewhat forward beneath large black eyes and eyebrows, and his lips are broad and full; his low forehead slants backward into a thin, oblong head that looks curiously canine. He looks as if he had stepped out of some other world.

He wears a strangely shaped cap that hides his ears. I don't know why I think this, but maybe if he took that cap off, I'd see that his ears are tall and erect and have pointed tips. Why do I think that?

Day Six

Anpu dug a trench today, along the entire length of where the wall will be going and has begun filling in the trench with smaller stones. Later in the day we discussed briefly some issues touching upon details about the wall, especially about the ending of the wall, where it will meet the driveway, and about the position and shape of a gateway. He has quite a few suggestions to make, and we'll have to make some decisions. We never discuss the general style of the wall. I assume that that matter is decided simply by what is more or less traditional in the area.

Stone walls around here all tend to look a certain way—at least if you're not looking at them too carefully, though, in recent months while thinking about a wall, I've learned to distinguish several variations of style. For the most part, the fieldstone is fitted together without mortar or any other joining substance or rigging, making what is called a "dry wall." Variations seem to be determined by how careful the fitting is—some walls are loosely fitted; others are precise. Some are thick with broad, level tops; others are only one stone thick with a thin, craggy ridge along the top. It's also amazing how nice these walls look, no matter what variations of style they exhibit or in what state of disrepair they happen to be. Many of the older walls have partially fallen down or settled and flattened out, yet they still look so attractive that people, as I've heard, sometimes instruct stonemasons to build new walls so that they look like these old, partially fallen-down walls.

In earlier days, I was of the conviction that the multitudinous stone walls of New England were simply piles of stone conveniently lined up along the edges of fields. Some of them were, but the most elementary sort of effort to repair one of these walls quickly dispels any illusion that building these walls didn't require a fair amount of skill. The walls were built by people who knew what they were doing. For the most part, they did it well. I've given Anpu no particular instructions about the style of the wall he will build. I assume the stone wall will look like—well, just like a stone wall.

Day Seven

The building has begun.

Stakes and strings have been set up and a row of stones placed along the outside of the base on either side. They look like a jagged little parade of two mountain chains running parallel to and facing one another. The sides of the stones facing outward from the wall are all flat. How can they all be flat? The stones up in the woods were round. They looked to my eyes like cannon balls of different sizes. I know he isn't cutting the stone, so where did all these flat sides come from?

I now think I know where I've seen Anpu before … seen him a thousand times. He looks like one of those figures in ancient Egyptian paintings, face presented in profile, shoulders at right angle to the face, dressed in a kirtle or short tunic, surrounded by hieroglyphs and papyrus stalks and lotus blooms, wielding tools, building temples and pyramids.

Could his name be Egyptian too?

Anpu? But that name doesn't ring a bell.

And Anpu doesn't seem to be using any tools, though he carries around with him at times a sort of iron rod with a crossbeam and a circle at the end. A crowbar of some sort? I don't know. I never see him actually using it.

I walked up to the woods this afternoon to check out how much of those original rock mounds are left. All of them still seem to be there. It doesn't look as if he's touched any of them. Where did all those stones come from?

In the evening, after he's left for the day, I go out and examine the heap of stones. I try lifting some. Most of them I can hardly budge, even though I'm physically much larger than Anpu is.

Day Eight

Sometimes when Anpu works outside, I'm practicing piano inside. I'm not very good at it and am only trying, desperately, to pick up where I left off about forty-five years ago. If I work at it persistently for a decade, maybe I'll get back to where I was when I was about fifteen. Frankly, I'm embarrassed by the notion of anyone hearing my practicing. Some of my neighbors hear it when they go for their daily walks and have indicated, without my asking, that they enjoy it — I can't imagine why. I think they're just being polite.

Anpu hears my playing (or, as I would put it, is the hapless victim of it) and has mentioned it to me, expressing some appreciation. I reply by saying that I'm glad that Beethoven and Mozart and Schubert and a few others are interred on the other side of the Atlantic so that they don't have to go through the trouble of turning in their graves, should my maladroit renditions of their work happen to assail their ears.

Anpu seems to like especially the second movement of the *Appassionata* (actually, it's the only movement of the *Appassionata* I'm able to play); but in its heaviness and slowness, alternating with sudden divagations into lightness and speed, it's perhaps like the joining of stones. Maybe that's why he likes it; or maybe he likes it because I play it reasonably well (unlike the rest of my belabored and belaboring repertoire).

I've noted of late that my interpretation of the piece has become unusually … lapidary? Marmoreal? Hmm — like travertine, like huge blocks of limestone fitted and angled precisely in an ascending line pointing directly at a burnished desert sky?

Day Nine

Pouring rain. Black clouds. Thunder and lightning.

Winds roaring and trees pitching fitfully backward and forward, turning their leaves upward in the thrust of the wind like corybantic worshippers raising and flailing their palms to and fro before an ancient idol.

Anpu works all day, unperturbed, in the storm. He carries stones back and forth through lashing curtains of rain. Often, I can't see him unless lightning crackles in the distant skies. Then he looks like a figure in an early black-and-white film moving in clumsily disconnected steps through darkness.

He carries the stones without effort and ignores the turbulence of the storm around him. The heavens thunder over him, but he works without stint—from early morning, when the sun never rose, unto this night that follows upon a day that, for all practical purposes, has been indistinguishable from night. Like a god he moves awesomely, solemnly, through the powers of unleashed elements and the forces of chaos.

Sometimes I have the impression that he's carrying titanic rocks larger than himself.

Sometimes lightning spreads over the far horizon in jagged spires, and I see him suddenly in silhouette, a sinewy presence, etched darkly against the momentary splatter of light, more mysterious than life itself, a face as pointed and black and lean as a shard of glossy obsidian, with arched eyes glowing fiercely opalescent through the darkness, and ears pointing up from beneath that cap, ears lithe and sharp.

At other times I see him on one knee, crouching backward on his heel, the other knee tilted up in front of him, his arms raised and his head bent slightly in his canine way, wondering, concentrated, as he meditates the tongue of an invisible scale, balancing stone upon stone, their sole bond and stay being an invisible gravitational plumb line, the subtle cosmic force that holds the teetering rocks firmly in place.

"I have come unto the House of Him whose dwelling is upon the mountain."

Why did I say that? Where does that come from?

Day Ten

I can't believe how much got done during the storm yesterday. A wall is rising out of the ground, as if it were growing out of the earth. It's a wall such as I've never seen before. It looks like a New England fieldstone wall, and yet it doesn't. It has a sculpted look about it, something architectural and monumental, yet simple and unpretentious at the same time. As is so often the case with arts that one appreciates but doesn't understand, it's possible to perceive differences and features but not be able to explain what accounts for any of these perceptions.

My wife is just as puzzled by it as I am. We've started calling it Hadrian's Wall, for lack of another expression, though it doesn't look at all like Hadrian's Wall. The neighbors walk by, and stop, staring at it in wonder. They can't quite believe what they're seeing. They like what they see, even as we do, but are mystified by it. Cars drive by and slow down as they pass. The town road crew, in several trucks, stops up the road a bit, ostensibly to work on the road, but actually to get a better view of the wall.

I decide to join them. I want to see how they react.

I amble up the road, having deliberately left my partial dentures in the bathroom. I've discovered, through long experience, that a certain measure of edentation greatly facilitates discourse with some coteries of the local gentry. One can loiter about with them, shifting feet, hands in pockets, staring at the toes of one's boots while pleasurably engaged in interminable wheezing, lisping, yapping, blabbering, and whistling through the open fissures of one's mouth. My gums are not quite as discolored as theirs, but that's okay. It would be unreasonable to expect perfection in such a circumstance.

They're laughing.

Of course they're laughing ... because they're *always* laughing.

Everything, for them, is funny. What people do and what people don't do is funny. Fauna, domesticated or wild or somewhere in between, is funny. Flora is just as funny. News is funny. Town politics is funny. Accidents are funny. Weather is funny, and extreme weather is extremely funny. And so on.

The new stone wall is funny—that's not a sign of derision; it's a sign of respect. They admire that stone wall, and they've never seen anything like it, as they repeat and laugh about it over and over again. Eventually, they go back to work (if that's what you want to call whatever it is they do) and drive off in their trucks.

Back at the house, with partials restored and now fully dentilated, I sally forth, brandishing checkbook and pen, and offer to make a half payment for the wall. Anpu is not interested. He says he will present a bill when the work is completed. He says that in a very curious way.

Day Eleven

Word has gotten around. Everyone's stopping to look at the wall. Cars pull up, and people get out with cameras and take pictures. Promenading neighbors are ever more astonished. Local contractors are coming by to gaze at it, though I think it's annoying them intensely. But that's their business — to be annoyed by others' work. If Michelangelo were out there sculpting this wall, they would still be annoyed. If Michelangelo were out there looking at this wall, he would be annoyed too.

I am, I must confess, a little disconcerted by all this attention, even though it seems favorable, indeed very favorable. When people work on my place, I always have the curious sense that I'm personally, even somatically, involved, as if I were being operated on by a surgeon, and others are witnessing this event. So I'm jittery, distracted all the time, unable to concentrate on anything else, watching things out of the corner of my eye.

Moreover, it's difficult for me, with Anpu out there, shifting those great stones back and forward, fitting them together with enormous precision, not to imagine myself complicit in some great archetypal event, something that resonates throughout history.

I'm not speaking merely of the stone wall building era in New England through the past few centuries, as amazing as that was: the glacial scree of the last ice age had, after all, to be picked up and stacked somewhere if pastures were to yield hay and orchards were to be planted.

I'm thinking of all that astonishing movement and cutting and fitting of stone that has transpired with time. Anpu himself makes one think of the lofty pyramids and temples mirrored in the waters of the Nile. And then there are the great ziggurats of the Euphrates lowlands, the jungle compounds of Maya and Angkor Wat, the city walls of Minoan Crete and, as Homer would have it, of golden Mycenae itself, perched so high above the coastal plains of "horse-pasturing Argos."

Again and again, I've thought of those ancient craftsmen — a race of giants, as the old Anglo-Saxon bards described them when singing of the Roman ruins at Bath — quarrying great blocks of stone, building tombs and citadels and theaters, castles and bridges and aqueducts, massive fortifications and monastic sanctuaries and elegant chateaux, guild halls and towers and amphitheaters and the retaining walls of marvelous terraced hillsides whose wavelike forms flow upward from valley depths into the skies above.

The world is replete with their work, much of it hidden from our eyes.

And, in my own front yard and at my own behest, another edifice of the mason's art is rising—like a natural wonder itself, carving the most obdurate sculpture of the earth into the most noble of earth's sculpture, arguably mankind's most enduring things. That, in itself, is the most astonishing thing of all, for these things made of rock seem to live, and to breathe, and to sing their existence through time.

Anpu's wall is already like that, even in its unfinished condition. It seems to be alive, to unfold and to transmute itself into a multitude of forms, and modulations of those forms, like a scroll of contrapuntal music, like one of those great cathedrals of medieval Europe as you saunter meditatively around and through them, and they respond to your gaze like partners in a dance, their exquisite recursive figurations shifting from moment to moment, by moving in unison with the dazzle of your eyes.

Now, some may disagree with what I'm about to say, but here it behooves me to pick a bone, or two, or three, in this respect, with our esteemed poet of New England, Robert Frost himself, who, I think, did our regional stonework something of a disservice when he wrote his piece on "Mending Walls." For therein he posits an impulsion that seeks to bring down what human beings have so laboriously put together and to restore, in the process, a balance and rapport conceivably more natural and humane.

"Something there is that doesn't love a wall," he sententiously asserts, and later adds, "that wants it down."

Granted: walls do fall down in time, erode, or just get lugged away (to build another wall sometimes); and there are walls that pen in, or keep out, what should by rights, progress back and forth through welcoming gates. Moreover, I'm not oblivious to the manifold social and moral ambiguities that have affected, through time, the building, preservation, and destruction of walls—even these stone walls of New England.

But I don't know what there might be that doesn't love our fieldstone walls in these latter times. Even the foraging deer, the birds, and the chipmunks love them as much as we do.

And when Roberto (as I affectionately call him — he wouldn't mind) brands his toilsome, wall-repairing neighbor "a stone-age savage armed," he hasn't seen Anpu, or ten thousand of his ilk, deftly joining for us the most adamant of nature's gifts. Nor is that work achieved by uttering spells or turning a blind eye and hoping it will work.

Fie on you, Roberto, you progeny of Rousseau!

Something there is that *does* love a wall and will keep building them, whether you approve or not. What else can bring neighbors in the spring to work together; what else can you lean against or sit upon so commodiously — morning, noon, or eventide — as you chat and smoke your pipe?

Of walls, I sing, and barriers and barricades (begging forbearance for my brief foray into rhapsody) and all they are and represent; of fences, railings, moats, curbs, and hedges; of banisters and balustrades and cloistered galleries; of natural rims and fringes of every kind — of riverbanks and beaches, of mountain ranges and craters and coasts and crested waves and horizons whose multifarious contours distinguish everywhere the earth from sky. I luxuriate in limits, bask in boundaries, delight in demarcations. Edges edify me, embellish me, exalt me, enrich me. Partitions purify me.

I rejoice in perimeters, frames, and borders. I savor distinctness and avow that, ever and ever, distinctness and distinctiveness walk hand in hand through all the aeons of time; for what is distinct is distinguished, and to distinguish is a mark of distinction.

I revel in divisions: in seconds and minutes and hours and days; in sunrises and sunsets and periods of the moon and seasons of the year.

I celebrate all that encloses and envelops and harbors and shelters: the roof over my head, the walls around and inside my house, the bark of trees and the rinds of fruit, furry hides and ornate garb and scalloped shells tumbled inland by the frothy surf.

The measures and movements of music modulate my soul in the rhythms of splendor. I indulge in the beginnings and endings of stories, of symphonies, of poems.

I relish the embroidered entities of speech itself: syllables and words, and phrases, and clauses, and sentences; paragraphs and chapters, verses and stanzas and cantos — all that delimits, all that segments, the flood of speech into tight-knit bundles that glitter like beaded jewels upon a necklace.

I know that wholes, to be wholes, require parts, and that parts, to be parts, require wholes, and that unity, to be unity, requires units.

And the glory of the wall, and all that resembles a wall, is nowhere more manifest than in its own internal divisions, the most important of which are its gateways, its windows, its apertures into whatever lies beyond.

I shall never cease to reflect upon that ancient memory of the Garden of Eden, which was surrounded by a wall, and the universal dream of Paradise, remembering at all times that the word "paradise" itself means, in its original Persian, "surrounded by a wall."

Something there is that truly loves a wall.

Me!

Tonight was a full moon. A pack of coyotes came down out of the woods and respectfully sniffed around Anpu's wall. They scurried back and forth along the wall, jumped over it, and one or two even ran along the capstones, where some have already been placed. None of the coyotes saw fit to "mark territory."

Then something set them off, I don't know what, but they gathered together in the moonlight next to the wall, crooked back their necks, and howled and yapped and clamored to their hearts' content.

A chorus of wonder.

A chorale of praise.

Day Twelve

Sometimes my wife complains about Anpu. She watches him from a window upstairs. He's just standing there, doing nothing, she says. She says he "ain't nothin' but a hound dog." Of course, she's not serious and she's making fun, too, I presume, of a song popular in her adolescent years. But I have noted Anpu's spells of inactivity.

I've also noted that he rarely places a stone in the wall and then takes it out again or moves it around very much. No trial and error. The stone goes from the heap to the wall and is an immediate and exact fit. He doesn't act until all the thinking about acting is done. Everything falls into place. That's what he's doing when he just stands there. He's doing that thinking.

But my wife is right. He does look like a hound dog, sort of. Lean and supple, strong and purposive, his head at times bent resolutely to a scent, his nose in the air at other times to refresh and retune the senses. Yet his face is more like the face of a jackal seen in profile, one great black-contoured eye affixed steadfastly to a far desert horizon, to the boundaries of a twilight world.

Like Anubis.

Like the jackal god.

Like the custodian of the dead, preparing their final passage, encasing them with gold and anointing them with frankincense and myrrh—the sacramental accouterments of entombment.

Like the *psychopompos*—as the Greeks would call it—the escort of souls into Hades, into the netherworld. Like Virgil leading Dante through the realms of the dead. The saying that came to my mind the other day—"I have come unto the House of Him whose dwelling is upon the mountain"—now I remember where it comes from: the Egyptian *Book of the Dead*.

I keep thinking about those coyotes that showed up here last night. Had they discerned a kindred spirit?

Day Thirteen

I've asked Anpu for, and received in turn, some advice on how to conduct a few minor projects in stonework. Not that I really have building a wall in mind, but I'm going to try to put some simple stone borders around the flower beds in the back of our house (where the neighbors won't see them). I can't say I really understood most of what he told me, but I'm setting to work anyway. I have a good supply of small stones, about the size of loaves of bread, to work with. They're not weathered fieldstones but, rather, were recently dug up from the soil in various drainage projects I pursued last spring.

As I work with these stones, I begin to understand, I think, one of the attractions of this métier to those who practice it. I've always been aware that craftsmen love the materials they work with. I've seen carpenters affectionately caress a wooden board and mechanics taking pleasure in the heft and the feel of a metallic bolt.

Musicians, I know, love musical tones—a G, or an F, on a piano, or violin, or guitar: what a lovely thing it is, just by itself. Then add something to it, and it's even better now, for that which is special about it is heightened by the contrast with something different—but not so different that the difference doesn't matter.

Poets love words. Even more, they love syllables, love the way they feel inside the mouth when they utter them, love how they cluster in little bouquets and garlands, love the rhythmic pressure in the throat and tongue as they navigate through those remarkable physiological straits like miniature armadas of vessels laden with spices and gold.

But I never thought that rocks could be lovable, both for themselves and in sequence with others. I soon learned that. Some of the rocks I found so lovable that I wanted to bring them into the house and cradle them in my arms and give them a sudsy bath in the kitchen sink the way you would bathe a newborn child.

So many of them, so different. No two shapes alike.

The astonishing textures—rough and smooth, grainy, soapy, mellow, ridged and sharp and serrated, solid, flaking, brittle, grooved, gnarled and knobby, flat and sometimes wavy and sandy as if an ocean breeze had, once upon a time, carved miniature dunes in a beach that, in turn, some other force petrified and preserved.

Many stones seem to be made up of several kinds of stone blended or molded together, so that they have many different textures in one surface. I love to touch them, run my hands over them, turn them around and examine them from different angles, and let sunlight and shadow play over their folds and furrows and brows.

The colors are beyond all description: thousands of delicate hues whose names I don't know—organdy and lavender and peach and bluish-gray and pastel gold and aubergine, like eggplants or damson plums.

Some stones are artist's palates in their multiform and sequenced richness. Many stones display webs of finely tinted veins, while others exhibit patterns of glacial scratches scored over their gritty surfaces. There are horizontally layered stones that split, even under as mild a pressure as from your fingers, and open up like thick, meaty sandwiches, revealing a medley of interior colors that even the most elaborately gourmet sandwich in all the world could scarcely emulate. There are stones that look like melons and mangos and Brazil nuts and pineapples and exotic squashes.

Why have I never noticed any of this before?

Ribbons of light spiral through the glittering facets of what I clasp in my wondering hands. I'm especially fond of the auburn and ruddy stones. Where do they come from? Did the earth pitch these up from its depths like all this quartz and granite; or did they compact as sediments at the bottom of an ancient sea?

Another stone common in this area is an amazing pale-pink granite filled with millions of small black dots. And then the silvery mica and the deep ruby-red garnets that shimmer in the fissures of the stone!

My house faces across a valley, at the eastern end of which is possibly the largest exploded volcanic caldera in New England. The sun rises directly out of that mountain-ridged kettle every morning, reenacting the blaze of its primeval glory. Is that the cornucopia out of which spouted such abundance, half a billion years ago?

Putting the stones together just in a single line—"pointing" them, or trying to do so, according to my instructions—reveals even more about color and texture and shape. Well, I can't say that I'm particularly successful at what I do—even at such a simple task (I'm not even engaged in putting rocks on top of one another to make a wall, which is the difficult thing to do).

But I am able, now and then, to sense the satisfaction when two utterly different rocks almost "click" into place. It is, I suppose, a little like the experience of finding the combination that unlocks a safe: hearing that subtle little "click" that says, "This much is done." The rocks that so overtly seem to repel one another, to be so intractable and stubborn, suddenly, even inexplicably, attract, invite, align themselves, as if, from the beginning of time, as different as they are, they were meant to go together. And yet a stone asks finally for one thing and one thing only: to be at rest; to be at peace so that it supports another and another and is supported by them in turn—an interplay of force, dynamic, harmonized, and serene—

Is that what we look for too?

In our lives, our relationships, in the course of events that we make happen and that happens to us, locking together our bits and pieces into their own inimitable happenstance? To be at peace, our internal force aligned perfectly with the forces of the earth, the forces of the cosmos around us, the forces of those we know and love?

I once asked Anpu, while observing him at work, if he enjoyed doing jigsaw puzzles. Laconically, without explanation, he said no. Later, and with a little experience, I could understand why the question was absurd to begin with. In a jigsaw puzzle, the pieces press in tightly, seamlessly, and, once in place, have no further function or importance as pieces. They vanish into a whole that finally has nothing to do with them as pieces. In a "dry" field-stone wall the stones retain their independence, even while coalescing into a complex and dynamic set of tensions and pressures. They're contiguous with their neighbors but don't fuse with them. Further, unlike the jigsaw puzzle, where only fit is vital, and not the dynamics of which I spoke, each combination of stones is a special case, for which no prearranged pattern is available. The making of the pattern is the same as finding it.

Well, I enlarge here upon matters about which I'm scarcely qualified. Meanwhile, my wife refers to my stone circles sardonically as "barbarian." Is that a compliment or not? But I know she's glad the neighbors won't see them. Actually, so am I; and I plan to deter Anpu, if I can, from making any exploratory forays to the back of the house to check them out.

Okay, so barbarian they may well be. I'm doing my little thing and feel my solidarity, however fleeting, with the stonemasons of Nineveh and the monument builders of Carnac and Tara and Stonehenge. If I've edged across the threshold of their immemorial guild with only so much as the somewhat disreputable toe of my boot, I shall have done at least that much.

Day Fourteen

Anpu didn't show up today. Or at least I don't think he showed up. I took advantage of his absence to work on and complete my stone circles.

While I was working, a fox clambered up over the old stone wall that borders the back field that rises high above our house, lay down in the high grass, and basked there in the sun, observing me and munching, now and then, on the wild blueberries that grow profusely in the thin soil along the brow of the hill. I could see his ruddy head above the grass, his pointed ears, his little eyes staring intently at me. He seemed to find what I was doing rather amusing.

I had the uncanny feeling that I knew this fox already; further, I had the even more uncanny feeling that I knew who this fox was. After an hour or so, he rose, turned, twitched his big bushy tail, mounted the stone wall where he stood, gazed at me again for a few moments, and then descended on the other side, trotting off calmly into the scrubby underbrush at the edge of the woods.

Day Fifteen

Anpu is back.

More and more people show up. Now they take photographs of Anpu, as well as of the wall. He seems not to notice them. Someone tried to take a photograph of me. Of me! Me — standing somewhere in the background: bemused, puzzled, a little quirky, after all! Ah, I do flatter myself!

At one point during the day, Anpu asked me how my stone circles were coming. I told him they were coming along fine, but I didn't offer to take him around to the back of the house to show him. His amused smile informed me that he knew all about them already and didn't need to see them.

He's putting finishing touches on the gate he created about a third of the way along the wall. He's adorned each side of the gate with small thin triangular pinnacles of stone.

Obelisks?

Day Sixteen

It's done.

Shouldn't there be, or have been, some kind of ceremony?

I knew that Anpu was finishing up because he had been cleaning up around the wall, removing unused stone back to the woods (or wherever it came from), and making some last minor adjustments, so I was keeping a close watch on his activities. He has a way of suddenly slipping away. He never says goodbye.

Meanwhile, I was engaged in a few desultory activities to keep me busy while I waited for the right moment to emerge from the house, inspect the finished product, congratulate him on his work, and present him with a check with the name Anpu (awkwardly) inscribed on it as well as the agreed-upon price (about which I now feel rather guilty). But, as so often these things go, I would watch for a while, then go off and do something, come back and see if things were ready yet, which they weren't, go off again, do something else.

I decided at one point to run through the second movement of the *Appassionata*. It would take only a few minutes. Then I would check again to see what was happening. Somehow, during those few minutes, while I was playing the piece on the piano, Anpu vanished.

One Week Later

Just vanished.

He hasn't returned. No one has seen him.

One Month Later

No one knows where he's gone. People drop in constantly and ask me how they can contact him. I tell them I don't know. He's never come by to collect. He's never sent a bill.

Three Months Later

He never did send that bill.

One Year Later

I've done the unimaginable. I've purchased a grammar of the ancient Egyptian language and am learning how to read hieroglyphs. I don't know how long I'll keep this up — it's a bit over my head. But I've learned something important already.

I have before me a hieroglyphic image. It's one of those hieroglyphs that function pictorially rather than phonetically. It shows a human figure, in profile, sitting on its heels with knees slanted upward at a forty-five-degree angle. Projecting from the knees, at the same angle, is a hand that holds a rod or scepter capped by the sacred *ankh*, which was later reverenced by Christians as the ansate cross, the symbol for life.

The head of the figure is canine with a sharp, thin muzzle and high, pointed ears. Yes, it's the sign for what we have come to know in a Hellenized or Greek variant as Anubis — the jackal deity, the Weigher of Destinies, the Escort into the God-World, the purveyor of Eternity. He's also the god of craftsmanship, of skill, of the perpetuation of the dead. His name is synonymous with wisdom and judgment. But the proper transcription for this hieroglyph is not Anubis. It's Anpu.

Could it be?

It can't be. My wife tells me I'm having delusions. That I've imagined most of this, dreamt it into being.

Maybe I have. But I don't think so. There's a wall out there in front of the house. It was built by a stonemason who said his name was Anpu. And Anpu never sent a bill.

People are coming from far and wide to gaze upon this wall. They've never seen anything like it. It's a miracle. It's a wall that must have been put together by a god. But there is no god but God. Therefore, it's a wall that must have been put together by God.

Last night, as the moon rose above the wilderness, I heard from afar the lonely shriek of a catamount and, soon afterward, the mournful howl of a wolf from the depths of the great forests beyond the mountains.

Quixote in Paradise

I rejoice among these scented hills,
Among these rivers of dark wine,
Among these fields of downy blooms
And heady spices, days unsullied
By the dross and drabble of age and time.
I, Alonso Quixano, erstwhile Don Quixote,
In La Mancha born and bred and buried,
Sifting my dust again into its soil,
Found gracious surety from my Liege-Lord
To journey hither to these blessed valleys.
It gives me leave to parse the filaments
Of my life, *of what was my life*; to bind
Its strands into one fine and plaited cord.
I was as I was warranted to be.
Who I was, even in my errant ways,
Magnified the seed that stirred my spirit
And the womb that gave me flesh of flesh,
Bone of bone, a proper investiture,
A place: in truth, a place upon the earth.
Shall I then grieve those dreams I entertained,
Dreams that bent my head awry, that led me
When it was I who should have been the leader?
I'll not reproach the vision that I had
Nor the course I traced amid its vagaries.
What more gorgeous vista could I traverse
Than when I, Rocinante, and Sancho Panza
Would tread the byways of serried Spain?
Stony outcrops crouched like tawny lions.
Skies were azure bays of glimmering light.
Rills were avalanches of chain mail

Glistering down through narrow mountain passes.
Aloes brandished thick and barbed blades.
Thunderheads, like wreathed bulls, scoured the plains.
Dawn would creep from bush to broom, day to day,
Stalking us, while the bleached and vaunting sun
Would thrust its golden targe across our paths
And the starlit snood of night would cull
Lush, earthly tresses in its purple snare.
We were all one glorious entourage:
Horse, helmet, burro, dangling sword and spear;
Proverbs, knightly lays, songs of love and longing;
Dulcinea, the beautiful, the proud;
Don Sancho, lordly viscount in the end
Of his demesne; Master Pedro's puppets,
Whose capricious antics I thought to tame.
But the swathe of my delirious sword
Cost me and others treasures bought too dear.
And I regret and shun the woeful day
When derisive chatelains paid homage
To my foibles, follies, confabulations
Grand, and not so grand. For I had fallen
Deep, and deeper yet, into boundless shame.
Were vanity, or madness, or contempt
My portion? How should I presume to know?
When trending homeward, raving in a cage,
Or taken sick unto my bed, I knew
The touch of mercy, the abode of grace:
By infirmity healed of infirmity
While my chivalrous deeds could yet attest,
Redounding in their very waywardness,
To what the faithful heart could strive to do.
How could I lament the gifts proffered me
Or the gifts I've given others in my way?
As the hyssop-sprigs of my repentance

I offer them to my sole Suzerain;
To Him alone, my valor and panache.
Who measures justly is Who measures me.
Beyond all fantasies, I've seen a star
Mark the heavens with its luminous trail.
This new world is more beautiful by far.
My quest begins again; I shall not fail.

Waiting for the Night-Train

It does seem late. I shall not worry.
The night-train always runs on time.
The stationmaster dozes in his office,
Tilted backward in his chair.
A yellow bulb dangles above his head.
He doesn't know I'm here or care.
No one else waits on the platform.
I have no luggage—I won't need it there.
A forest rises high on either side;
An owl hoots now and then.
A breeze stirs branches overhead.
I sit upon a bench and watch the tracks.
I've done my work, my day is over;
It was filled with ruts and rain
And sunlight sometimes harsh to bear.
But I have left my things in order,
Said goodbye to those I've loved,
Wished well, at last, to those I didn't.
Twilight was a blessing and a burden.
I hear the locomotive whistling far away;
I'm not afraid. I'm not alone.
The night-train comes to take me home.

Envoi

To thee alone, of whom I here indite,
I commend these modest verses; to thee,
Master of true Revels, who yet beguiles
That sovereign pith and balm of all our days,
I extend my tribute; to thee, none other —
Friend, fellow guildsman, "Sweet Swan of Avon."

Sources of the Stories and Poems

Aunt Jennie's Christmas Pie: *Love of the Blossoming Hills: New England Stories and Sketches*

Berceuse: *Most Ancient of All Splendors*

Bordeaux, A.D. 408: *Most Ancient of All Splendors*

Brünnhilde: *Tutelary Presences: And Other Stories*

The Bulls of Bashan: *Farewell . . . and if Forever: And Other Poems*

Canso d'Amor: *Farewell . . . and if Forever: And Other Poems*

Envoi: *Late Autumn at Dumbarton Oaks: And Other Poems*

Estampie: *Farewell . . . and if Forever: And Other Poems*

Galileo: A Letter to His Daughter: *Most Ancient of All Splendors*

"Good Night, Sweet Prince": *Farewell . . . and if Forever: And Other Poems*

Harry Wiedenhausen: *Tutelary Presences: And Other Stories*

"Je te veux": *Farewell . . . and if Forever: And Other Poem*

A Lament: for Gilgamesh of Uruk: *Most Ancient of All Splendors*

Leander Baxter and the Foxtowne Races: *Tutelary Presences: And Other Stories*

Le Danse du Diable: *Tutelary Presences: And Other Stories*

Leviathan: *Tutelary Presences: And Other Stories*

Maura Briscoe: *Love of the Blossoming Hills: New England Stories and Sketches*

Maître Renart's Shrovetide Confession: *Farewell . . . and if Forever: And Other Poems*

Old Gander's Weeping: *Most Ancient of All Splendors*

Pup: *Late Autumn at Dumbarton Oaks: And Other Poems* Quixote in Paradise: *Late Autumn at Dumbarton Oaks: And Other Poems*

The Stonemason: A Journal: *Love of the Blossoming Hills: New England Stories and Sketches*

The Story of My Life: *Tutelary Presences: And Other Stories*

Three "Friends": *Love of the Blossoming Hills: New England Stories and Sketches*

"The Triumph of the Human Spirit": *Love of the Blossoming Hills: New England Stories and Sketches*

Two Sisters: *Love of the Blossoming Hills: New England Stories and Sketches*

Waiting for the Night-Train: *Farewell . . . and if Forever: And Other Poems*

Wobbly Jane: *Tutelary Presences: And Other Stories*

About the Author

Johann M. Moser was born in Cambridge, Massachusetts, in 1940. He grew up in New York City and later in New Jersey. At Dartmouth College he majored in philosophy and studied with the poet Richard Eberhart. In 1970, he received a Ph.D. in comparative literature from the Catholic University of America in Washington, D.C., where he specialized in poetics and medieval literature. From 1970 until his retirement in 2000, he taught literature and philosophy at St. Anselm College in Manchester, New Hampshire.

Moser published a volume of verse titled *Most Ancient of All Splendors* with Sophia Institute Press in 1989, as well as edited and translated for the press both an anthology of classical Nativity verse and, in collaboration with a colleague, Robert Anderson, an edition of St. Thomas Aquinas's hymns and prayers.

Moser has recently published two additional collections of verse, as well as two full-length novels and two collections of short stories. He is now embarked on bringing together his various scholarly works, which are being published by the Diamond Ledge Press in a series of volumes. The studies are the results of forty years of teaching, of public lectures, presentations, and seminars, and of writing, in the early 2000s, for a website he once managed. Further volumes may be provided in the future as the occasion requires.

Academic Works
by Johann M. Moser

A Philosophical Lexicon
of Literary Terms

A Treasury of Essential Quotes
on Form in Literature
and in the Fine Arts

Elements of Beauty
Or What Makes a Thing Beautiful

The Primacy of Form
in Literary Works
An Introduction to Classical Poetics

Disputed Questions
about Classical Poetics

Essays on Literature
and on Particular Literary Works

www.ingramcontent.com/pod-product-compliance
Lightning Source LLC
Chambersburg PA
CBHW032223050726
47591CB00001B/243